AN AFFAIR ON THE APPIAN WAY

by

Michael Levey

Hamish Hamilton
London

By the same author

TEMPTING FATE

First published in Great Britain 1984
by Hamish Hamilton Ltd
Garden House 57–59 Long Acre London WC2E 9JZ

Copyright © 1984 by Michael Levey

British Library Cataloguing in Publication Data

Levey, Michael
   An affair on the Appian Way.
   I. Title
   823′.914[F]   PR6062.E91/

ISBN 0–241–11315–6

Phototypeset by Input Typesetting Ltd.,London SW19 8DR
Printed in Great Britain by
St Edmundsbury Press, Bury St Edmunds, Suffolk

In the peaceful, assured, even smug Rome of around 100 AD, discovery of the strangled body of a young patrician woman creates a mystery — and very soon an incipient scandal.

Such is the 'affair' that opens this highly unusual and intriguing novel. The story is told by no less prominent a figure than Julia, the Chief Vestal Virgin who is drawn into the investigation half against her will. She commands authority and respect, yet her position of power is a lonely one, loveless and, as she begins to sense, vacuous. In seeking to uncover facts about the murder, she uncovers facts about her own emotions; and the very tomb on the Appian Way where the corpse was found sees the start of a rather different 'affair'.

It is this relationship, tender and stirring, which is at the heart of the book. Whatever else he may do or be, a good-looking young Gaul nicknamed Rufus restores Julia to life. And when it turns out that his own life is in danger she, as Chief Vestal, is uniquely placed to save him. But at what price to herself?

What began light-heartedly ends poignantly. In his second novel, part murder mystery, part love story, Michael Levey transports the reader to an authentic Roman world populated by a cast of living — and lively — characters, from the crafty entrepreneur Afranius Dexter and hypocritical Prefect to the formidable figure of the Empress. And behind them all, like the Tarpeian Rock, looms the Roman state against which no individual can fight and hope to win.

Soles occidere et redire possunt:
nobis cum semel occidit brevis lux,
nox est perpetua una dormienda.
                              Catullus

Suns, that set, may rise again:
But if, once, we lose this light,
'Tis with us perpetual night.
                              Jonson

For
ANNE GRAHAM BELL
With love and gratitude

'Men,' said Gemma, my lively jewel of a maid. She bounced in so hastily that there was no time to dispose of the linen strip I had been guiltily poring over.

'Men? Here? At this hour?' In response to each question she nodded cheerfully.

Only that December morning had there appeared a rash of strips stuck ingeniously on porches and pillars throughout Rome, proclaiming the advantages of a winter cruise to Carthage. It was something new, as Gemma herself had pointed out: an advertising campaign. Celeriter Tours offered everyone the opportunity, for a price, of following history's trail to Queen Dido's capital.

'Men,' I repeated thoughtfully. Yet the word failed to take flesh. I could think only of Aeneas, who had quitted Carthage and the despairing Dido, seeking Italy while she was left to seek death.

Centuries ago, had some Carthaginian Gemma bounced in as cheerfully to her mistress one evening, announcing the arrival of strange men? Whatever the poets might feign, I could see it happening like that.

'But this is disgraceful, Gemma.' I was indignant with my own imagination. 'Almost a sacrilege. This house was sufficiently profaned by that, that—'

'Advertisement, mum?'

'Exactly. You know it required a ritual lustration and the girls out with mops in this weather.' Off me it seemed to have washed less easily. 'Who are these men? Are they selling something?'

'Can't say I'd buy, if they are. Three of them — and one asking for you ever so loudly. Chief Vestal, he starts bellowing as soon as he catches sight of me. Oh, yes, indeed, I said.

Thank you very much, but I'm nothing of the kind. Take me to her, he says, adding something I'll not repeat, mum. Even down in Butunti we don't use words like that, not to ladies anyway. Pipe down, I ought to have told him and mind your language when you're visiting a goddess – uninvited too.'

'Well, I'm not divine, Gemma, and perhaps I shouldn't even be curious. Didn't he give you his name?'

'Oh, Prefect, he claims to be. Publius Inflatus something – he gabbled it off before I'd got my breath back. Ebriolus, if you ask me. He's been at some party, I can tell. Shall I send them packing, mum? The youngest has ever such a pale face. I'm sure he's foreign. And the other two are old enough to be your father. You'd think they'd know better than to stagger in here, and at this hour of night.'

'Thank you, Gemma. If it is the Praefectus Urbis himself, I shall have to see him.'

'Do you think it's safe, mum? Urbis or not, men at night can be no joke. And you've the girls to consider, as well as yourself. We don't want a scandal, do we? I didn't like the look of the big talkative one – inflatus his nose is, all right.'

'It sounds as if it must be the Prefect. I think you may trust me to see he doesn't misbehave.'

'Oh, I don't mind for myself, mum.' Gemma giggled. 'He's not my type. Never mind his age, he's far too stuck-up and civic for me. I suppose the foreigner's not too bad-looking. But that big one – ever so *Roman*, he is.'

Outwardly Roman myself, and as marble as the vestibule, I entered it calmly and gravely, to find the trio of men huddled like malefactors on a bench from which they hastily rose.

'My dear Julia.' Publius appeared to swell and fill the space aurally no less than physically, blocking out the other two as he bowed and boomed at me. 'For this intrusion – '

'It's quite all right. I wasn't in bed.'

'I was about to say,' he said, deflating somewhat, 'I make no apology. Disturbed myself at a supper-party, I hesitated over the propriety of disturbing you. But I believe – and I believe you too will – that the situation is one where any personal inconvenience sinks before the demands of the state. You and I, my dear, are not likely to forget what we stand for in the public eye. Others may pass their time in pleasure. Duty, with us, must always be the prime consideration.'

He hunched his heavy shoulders and lowered his head, as though about to charge or, rock-like, absorb the waves of applause his conclusion would have stirred in the Senate. After a pause and the silence, he lifted one hand to smooth his thick white hair, itself impressively shaken by his words, and encountered a lop-sided crown of what looked like winter violets. As he resumed, he slid the flowers deftly off the back of his head, crumpling them in a fat, red fist. 'Delicate – delicate and distressing the affair is, I regret to say. And its implications could reverberate in ways that are frightful to envisage. Privacy and discretion are at this moment paramount. If for no other reason, my dear, I thought of you. Might we retire to your apartments?'

Seeing my hesitation, he added, 'The two of us, of course, I meant. These, er, others – officially involved – may wait outside. The sacred repute of this house must be upheld at all costs. I am the first to insist on that.'

'As you feel so strongly,' I said, 'wouldn't it be better if they stayed inside? Being seen on our portico as late as this isn't likely to do them, or us, much good. Besides, I'm sure it must be cold out there.'

'Freeze the –' one of the other men started to say. 'Well, cold enough for snow, madam.' He was thin and dark and sharp-faced, I saw, before a prefectorial gesture by Publius pushed him into the background, where the third man stood silently.

'Rome does not expect snow,' Publius intoned, turning reassuringly towards me.

'Quite a lot it doesn't expect, does it, sir?' the sharp-faced one put in. 'Or we'd hardly be troubling the lady in the middle of the night.'

'Shadows, my dear, awkward ones,' Publius began sighing and explaining, as I led him away, having told the other two that Gemma would get a servant to bring them something warm to drink ('women and wine,' I heard the dark man saying to his companion with slow ennunciation of each syllable. 'If it's mulled Falernian, don't touch it.')

'A bad year for aediles,' Publius went on confidentially. 'And this one's commoner than most. On top of which I've been landed with that young Gaul. He's training for some

3

post in Marseilles, or somewhere, and is meant to be seeing how we run things in the capital. Now this has to happen.'

'Do sit down,' I said. 'Some of the stools are not as uncomfortable as they look. You must forgive the primitive appearance of this room, but—'

'Forgive it? I approve of it, honour it, my dear Julia. It recalls the plain, simple ways of our ancestors. It is a lesson in how we ought all to live.'

'Would it spoil the lesson if I offered you a glass of wine? I know the room suggests nothing but cold water in an earthenware beaker. We have that too, if you'd prefer it.'

'Well, in the circumstances . . . a thimbleful – no more – of wine. To calm the nerves.'

'You won't mind Samian? It just happens to be at hand.'

'Delicious, delicious. Ah, it's good to see you, my dear.' He leant back on the rustic stool and almost overbalanced, spilling some of his wine. 'Now, to this most deplorable affair, which is bound to come, I fear, as a great shock to you. Of course you know whom I mean by Pontilla Pilata? Widely respected, I'm sure, and religious and sadly widowed, though still quite young. One of our leaders in piety and good works – and extremely well-viewed up on the Palatine. Quite an honorary Vestal, if I may put it like that.'

'I hardly know her, except by reputation.'

'Nothing could be more unfortunate than the Emperor's absence. To think of him away fighting the Barbarians at this moment while here in Rome. . . . Oh, altogether it's a disaster.'

'Unless there's a time difference, I suppose it'll be too dark by now for much fighting in Dacia.'

'The fact is,' he went on, ignoring my remark; 'Pontilla Pilata has died – quite suddenly. Of that I am afraid there can be no doubt.'

'I'm sorry.'

'Her body has been discovered. It was not by any means a normal death. Violence had been used. In brief, she appears to have been murdered. Murdered. She was found strangled with one of her own scarves – a crocus-coloured one of which they tell me she was particularly fond.'

'Perhaps I'll join you in the wine.' I got up. 'Would you care for another thimbleful?'

'Well . . . if you yourself are partaking. But these glasses are really larger than I would quite designate as–'

'We call them Vesta's thimbles.'

'Most charming and apt. Or, at least, diverting. We must not assume the goddess's fingers. . . . Ah, my dear Julia, how good life seems within these walls. A haven of peace and calm you have created, with a consciousness of sacred duties done and some modest relaxation as reward at the close of day. Do you have this Samian specially shipped?'

I forgot to answer that it had been an unexpected gift from the Empress – 'the dear Empress' was the form in Palatine circles.

It was not easy settling on my own rough-hewn backless stool. I could have done with some support, physical as much as emotional. Although it was true I scarcely knew Pontilla Pilata, I still felt a sense of shock. Violent crime was nowadays rare, apart from the odd tavern brawl. It was a long time since the murder of any patrician.

'And the murder of a woman,' Publius boomed out with unusual matching of my thoughts. 'Of, I should say, a lady, makes this case the more horrifying. I recall no precedent for it. It raises the very greatest problems not only of public morale but of – of, er – procedure. Although I have arrested all her household slaves – the least I could do – I may not have apprehended the murderer. But he must be caught. Rome requires it.'

'I'm sorry,' I said slowly. 'I suppose you thought we had her will here. We haven't. If she made one, she didn't deposit it with us. I can't help.'

I waited for him to get up, fixing my eye on his large foot, wrapped in a gilded-leather boot, with one horny toe-nail protruding from it. The firm senatorial façade seemed dissolving in a mixture of intimacy and uncertainty. I hoped he would leave before it melted further. I preferred Publius official and in control to the private man whose hand sooner or later sought my knee, while he declared we ought to be closer since we were twin pillars of the state.

'I'm not a proper pillar,' I had said on an earlier occasion, shifting his heavy hand. 'At best only a caryatid.'

'Let me take the weight, my dear Julia, by all means. Yours the role of decorative support – yes, I assure you, I intend the idea to have more personal application, without creating anything that could give rise to scandal. Simply, in society's eyes, we would function as twins.'

'Romulus and Remus were twins. And look what happened to Remus.'

'The analogy, my dear, is poorly chosen. What do we know of Remus, to begin with? Nothing, except he was obviously a person of jealous, unpleasant temper. He made fun of his brother's plans—'

'Exactly.'

'Made fun of them, as I say, and suffered the consequences.'

'Romulus, I suppose, was the first Italian murderer.'

That fragment of conversation floated back into my mind as Publius sat on. Then he had frowningly halted our exchange, removing the hem of his toga, metaphorically speaking, from the unsavoury aspect of the topic, having reminded me that the mother of Romulus and Remus was a Vestal Virgin.

'I prefer,' I had explained, 'not to let today's Vestals dwell on the fact. They're nice girls, if rather dim, and I don't want to encourage even a phantom pregnancy. Still less would I suggest that a wet-nurse service is always available from wolves.'

This evening it was Publius who was talking of murder, and not as something in the near-mythical past. I listened, half against my will, while he seemed determined to describe in detail the circumstances. It was an aged workman who had only that afternoon come across the body of Pontilla Pilata, lying in her family tomb on the Appian Way. At her request he was checking some cracked masonry; he had intended to do so some days earlier but other tasks intervened and he had almost forgotten about it. Afraid he would be punished, he had hurried out to the tomb.

On the threshold, not far from the shelf that held the vases of her ancestors' ashes, she was lying strangled, elegantly dressed, her ear-rings and necklace untampered with.

'She had some lovely jewellery, you know,' Publius said. 'Lovely pieces – several of Eastern workmanship brought back by her grandfather. And there's piety even in the sad circumstances. She must have gone out for the anniversary of some family death – may have meant to make a vigil, because there was food in the room.'

6

'Had any been eaten?' I asked, interested in spite of increasing tiredness and my wish for Publius to leave.

'That I have not ascertained,' he said, in a tone implying the irrelevance of the question. 'But I had the workman taken into custody at once. He's a doddering old fool and probably also useless as a mason. Still, I am bound to say he appears most unlikely to have committed the crime – awkward though it is not to settle matters so conveniently. If only he'd robbed the body, I should have had no hesitation in prosecuting him. As it is . . .'

The discomfort of the stool must soon make him get up, I hoped, as I ostentatiously re-arranged my dress and came as near fidgeting as I decently could. But before the silence could accumulate meaningly, he had begun again.

'If it was a political crime, I should to some extent feel happier.'

'Political?' I said, after a pause, annoyed with myself for speaking at all.

'Revenge by that sect whose ringleader was dealt with by her grandfather when he was procurator, wherever it was exactly. They're still active, you know, in an underground way and probably have long memories. It wouldn't altogether surprise me.'

'I wonder.'

'My dear, I'm glad to hear it. This is a case involving a woman after all, where I feel a woman's aid could be invaluable. An investigation in your hands – with your discreet access to people. . . . It would have my full official support, and of course you could delegate the – er, shall I call it mule work? I'd second some capable fellow for that. There's that young Gaul, as a matter of fact. It might be a fine opportunity for him to see exactly how Roman justice works. Or would a lady assistant be more suitable?'

'Thank you, Publius.' I got up with finality. 'You honour me, but I'm simply not qualified for the task. I am not an inquisitor and anyway I shouldn't know where to begin. If you care to consult me as your enquiries proceed, that's different. But it's not for me to take on such a case.'

'A woman's intuition . . .' he said wistfully, without moving.

7

'Is a convenient piece of male legend, a kind way of saying we can't think.'

'Your duty to the state . . .' he said sternly.

'Requires me to preside over this household and the temple.'

'Julia, I appeal to you.'

'No,' I said.

Of the two of us I seemed – I was displeased to note – the more perturbed. As he boomed on, begging me to reconsider, to reflect, the verbs bounced like unwelcome hail on the weak surface of my determination. I tried to let my mind drift away, go cruising to Carthage, even while I kept reiterating aloud phrases about hearth and Rome.

I was on the point of yielding to Publius – until he came close and put his arms around me. Under the thin robes, faintly redolent of now stale scent, the block of his body was heavy and shockingly palpable: harder than lard, I felt, yet greasy. Only too vividly could I sense – virtually see – it, as though heat was dissolving the fabric and soon his bristly, porcine flesh in its full intimacy would be bared before me.

'My dear Julia.' It had become a whisper, with his pursed lips snouting wetly at my ear like some too-large, over-affectionate animal. I could hardly hear the words, only intermittent nuzzling sounds: 'Investigating together . . . every confidence . . . delightful proximity. . . .'

'Your duty,' I started to say.

'Say ours,' he breathed.

'Your wife.'

'Unusual. Even unexpected.' He drew back his head and smiled at me. 'But with the Emperor's permission, it could be arranged, I am sure. It would make me very happy, my dear.'

'Don't be absurd, Publius. I meant you ought to remember you have a wife.'

He nodded unenthusiastically. 'In Naples at present, but a divorce could easily be arranged. No scandal need arise. Indeed, the possibility has often, I am bound to say, occurred to me, but out of laziness I have taken no steps. You give me an incentive.'

'No, Publius. I give you nothing.'

'Worse.' He looked sulky, dangerously so, with nothing

now of playfulness about his heavy, lowering features: a boar had replaced the sucking-pig. 'You leave me with a problem, and with a strong sense of disappointment, Julia. I shall say no more – except this. No one doubts your ability as Virgo Vestalis Maxima, and the Vestals of today are a tribute to you. But is this simple, blameless life – excellent example though it be – all you want? What I offer you is the opportunity of . . . of a fuller existence, richer in many ways. You spoke of the hearth, but with the right partner, my dear, there could also be the joys of the home. There is still time for that, for both of us.'

'I'm confused,' I said. 'I thought you came to propose that I investigate a death. It seems to have become a rather different proposition. It's very kind, of course, but–'

'The investigation will proceed and, I have no doubt, speedily terminate with justice done. You need not concern yourself further about it. I quite understand your reluctance *there*. The other matter into which I was led deserves perhaps greater reflection than you have yet given it. You do realise I am prepared to make you my wife? Assuming the Emperor's permission, I should add.'

I wanted to look anywhere but at him, though the room provided little distraction. However calmly I responded, I felt as shaken as if he had physically assaulted me, as vulnerable as the glass flask on the wooden table beside us. His incursion into the house and his attempt to enter my life could be dealt with; he too might regret both by the following morning. More painful and disturbing was the effect of his resentful questioning – far more so than he would ever guess.

The ostentatious austerity of the room seemed to mock me. For a moment I even had the extraordinary sensation of being sealed within it, condemned to linger there for the brief remainder of my life, accompanied by one last ironic luxury in the shape of the Samian.

'You will reflect on what I have said?' Publius asked anxiously, moving closer to me.

'Certainly.'

'I felt sure you would do no less, my dear Julia. I admit I may have taken you by surprise. Perhaps I've surprised myself, but I'm very happy to have done so. If Pontilla

Pilata had not died in sad, unexpected circumstances . . . who knows?'

'Publius.'

'My dear?'

'Don't go away,' I began, only to be interrupted by his murmuring tenderly. 'No, Publius, let me finish. Don't go away expecting anything. It isn't really possible for us to get married. Oh, I'm honoured by your proposal. I just don't want to discuss it − or you to leave expecting any response from me.

'Now, hadn't you better collect your subordinates? They must be rather curious about our prolonged talk.'

'Let them wait.'

'There's nothing to wait for.' As I said it I felt its terrible application. 'Nothing,' I repeated sadly, then was ashamed at the emotion I was betraying.

'Have you ever been to Carthage, Publius?'

'To Carthage?'

'Yes, Dido's capital, where−'

'I am fully aware of Carthage and its history, though I have not in fact visited it. I cannot say I ever thought of going there. Still less would I consider it after the vulgar campaign of advertising which broke out all over Rome this morning. But forgive me. Such trivia are not for your ears, my dear.'

I ought to have been able to smile, at least when I reached my own room after his departure.

'Gemma,' I said, more curtly than I quite meant to. It quenched her incipient gaiety and eagerness to talk while she helped me to get ready for bed. 'Please remove that piece of disgusting rag and see that it's burnt − at once.'

II

In the darkness I lay too disturbed to sleep.

The silence of the room, and the household beyond, had lost its usual power to soothe, though I knew there stood close at hand the familiar few objects, friendly presences, that constituted my possessions: the carved lamp, a statuette of Good Fortune which had been my father's, the ritual vessels of earthenware that tradition required the Chief Vestal to use (even while I at least preferred to use silver).

I did not mean to think again of Celeriter Tours and its beguiling, almost flaunting phrases about Africa's fabled hospitality and the delights of underwater swimming and trips out to the so-called Lovers' Cave, the very spot where Dido and Aeneas had consummated their passion in a storm. How can anyone possibly know, I wondered. It was so long ago.

And instead of thinking about Publius and his visit, I found I was thinking about my own past. That too seemed long ago and buried.

Today, under the Emperor Trajan, we were enjoying a peaceful, settled regime. Frugality and decorum were the imperial preferences. Some people unkindly described the court as being as deadly as that of Dis, but its respectability provided an example for all Rome.

When my turn came to be Chief Vestal, I had chosen not to occupy the comfortable and convenient quarters of my predecessors – for several reasons. The apartments I had, with their plain, ilex-green walls, were smaller and more austere. I made few alterations, and only after I moved in did I discover an outer doorway leading from a storeroom nearby, piled with discarded furniture. I left the door blocked with a beam. In today's peaceful city nothing was less probable than a break-in, even supposing anyone noticed, from the exterior, the modest entrance well-concealed in a blind alley.

Plenty of girls sought to serve Vesta. The round of pseudo-household tasks happily absorbed them, and routine was broken for them by preparations for religious festivals. I need never fear a scandal of the sacred fire going out through the inattention of these Vestals. My task seemed rather to restrain a devotion that fed the flame so generously that there was danger of a conflagration.

'Our duties,' I had had to murmur, 'exclude fuelling a whole hypocaust system for the city. Nor is there any reason to sit up late at night grinding ears of corn in the dormitory – of all places. The goddess does not expect it, and we certainly do not want it.'

Indeed, the nearest we had come to an intruder might, I thought, well have been caused by such unhygienic zeal.

Once, one morning, unaccustomed shrieks from the dormitory woke me unpleasantly, and proved to come from the discovery in the communal water-jar of a frisky mouse. Otherwise, the placid tenor of our lives echoed that of the city outside and the state itself. If any coupling took place within our walls, it was no more than that of two sandals, playfully tied together and left for the owner to fumble for under her bed.

Once I too had been as innocent – even, perhaps, more so. A motherless child, I had early enjoyed the sensation of ruling in my father's household.

'A little Empress,' he liked to call me, but I was not fated to be an Emperor's bride. Marriage was a yoke I knew from the first I was too independent to tolerate. Vowed to Vesta, I saw myself as paradoxically more free. There were the privileges not otherwise given to a woman in Rome.

I should never forget the first occasion I had passed, dressed in white, carried in my white litter, through the crowded Forum. It had been hard to restrain the childish glee I felt at the people falling back at my approach. And it was crowned by the happy chance of an encounter, hoped-for even while I impassively reclined on the cushions, with a high-ranking magistrate, whose lictors immediately lowered their fasces in respect. All that was lacking that bright April morning was my meeting a criminal on the way to execution. Firmly assured of a Vestal's unique status, I should have exercised my right to have him pardoned.

Today I would be less eager and less confident. My hopes are, rather, to pass unperceived. I count myself lucky never to have met a criminal in that public way, never to have had the dilemma over whether to exercise that right. As for respect, how could I have guessed how stultifying it becomes? Slowly, it robs one of any sense of being an individual, thinking, feeling – even existing. Sometimes I see myself as another, much more hopeless Andromeda exposed, chained to a rock of my own choosing, and unable to take advantage of any Perseus who might happen to fly by.

What an irony that some of my oppression comes from being ringed by such docile, contented, perhaps truly religious Vestals as serve the goddess today. Increasingly I wonder if I can match their instinctive estimate of me. And perhaps their effortless obedience is now as shocking to me as were once the outlook and practices I slowly discovered in the community that I joined.

Lonely then, an over-solemn if not priggish girl, barely past puberty, I was ready to respect the stately, aged (as she seemed) presiding figure of Cornelia, Virgo Vestalis Maxima. I was even more ready to admire and be friendly with the Vestals nearer my own age.

The liveliest were the two Oculata sisters. The younger, the prettier, was about sixteen. Everyone laughed at the stories they told, and I too laughed dutifully as they rolled their dark eyes and vied in anecdotes I often failed to follow.

'Try having a lictor in a litter,' the younger declared. 'Just try. So when he thanked me, I said, "It's my privilege – I really mean it." What's so funny about that, young Julia? I'd advise you to learn the difference between your litter and your lictor, and here's one tip. Litter's feminine.'

I expect my smile was tremulous, because she quickly dismissed me – 'banishment to Tomi,' it was called – to the far cold end of the supper-room.

I should never forget the Oculata sisters, nor Varonilla, the Vestal who had the bed next to mine, a plump, pale, self-satisfied girl who enjoyed bossing me.

'Oh, you didn't,' I said horrified, when early one morning she told me that overnight she had let the sacred fire go out. 'It's our job.'

'Yes, dear, but I can think of better jobs,' she replied. 'As a matter of fact I was enjoying one when it happened.'

'What do you mean?'

'Oh, you're too young to grasp it. Or too good to be here, wasting opportunities another girl would be really glad of. We're above suspicion – *and* it's a criminal offence to touch us. Ha, ha.'

'I know. It's Lex–'

'Never mind the lex, dear. Ye gods, you're dim, Julia, aren't you? I suppose your idea of a hot night is sitting there fanning the sacred flame with your skirt?'

'But, Varonilla, seriously, if the fire goes out, the city's fate–'

'You goose. Even you can't believe Rome runs on a couple of sticks of firewood, in this day and age.'

'It's the felix arbor,' I said. 'The Pontifex Maximus himself has to come and specially re-kindle it with two pieces of that. Oh, and Varonilla, the punishment is awful, if you're found out. It's scourging – by him.'

'I expect he'd love the chance. But he's not getting it from me, I can tell you. Not to worry, dear. These things happen. Rome wasn't burnt in a day. Hey, isn't that good?'

We were sitting on our beds in the dormitory, I staring at her while she smiled provocatively and pleated and re-pleated the folds of her dress.

'But–' I stammered.

Even if somewhat casually, the other girls and women often made a point, especially in the evenings, of remarking when they were off to the temple: time, as they put it, to see the fire got a blessed poke. More than once I'd been told I need not trouble to take my turn in going along the underground passage that led from our house to the temple precincts: instead, I could do an early morning duty.

'No reason to bother old mother Cornelia,' the younger Oculata sister had said, with a wink, the first time it occurred. 'I happen to know she's discussing Vestal affairs with a new flamen.'

'Wake up,' Varonilla said, as I went on vacantly staring. 'Or, anyway, grow up. You ought to have twigged most of the lingua sacra by now – even you. It's not "go to the lavatory", is it?'

'Oh, no,' I said earnestly. 'It's "see the goddess about an offering".'

'And the curse?'

'On the hearth.'

'Well, then. . . . Look, I can't sit here all day gossiping with you. In fact, I must dash and see the goddess. You'll learn some day.'

I had indeed learnt, eventually. Rome, too, was to learn.

14

After a year or two Cornelia assigned me a pontiff for initiation. I shall never know if she foresaw, intended or at least suspected what would happen. Chastely aloof and faintly smiling, she had announced that it was time I entered the inmost sanctum of the temple and was permitted to handle the mysterious precious relics there. 'You are no longer a child.' It was the phrase she had used once before when, as ever aloof yet grave, she had informed me of my father's sudden death from apoplexy.

The pontiff was squat and balding, dark-skinned but made darker in the face by heavy, permanent stubble. I felt it must be ploughing my own face bloody as he forced his against mine — it was the second or third step in my initiation — wrestling briefly before his rape succeeded. I had not even struggled much: inert, sore, resigned.

I told no one and I went, indifferently, to my next session with him. I had settled nothing with myself, but I found him subdued, trembling so badly that I thought he would drop the sealed clay vase — 'most sacred single object in Rome,' he said hoarsely — that reputedly held the teat of the wolf that had suckled Romulus.

How light it weighed, I thought: perhaps it was actually empty, though of course the piece of skin must by now be dried and shrivelled, if not mere powder. Solemnly I handed it back, and he made a great show of avoiding any contact of our fingers.

'With regard to the making of Vesta's cake,' he began.

'Mola salsa,' I said knowingly.

'The sacrificial cake is composed—'

He stopped, sweating profusely.

I did not then know that on that very morning some ex-lover of Cornelia's, angry at her dismissing him, had denounced her before the Emperor, the never-deified Diocletian. An investigation was already under way, despite Cornelia's confession of her own guilt in an attempt to prevent exactly that. The whole scandal of the household was revealed.

I never saw her again. We were not told her fate, but everyone recalled that the traditional punishment was to be buried alive; and a ritual existed for it. The utter silence of the house was horrible enough. Down the dormitory the narrow beds stood like empty coffins, and my eye glanced across not so much at what had been Varonilla's but to where the younger Oculata girl had sprawled and laughed. The few of us remaining heard the whispered report of the Emperor's special grace for the two sisters: that they might choose the form of their own death.

It was the younger who had cried out to be stifled by roses. Although it was autumn, the Emperor had sent to Paestum for the largest, late-blooming flowers, the thick petals of which served to smother her. And over the bier-like stillness of her bed, I went on seeming to see pink petals shaken and falling.

To her, though no doubt she would have laughed, I might have confided my experience in the temple. Now, it was impossible. No one thought me worth either interrogation or suspicion. But when there arrived a sour, elderly woman, hastily installed in Cornelia's place, having previously been a priestess at the temple of Vesta in Milan, I sought her guidance over the progress of my initiation.

'Rather too gifted for you, is he?' she said sharply. 'Or is it you who's slow on the uptake?'

'The latter, I'm afraid. The pontiff has been most kind, of course, but I fear he finds me very dim.'

'All right, my girl. I'll speak to him myself.'

Two days later she told me the pontiff agreed. I would benefit from a different initiator. He had spoken approvingly of my discretion; he praised my sense of vocation and simple faith.

'Not been too much of that around here,' she said grimly. 'So let's see you keep it up.'

III

After the climb, the crowds and the noise, the hush achieved at the Palatine was always impressive. As those tall ivory doors closed silently behind me and a major-domo, somehow

16

set in motion at the same moment, approached slowly along the corridor, I felt soothed by the familiar ritual and yet intrigued by the summons that had brought me there.

It had been a surprise to find the Empress's tablets intimating the wish for, without exactly requiring, my presence on the morning after the visit of Publius. When the Emperor was away from Rome she saw few people apart from close friends, and I was not one of those. Although we often enough met officially and probably felt much of the respect we each took care to display towards the other, we found little in common when alone together. Perhaps neither of us could quite ignore the whisper that we ought to change places. No doubt she thought me too imperious for my role; and I certainly was puzzled by such resolute, retired domesticity and economy practised from the throne. Weaving and plain cooking – sometimes for the imperial circle – occupied the Empress possibly in place of the children she had never had. Her gifts of squares of woven, woollen material were, I knew, greatly esteemed by those so favoured, as was her dish of beans cooked to a recipe that avoided flatulence.

Smooth as ivory himself, well-jointed but scarcely animated, the aged major-domo bowed before me (Marcus was all I could recover of his name) and spoke in the recognized oblique style that characterised the palace staff close to the Imperial couple.

'It will be greatly appreciated,' he murmured, indicating I should precede him down the corridor, the walls of which were painted with simulated lilac-coloured drapery, eye-deceiving by intention but patently unreal. At the end of it the Empress had recently arranged niches to exhibit gifts sent from the provinces. 'Gorgon Corner' it had been unkindly termed, and some of the cruder handicrafts, bearing such labels as 'made in Vectis', forced one to halt, if not exactly turn to stone.

A grey-haired, homely lady-in-waiting appeared beside a niche, almost as though the stall-owner of the basket-work and unglazed pottery piled within it. She smiled as she took adroit possession of me.

'Too cold for rain, I think, so it's a blessing really, isn't it? We do hope you had a good journey – not that it's far for

17

you to come. But the mornings are turning nippy, I find. Still, we mustn't complain. Your dear girls quite well?'

'Quite,' I said. 'And the dear Empress?'

'As well as can be expected.'

I must have looked rather astonished, for she added even more mournfully and emphatically, 'In the absence of the dear Emperor.'

'Of course.'

'Needlework has helped so much.' She gave me a brave glance, with chin uplifted. 'We have been so glad, especially as the days draw in early at this time of year.'

She stopped at a curtained doorway I recognized. It was impossible not to check oneself as presentable, mentally and physically, though most people liked to pretend otherwise. As I paused, thinking of what might lie ahead, recollections of the previous evening came back to me more clearly.

'I hope the Empress was not too distressed by. . . .' In the intense, almost attentive silence, I lowered my voice, conscious that such an enquiry verged on a breach of protocol.

'Looking forward so much to the warm spring weather,' Marcia broke in resolutely, pulling back the curtain with a single, swift, noiseless gesture. 'And the days drawing out again.'

The Empress was alone, not reclining but seated on a couch, holding some needlework that she placidly put aside as we entered.

'This is good of you, dearest Julia,' she said in her rather guttural voice. She half-embraced me as I bent before her and pointed to a facing couch.

It was always a shock to realize how short she was, and if not fat at least plump: in a homely, reassuring, oddly natural way, like a well-baked loaf planted in rough female form as an offering at some rural shrine. Her swarthy features were as impassive as ever and her minute dark eyes had their usual sly, Spanish look. It was hard not to wonder where the Emperor had found her, and what, in a vulgar phrase, he saw in her, but I was conscious also that she seemed aware of such thoughts and not unamused.

Barely a glance from her, without a gesture, had the lady-in-waiting retreating from the room.

'I don't,' she said after a pause, smiling at me, 'ask you to

18

admire my needlework. That would be a pretext were I talking to some other woman. Besides, though you might not be prepared to say so, I'm still rather clumsy.'

'Your Majesty finds it a consolation, I was glad to learn, in the Emperor's absence.'

'Not much of one, Julia, to be frank. Nothing could make up, you know, for the absence of my man. And Hadrian being away with him makes me feel lonelier.'

I murmured something sympathetic.

'But I didn't invite you here to moan at you. I always feel grateful for the speedy, sensible way you handled that matter of my new clothes. Do you remember?'

'There was nothing in it, ma'am.'

'Exactly. But there might have been. Can't you imagine the scandal, in Rome of all places? The Empress's new clothes – first they cost the earth, then they've disappeared and finally it's discovered they don't exist. I should have lost my reputation for being thrifty. And that I can't afford.

'Now, I need the benefit of your advice again. You heard of course about the death of Pontilla Pilata?'

'Indeed, ma'am, and I must offer you my condolences.'

'Julia,' she said. 'I hope you will offer me more. It's been sudden and shocking. But she's dead. What I want to know is how it happened. Will you help me?'

I longed to be allowed to move or at least for the distraction of a lady-in-waiting blundering in, perhaps with a tray of refreshments. Outside, unseen, was the teeming, daily life of Rome (a book in itself, I always thought) but we sat as though sculpted in total, silent decorum, facing each other in a proximity without real intimacy. Silence oozed over us as firmly as if it were volcanic lava, and I felt it oppressing me almost as palpably, so that soon I should be unable to move or speak. No doubt it outwardly looked as if our roles had become reversed: I the Empress, tall and distinctively dressed in flowing robes, and she a humble petitioner, in some nondescript darned garment, awaiting my decree. In reality I was the one dominated, with only the poor little freedom of declining, if I dared, to obey her. And she knew the pressure silence could impose.

'You're very kind to suggest it, ma'am, but I doubt if I could help,' I said at last. 'I scarcely knew the – er, deceased.

Our circles did not touch, and besides I understand the Praefectus Urbis himself has the matter fully in hand. Distressing though the circumstances indeed are, I feel sure there will be a speedy solution.'

'Do you really believe that, Julia?'

'Well, I very much hope so.'

I spoke in such a way as to make my words leave behind their own cloud of silence. It seemed settling effectively over us until the Empress rose, too abruptly for me to be on my feet first. Half-relieved, half-disappointed, I awaited my dismissal. If there had been an unspoken contest, I had not exactly lost. And I made a vow – to Vesta, it ought to have been, though consciously I addressed it less specifically – to live more contentedly within the restrictions of my existence. I saw myself astonishing Gemma by requiring her to reinstate the wretched ritual earthenware, and going on to achieve a purity and austerity that would become a legend of Rome's. The reign of the Emperor Trajan, I could almost read in future history, was further made remarkable by the example of one woman. Her uprightness, chastity and benevolence cast even on that most liberal age an agreeable light. . . .

'Did I what, ma'am?' I had awkwardly to ask, aware that the Empress must, perhaps more than once, have put a question to me.

'See this?' She was standing, holding out a sheet of the *Acta diurna* and gesturing me to take it. It looked at first glance much as usual: cyclone hits Sirmio (several feared drowned); soothsayers close to the Capitol prophesy military coup in Thrace; after a brisk opening, the denarius rallied. I just caught sight of something about a sow running amok on a Sabine farm before I turned to the back. At once official and trivial, the *Acta diurna* was unlikely to be allowed to alarm its Roman readers, but even so there was a hint of worry behind: 'Patrician lady's demise poses puzzle for Prefect.' Still, it was reassuring for citizens to read that the authorities were convinced that this was an isolated case: the idea of an Appian Way strangler was firmly scouted by a senatorial source last night.

'Yes.' The Empress's guttural voice came from close beside me. 'You see, it must be thought a possibility for us to have to deny it. Another such death and the scandal sheets will take it up, whatever the *Acta diurna* tries to do. In the absence of the Emperor, I have a grave responsibility, Julia. It is Rome, you realise, not the death of a friend of the family, that most concerns me. Does that sound heartless? I like to tell the truth and I want to find out the truth of this affair.'

'That could perhaps have its own dangers, ma'am, don't you feel?'

'You surprise me,' she said stiffly. 'It's the sort of phrase I expect from our esteemed Publius. Did it ever strike you, incidentally, that his fine head of hair might be a wig?'

I smiled, little though I felt like it. A few words about the imperial discernment would drop better from the lips of a lady-in-waiting, yet I was tempted to offer the tribute as I thought again of the physical unease Publius always caused me.

'But the murderer of Pontilla Pilata,' I said, rather assertively, 'accepting she was murdered, might come from any stratum of society. Discovering him could have a disruptive effect, could it not?'

'I'm prepared for that,' she answered grimly. 'I'm even prepared, Julia, to consider that she was murdered by a woman. Or at a woman's instigation.'

And so, I thought, it seemed a suitable task for me.

'Your majesty honours me by her confidence,' I said, 'and I am sorry to disappoint it. But I don't feel I can help. Indeed, I wouldn't know where to begin. In the case of your majesty's clothes, of course, it was easier. After all, that was not a public matter.'

'You would have my support no less on this occasion, Julia, and that of the Emperor, I assure you.'

'I am deeply honoured,' I began.

'But you decline? You leave me with some clumsy, stupid men, more afraid of scandal attaching to them than anxious for the truth? What a pity, my dear, that we have never been friends – just respectful rivals, I should say. Still, I understand, I hope. You look on it as my affair. Perhaps I ought to dress up as a man and conduct my own investigations.'

'I'm sure, ma'am, they would be conducted admirably.'

'Efficiently, at least. I should enjoy it, too. The dressing-up anyway. Has a Roman Empress ever done that before?'

'Not that I can recollect. I suppose Clodia of infamous memory may have done so. She certainly did everything else, if one believes Cicero. And her brother notoriously dressed up as a woman.'

She shrugged. 'Before yesterday I thought we had finished with all that – scandals, orgies, sudden deaths, the typical history of this city and its aristocracy. Well, I must not keep you any longer, Julia. You have listened to me, and for that I am grateful.'

'You are most kind, ma'am. And if on another occasion I can usefully listen–'

'No.' She said it unaggressively but firmly and finally, not trying to appear gracious. I had to admire her for that.

I backed away towards the draped doorway, to find I was almost colliding with the grey-haired lady-in-waiting who had burst in, robes agitated and the curtains set swaying.

'Your majesty,' she gasped.

'Yes, Marcia dear?'

'A message from the Prefect. Most urgent. Otherwise I should never have presumed. . . .'

Ignoring me, she fumbled for the tablet while making a confused obeisance and trying to gather her robes around her. The palace weather – like the weather convention – had, it seemed, abruptly broken. She virtually lay on the floor, glad of the rest, panting heavily, her hair dishevelled. I thought of her running down that long corridor, knocking protocol flying at every corner, as the Empress calmly cracked the seal and read.

'Good news, ma'am?' Marcia ventured. She had started to attend to her hair, and I realised from her tone that she knew something of the message. She was a messenger who might be distracted but did not expect to be punished.

'Very good,' the Empress said. 'Send back at once my thanks and congratulations to the Prefect.'

'Your majesty's warmest thanks, perhaps?' Marcia had got up, recovered, and was again bright, it appeared, with atmospheric observations.

There was a pause. I felt it, if only on behalf of the slowly congealing Marcia, growing cold, I suppose, where before she had been hot and excited.

'Shall we keep to the words of my message,' the Empress

stated rather than asked. 'If you will be so good as to have it conveyed to the Prefect.'

As soon as Marcia stumbled from the room, the Empress came up to me, her little eyes black as olives but far harder. No longer could I think of her as a squat, confortably-shaped loaf. Now she suggested a lump of iron, rounded, unanimated, yet oddly menacing.

'You hoped for a speedy solution, my dear Julia, and we have one.' Her voice was harsher than usual. 'Our good Publius tells me that all is over. The old workman has proved his guilt by committing suicide. We may consider the case closed.'

I stood there unmoving; inwardly I was agitated, almost trembling.

'It is closed,' she repeated. 'I troubled you unnecessarily. We shall be able to read the details in the *Acta diurna*. It is a triumph – of something. Of Roman behaviour, I suppose.'

'I don't believe it.' I forgot any of the due forms in my agitation. 'Do you?'

'The thanks of the Empress are being conveyed to the Prefect, and that will become public knowledge. Ought anyone to seek further? You yourself reminded me of possible – reverberations, should I call them? Very well. Now they will not arise.'

'But the truth? You, ma'am, spoke of that. Is it likely that that wretched old man strangled Pontilla Pilata, for no reason at all? Do we even know he really committed suicide? He could have been killed, conveniently, or forced into killing himself.'

'My dear,' she said, 'we know only what the Prefect has chosen to let us know. How could I order an investigation now the matter has been resolved to the general relief? It would hardly redound to the credit of the city, or of me. And what could I tell my man on his return? No, it is over, finished, done with.'

'And wrong,' I said angrily. She, I felt, had become the obstacle to justice.

'Ah, yes – probably. Perhaps if it had been in your hands, dearest Julia. Still, you saw further than I did when you declined.'

'Now I accept.'

23

'Too late.' She spoke sadly. 'I cannot forbid you yet I can hardly help you.'

'But, ma'am, if I should discover the truth, and it's very different?'

She reached out and gripped my wrist with her hard, wiry little fingers, made for something far tougher than needlework.

'The real criminal, do you mean? For him, her, high or low, young or old, punishment. Death. Yes, the Emperor will allow me that.'

'His majesty's notorious clemency,' I started to say, chilled by her sombre tone, but she shook her head impatiently, imperiously.

'Swear one thing, Julia. If you go forward – and I don't ask to know, should not know – you must give me the truth should you find it. I command it. Even if my own brother turns out to be the criminal.'

For no clear reason, I remained hesitant. Her implacability had the effect of shaking my resolve. She seemed, as she stood there, chaining me to her, to see further than I could and to take pleasure in a vision of death as much as truth.

'Well,' she said, releasing my wrist. 'I am waiting.'

'If, ma'am, by chance I should–'

'You swear to tell me? I ask no more. And I know an oath by you – of all people in Rome – will be sacred.'

'I swear,' I said solemnly, feeling suddenly the irrationality of my previous hesitation. There was a pause, and then she moved away.

'How far we have gone in hypothesis,' she said, quite lightly. 'Rome must be rejoicing, and so should we. An ugly case is closed, and it is time for us also to conclude. I am happy to have talked to you, Julia.'

No longer flustered, Marcia reappeared. I had often wondered if there was a Palatine device for summoning attendants by the pressure of a floor tile, perhaps vibrating some signal located outside the room. One never heard a bell ring or noticed the Emperor or Empress make any movement to have one escorted from their presence.

I was still faintly thinking about that as I got into my litter. But what seemed important was to reach the house again, and it was infuriating to be halted at the bottom of the hill,

24

while becoming conscious of a pervading stench in the chill air. Nothing should have halted us. I drew back the curtain, only too anxious to berate and even beat my bearers.

'The beasts, mum,' muttered one of the men behind me.

'The what?'

Then I saw the slow-moving line of huddled, chained animals being driven across our path – thousands of them, it appeared. And I remembered hearing that special consignments had been ordered in anticipation of the games to be held on the Emperor's triumphal return from Dacia. That it would be triumphal was not in doubt.

I was glad to drop the curtain on the sight, though that did nothing to exclude the rank smell. Perhaps it was the sheer number of heaving backs and bewildered swaying heads that oppressed me. Had the *Acta diurna* really spoken of the spectacle as likely to include the slaughter of as many as eleven thousand animals?

Immediately I reached the house, I sent for Gemma. The slight delay on the way back must have affected my temper, I realised, as I sat waiting for her and barely listening to a childishly round-faced Vestal who had followed me inside to ask respectfully about the detailed arrangements for the Lupercalia.

'It's months away,' I said impatiently.

'Still,' the girl bobbed a smiling curtsey at me, 'It's nice to be thinking well in advance and we do want it all to go well.'

When you've been involved in the Lupercalia for twenty-seven years, I might have begun, yet perhaps I didn't wish her eyes to grow as round as her face, in wonder or pity at the length of time.

'But not too well. The festival has its less decorous aspects, you must remember,' I said reprovingly. Young men running around with bloody foreheads and girded provocatively with such fragments of goatskin as they hadn't torn into strips for whipping nubile women. . . .It was a good thing that the Vestals traditionally retired before things got out of hand.

'You may retire,' I added aloud, seeing the girl still beaming at me.

'Could I just ask one thing? It's awful cheek, I know, but you had to shoot off to the Palatine this morning, didn't you? I wondered if you actually saw the Empress and how she is.

On her own, you know, in the Emperor's absence. She must feel awfully down in the mouth.'

'Valeria.' I had recovered her name. Her father was one of the most stupid Senators, though also one of the most loyal; he and his wife had created an imperial cult so unremitting that the Emperor tended to avoid them.

'The dear Empress,' I said, while Valeria nodded at each respectful syllable. 'The dear Empress, whom I saw, is as well as can be expected.'

'Oh, I'm so glad. What splendid news, and isn't she brave?' She paused on the threshold to give me a last, thrilling, artless smirk. 'They say she makes all her own clothes.'

Gemma's entrance saved me from any response. Once Valeria had left, I told her to sit down. She folded herself neatly onto a stool, without speaking, looking as wise and cheerful as a good-luck charm, and not much bigger.

'I've decided to investigate a – a death, Gemma,' I said slowly, watching to see if she understood, and wondering if I quite understood myself. Even my decision seemed made only now as I uttered it. 'It's going to be difficult and possibly dangerous. I don't know that anyone has done anything like this before, and I won't have much aid, anyway officially. I'm not even sure how to begin. Don't be alarmed. But I may need to ask you to help me – without getting involved, of course. Nobody else here – and few people outside – must know what I'm doing.'

'Doing it on your own, mum, are you?'

'Yes, I have to, now. You see, Gemma – no, the less you know the easier for you if anything should go wrong. It's not that I don't trust you.'

'Oh, yes,' she said thoughtfully. 'That you've got to do.'

'I'm sorry not to feel able to tell you more.'

'That's all right, mum. Perhaps there are things I can tell you.'

I laughed. It was the first time I had felt entirely relaxed since I had woken that morning. But I could see Gemma's cheerfulness vanished at my laughter.

'Gossip, in moderation, in a house of women like this, I've never objected to,' I said. 'Even your tales, Gemma, though I don't know where you pick them up.'

26

'Have I ever told you wrong?' she asked indignantly. 'Who told you first about the Carthage cruise campaign?'

'Well, you didn't tell me exactly what it was a campaign for, did you?'

She looked at me as if I had suddenly struck her – something that had never occurred.

'I can't read, mum,' she said reproachfully. 'But I can listen. And I pick things up quickly, so there. I could tell you plenty, if you'd pay attention.' She added some phrase I couldn't catch; once or twice I had noticed she used what must be dialect words or idioms, especially under stress.

'Pin your ears back,' she half-mumbled shyly, when I asked her to repeat it. 'It's what we say in Butunti when we want someone to listen carefully. I'm sorry. I didn't mean to use it to you, mum.'

'It's vivid, I grant. And supposing I pin them back for you, Gemma, what might I hear?'

'This is the Pontilla Pilata business, isn't it? Oh, that's easy. I heard those two fellows chatting over the wine I served – made it nice and hot for them I did, with it being such a cold night last night. Though why you want to get mixed up in that, I can't for the life of me grasp. Nasty goings-on, I'd call them.'

'A murder, and I very much fear it was a murder, is bound to be nasty,' I found myself continuing calmly, telling her what I had surely not intended to: what had happened at my meeting with the Empress.

'You see, Gemma,' I finished by saying in a kindly way, 'although I never met the lady myself, she was a close friend of the Empress and the Emperor, extremely pious and very widely respected. You could say she probably hadn't an enemy in the world.'

'Oh, I wouldn't say that, mum.'

'Why not?' I asked, smiling at her literal, sharp reaction.

'I know one she had – that's for certain.'

'You know one?'

I was too astonished to conceal my amazement. Gemma grinned at me from her stool.

'Know of, I should put it. Like to meet her, mum, would you? That's easy enough, and it could give us a handle, as

27

you might call it – a clue, sort of. I can't find the right word, but you take my meaning. Why don't we start there?'

'A clue,' I repeated thoughtfully.

'Oh, mum, I just called it that.'

'Was it a clue Ariadne gave Theseus to the labyrinth?'

'Not knowing, can't say,' Gemma replied tersely. 'She and he, were they? I expect she gave him more than that before they were done.'

IV

'Best wear a big cloak,' Gemma advised. 'It's quite near but you don't want to be spotted.'

'Spotted?'

'Seen,' she said impatiently. 'Anyone twigging who you are. Keep your hood up and leave any talking to me.'

'Gemma, I must know where we're going. Of course I realise you're trying to be helpful, but on that I insist. And how, anyway, is this connected with – well, with the case?'

'Tell you all as we go, mum.'

I ought, I felt, to demur, if only for dignity's sake, remembering who I was. Yet as I went on standing there, letting Gemma drape me in the folds of a coarse grey cloak, the sense of exactly who I was seemed receding from me, in no unpleasant way. Something comforting as well as enveloping was conveyed by the bulky, anonymous drapery – and something exciting too. I was another, much less sorrowful Demeter, going out into the world on a quest, not to seek a missing daughter but to solve a crime.

Yet when Gemma paused on the portico, staring up at the sky now as thunderously grey as my cloak, I also paused. This step – stepping off, more properly – would be significant, I felt certain. I had only to murmur that I had changed my mind. We could go inside again. The calm domestic tenor of

28

the house and temple would at once surround me; it even seemed murmuring as I stood hesitantly poised, lulling me to return and risk nothing.

'Let's make a dash for it,' Gemma said, plunging down the steps. 'It's going to start pissing down before long. We've got to get near the river, behind old Balbi's theatre, and it's not Rome at its poshest, mum, I may as well warn you.'

'Yes, of course,' I said kindly. 'After all, we don't live so luxuriously ourselves, do we?'

She looked to be smiling, I thought, as I hastened after her small, energetic figure which had already begun striding up the road.

At first I found it merely unusual to be walking in the urban, open air, conscious of slabs of smooth paving-stone under my feet. Hurrying to keep up with her, while managing my voluminous cloak, I was conscious too of the discrepancy in our respective heights, and the difficulty of hearing what she was starting to tell me of the old woman – 'must be nearly a hundred' – whom we were going to meet.

'Still got wonderful eyesight,' I just caught her saying. 'Comes from my part of the world, Butunti, and does really lovely needlework.'

'Butunti always sounds–' I began, but even I could not hear my own voice.

What I knew so well as the familiar buzz of the city's noise, sieved aurally through the curtains of a litter, was rising around us now in a way quite confusing enough, apart from the jostling and cries of tradespeople and the uneven, broken paving over which I stumbled. We had left the Forum and the streets I knew. My cloak dragged. I was bending lower, still muffled, straining to distinguish Gemma's brisk comments or exclamations until I must have appeared some bewildered ancient crone, unfitted for survival in this crowded environment.

'Step lively, auntie,' a shrill voice urged – surely not Gemma's?

In my anxiety I felt my foot slip on a disgusting dampness I did not pause to investigate. The vigiles, I recalled, were meant to be responsible for the state of the streets, recently described in the Senate, and so reported by the *Acta diurna*, as a credit to our enlightened civic authorities and so clean you might dine off them. Certainly I could detect enough offal littered about to give meaning to the claim – not that any Senator was likely to have penetrated to the narrow, smelly alley down which I was making my buffeted progress behind Gemma.

As I collided yet once more with a body, that of a solid, leather-clad workman who actually steadied himself by clutching me, I was tempted to throw off my cloak and reveal my identity. I could envisage the sudden stillness, the crowd pressing backwards, almost into the grubby walls, and a pathway magically cleared.

But I knew, even while I raised my head, prepared to annihilate impiety with a glance, that a pathway achieved by those means would lead nowhere, as far as my quest was concerned. I was living without authority – on, as it were, my wits. Here one did not command, still less assume, any privilege. To progress, one pushed and shoved, human being against human being; and with fresh vigour I dug my elbow into the nearest mass.

'Ooh.' It was a moan from the workman, an old man I now realised with shame, who was nursing his stomach and staggering against a piece of projecting gutter. 'Ooh, you nasty old cow. And I thought I'd hurt you. Felt sorry, I did.'

His gasping had turned into a coughing fit. I paused, unsure whether to expostulate or apologise. Two or three people had stopped, smirking hopefully, and a fat peasant woman, waddling by with a basket, called out something that sounded like a cheerful obscenity. My arm was grabbed – by Gemma, I noticed, with relief.

'Shut up, you old moaner,' she snapped at him, tugging me away. 'And look where you're going in future.'

'But, Gemma,' I whispered.

I half-turned back, reluctant to leave and yet uneasy under the stares that followed us. The workman had straightened up. He was stout and brawny and had got his hands placed firmly on his hips. Even as I saw he was recovered, he saw, perhaps misunderstood, the expression on my face. His own contorted abruptly – he's ill, after all, I thought – and from it there flew towards me a stream of spit.

'Come on,' Gemma said urgently.

Now she kept me beside her, and every so often I heard,

as we turned another corner and encountered fewer people, fragments of information which gradually calmed me. The old woman could scarcely be as old as a hundred, I decided, listening to Gemma say how popular and in demand she and her work were in certain female patrician circles. Pontilla Pilata it was who had taken her up – 'in a big way' – had her sewing shown-off at ladies' parties, encouraged her to come and go like a household pet. It sounded one of the typical acts that had given Pontilla Pilata her reputation. An exclusive group of high-born women who devoted their leisure to a harmless, indeed laudable and homely activity: the 'White Hen' set, they called themselves, and their favourite coop was Pontilla Pilata's house. It was almost a reproach to any other activity for Roman women, and the more praise-worthy in Pontilla Pilata since she was the youngest of the Hens, and easily the prettiest.

'Then–' Gemma stopped, gesturing to a cliff-like row of large tenement blocks ahead of us. 'Nearly there. Then, about six months ago, quite suddenly, she dropped the old lady. Just kicked her out, without more ado. The servants got orders to bar the doors against her, if you please, and one of them pushed her down the steps so roughly she bruised her thigh. Nobody upper-class wanted to have her work for them after that – all thanks to Lady Pontilla Poison-pot. And her thigh hasn't healed properly. No joke at her age, so I shouldn't think she'll have wept much when she heard about Lady P. getting hers, as you might say.'

'All the same, Gemma, there must have been some reason,' I said thoughtfully.

'That sort don't have reasons. Anyway, the old lady can't think of one. You can ask her yourself.'

'I shall. It's a nasty story, but it doesn't quite make sense. Perhaps she had been rude or disrespectful in some way. What surprises me is that it didn't harm Pontilla Pilata's reputation. After all, it's not how we behave nowadays in Rome.'

'Some do; some don't.' She halted. 'We're here, mum. I shouldn't speak, if I were you, as we go up.'

'Here?'

We were standing at the base of a tall, conical building of mouldering brown brick, pierced with holes that might have been for drainage, though the ones at ground level were occupied by crude stalls, round which an animated crowd of poor people jabbered and gesticulated. A smell of something rank, stale, decaying, seemed floating almost tangibly in the darkening, oppressive air. It was like entering a bath of dirty water, I thought with distaste, displeased by the vividness of the thought and feeling my skin start to shrink and contract. Yet nobody around appeared other than lively and feverishly occupied with their own affairs. Nobody bothered even to glance at us, as I clambered after Gemma through a ragged aperture and up steep, lop-sided stairs where the stench was stronger still, mingled with cooking smells.

Pitiable figures crouched there, ugly if not positively deformed and so scantily dressed that I felt I ought to avert my eyes from them. Yet, surprisingly, they too were busy, almost cheerful, uncaring as we stepped past them. They bent over pots of food or unrolled bundles, pausing occasionally to shriek at the children who shrieked back and hopped and chased each other up and down the precipitous, crumbling stone of the staircase.

As I toiled, strangely out of breath, behind Gemma, there broke at times from the anonymous folds of my grey cloak an incongruous wave of white-pleated dress, somehow suggestive of the fluting of a column. A great distance separated me from the white façades and colonnades of public Rome, though it lay quite close at hand. I thought of the Emperor fighting far away in Dacia, and how he would see these people of his only as a blurred mass of faces and raised arms when he returned in triumph.

To me they were hardly even a blur. Until now, if I thought at all, this Rome where I trod so uncertainly, in every way, had existed in terms merely of some pungent epigram I probably smiled over as too satiric. Perhaps I was nearer to Publius than I quite cared to realise; and almost with a sting of envy I could see the Empress at ease in this foetid, raucous atmosphere. She might indeed be one of these swarthy women spreading a patch of filthy blanket, cuffing a too ebullient child and handing out bowls of some steaming, yellowish, clotted substance. I could only resolve to ask Gemma later what it was.

She had stopped and was tapping at a plank of wood

serving as some sort of door or shutter when a wrinkled face peered out from a fissure in the wall beside me and a skinny hand beckoned us over.

'All on her own, poor thing.' The voice hissed at us accusingly. 'Nobody been near since it happened. Family, are you?'

'From the same part of the country,' Gemma answered, broadening her accent as she spoke. Under the scrutiny of the suspicious, glinting brown eyes in the face fixed like a grotesque mask in the masonry, I felt myself insufficiently rustic. I hunched up a little and tried to look at least fragile, even coughing slightly to convey frailty.

'About time somebody bothered. It's a disgrace, I'd say.' The old woman's lips pursed disapprovingly, while Gemma went back to her gentle, resolute tapping. 'Being left in that way, and at her age too.' Her fingers reached out suddenly and seized mine. 'You look nice, anyway. Somebody's mummy are you, dear?'

I stared back at her, unable to speak. From behind I could hear at last a noise of the plank being awkwardly moved, Gemma's voice and that of a girl talking in soft, urgent tones.

I pulled my arm from the restraining, bony hand, turning to look at the girl – child, really – who stood in the doorway, gazing mildly at me with unusual, pale blue eyes. Her very long fair hair was pale, and her skin seemed unnaturally white, but she was beautiful in some sad, statue-like way.

'This is Tibicina, mum,' Gemma said gently, as we moved inside, with Gemma holding the girl round the shoulder. 'The old lady's niece. She's just told me, I'm afraid.'

I looked about the bare room, hardly more than a cell with an aperture for a window. On the dusty floor was a discoloured mattress and beside it a stool on which rested a handsome, ivory double-flute.

'Told you?' I said, half-irritated by the lethargic girl who seemed to have infected Gemma with her lethargy. I stood at the opening, only now appreciating how high we had climbed as I saw the city spread out below in the thundery dusk. The Forum gleamed vaguely, and the mass of the Palatine hill rose darkly behind. I strained to see our temple, if not our house, but an abrupt growl of thunder made me draw back my head.

'She's dead, mum – the old lady. About a week ago,

33

Tibicina says. Sorry, mum, but there we are. Just went out like a light. No pain or anything. The best way to go.'

'No doubt.' My tone was dry. It was not the moment for sententiousness. My chief feeling was frustration at the journey, the effort, wasted. 'I'm very sorry,' I told the blankly staring girl, who seemed waiting for me to speak. 'It must have been sad for you.' Still she did not move. 'Your view,' I went on rather desperately, 'is very fine.'

'She's blind, mum,' Gemma said softly.

To feel annoyed she had not told me before (or had I failed to hear her as we hurried along?) was only an additional shame. I was not accustomed to the tang of humiliation I seemed positively to taste on my tongue. Even the very shabbiness of the room was a rebuke to me – never mind the girl herself, who yet failed to stir any instinctive pity: too cold, too self-contained, for that.

I moved away from the window, an additional instrument in my humiliation. Uselessly smiling, I spoke to the girl directly, forcing my voice to express what it was only natural to express in the circumstances.

'We could take care of you, my child.' Nothing should be easier than to catch the right tone. It was obviously my duty to remove her from the dust-heap of this tenement and protect her ivorine beauty that had been fashioned so unexpectedly there. She stood posed more statuette-like than statue, immobile and apparently unresponsive. There must have been the shock of grief, of course, and the bewilderment.

'We–' I began again.

'I don't need care,' she interrupted calmly. 'Thank you, madam. I am a musician.'

'In demand a lot, aren't you?' Gemma said. 'Lots of posh supper-parties and so on. It's a treat to hear her play, mum, it really is.'

'Now I am playing at the Blue Toga Club Baths.'

'Well.' Gemma giggled. 'You'll be safe enough there, anyway, if you know what I mean.' She held up for my inspection a strand of the girl's flaccid, yellow hair. 'Lovely, isn't it, mum? You don't find many girls with hair like that. Now, Tib dear, if there's nothing we can do for you, we'll be off.'

That seemed too crude, and I mimed that we ought at

least to send someone back with money, having none with us. Gemma firmly shook her head. Yet to leave the girl like that could not be right, even if it was something of a relief. Later, perhaps, I would send for her to play one evening. It was a pity, I reflected, that the Vestals tended to be so unmusical; it was hard to say why, but I suspected that an evening of flute-playing would leave them as unresponsive as Tibicina herself, even if it accompanied a hearty meal.

Still smiling, I approached the girl on my way out, nerving myself to give a reassuring touch to that pale, waxen skin. The room was now so dark it was not easy to distinguish where she stood.

'You wanted my aunt?' she said suddenly out of the penumbra, addressing me to my face with uncanny directness.

'We just wondered if she could help us a little,' Gemma answered for me. 'Don't you worry yourself about it, dear. It was one of my bright ideas. Not to give it another thought.'

'How,' the girl asked slowly, as if speech was not quite normal to her, 'could my aunt have helped this lady? Was it work she wished her to do?'

'Nothing like that – just tell us a bit about someone we're interested in. Now keep in touch, Tib, won't you? And watch it. Don't get too breathless playing the old flute.'

Gemma followed me out, both of us groping towards the staircase, where a feeble oil lamp flickered, almost more alarming in its wavering light and deep, shaggy troughs of shadow than would have been total darkness. There was another, louder rumble of thunder, and I found myself angrily echoing it at this useless, embarrassing visit.

'What person?'

Tibicina's voice, coming after the thunder, was oddly sibilant and haunting. It made me stop. Thus might an oracle begin its message, though from a human source I would hope for something less obfuscating and involved.

'The lady Pontilla Pilata,' I said formally, turning at the top of the stairs and feeling nearly as blind as the girl.

'She sent you? Is she still pursuing me? Tell her my aunt is dead and then she'll be glad. Now, I'm on my own. And I can no longer get a decent job. Isn't that enough?'

In the smoky dusk her voice rose and wavered like the wretched, guttering wisp of light that made her look so ghostly and even paler than before. She tottered forward impulsively, excited, where earlier she had been passive and graven.

She will trip and fall, I thought. And at that moment Gemma caught her.

'Listen, Tib, you've got it all wrong. Of course we're not here on her behalf. We wanted to know about her – that was all. Now calm down, please. This isn't like you.'

'Go and ask her what you want to know. Let her tell you. How kind she is, and so good and pure. And they say she is very lovely. Even my aunt said that was true.'

'You needn't be afraid,' I said. 'Pontilla Pilata cannot harm you – nor help us. She is dead.'

'Strangled,' Gemma put in impressively. 'So serves her right, doesn't it? Tit for tat, you might call it, from your point of view.'

'It was I she hated. She did what she did to my aunt to punish me. I never dared confess it before.' Suddenly she put her arms round Gemma's neck and burst into tears. 'Oh, Gemma, Gemma, my aunt died because of me. And I hadn't meant to offend. I said nothing, but somehow she knew. She knew I had heard something. She knew.'

Over the girl's shoulder, I briefly saw Gemma's face, sympathetic yet stirred, half nodding at me to speak. Then, from some draught of damp air perhaps, as the thunder rolled frighteningly close, the lamp expired.

'Tibicina.' I spoke solemnly. 'A poor aged workman happened to discover Pontilla Pilata's body. He was arrested on suspicion of murdering her, and has killed himself. He was innocent, I believe. I want to find who really did it.'

'I would have done it,' she cried. 'For my aunt's sake. Yes, I did it. You are right, lady, to come and ask me. A poor person did it – not an old man but a young girl. I am guilty. Poor people always are, aren't they?'

'Not always, by any means. But the offence that might interest me is yours in Pontilla Pilata's eyes. Tell us, please, what happened and what you heard that upset her so much.'

I was prepared for her silence but also to be stern. The dark and the discomfort no longer mattered. There was something she could tell me, however biased or trivial it was.

'Is she really dead?' she said at last.

'Really and truly,' said Gemma.

'Because my aunt talked of me, I suppose, she had me to play at some gatherings of ladies, and after that the servants got used to me. I was often left somewhere like a piece of furniture – even in her bedroom, once or twice. She hadn't been well, and she wanted music, they said.'

I listened intently to her voice, still quivering though much steadier, almost sinister-sounding as it came out of the darkness. It was fortunate for her that she could not have gone along the Appian Way and lain in wait for Pontilla Pilata, carrying no scarf but a dagger. Certainly her tone suggested no less deadly emotions, hard to relate to my image of the ivory-pale, listless creature who had confronted us on our arrival. I tried to recollect if I had ever seen Pontilla Pilata. Was she, too, fair-haired, but animated and charming, slightly ostentatious in her good works, rather humourless in her notable modesty and marked preference for a circumspect life with women older than herself? Amid the White Hens she must have somewhat consciously stalked, not strutting exactly, a mere chick and yet very much their leader.

I began to foresee visits odder than this one, though the locations would be more agreeable. I had to suppose afflicted friends, horrified at what had happened, though only too willing to talk about it. And I should be present to condole.

'The rooms each had different smells for me,' Tibicina was saying, 'though they all smelt of her. You knew she lived alone – I knew it, anyway. It was clearer than seeing it. The bedroom was lovely. It must have been sprinkled with rosewater, and once I touched the bed itself. It was like stroking a soft, warm animal – all fur and silk. When she wasn't well – she suffered from headaches, because of her thinking so much, they said – she just lay there, and sometimes I didn't play a note or speak.

'One hot afternoon, it was, she was lying and dozing. I heard someone approaching hurriedly and the curtains swishing, and then murmuring to her – over her, I think. They talked and laughed for a minute. And then I got so nervous I chinked my flute against the foot of the bed. She went rigid, I could tell. Suddenly she started babbling about dearest Sempronia and how delightfully unexpected this visit of hers was, and before I knew what I was doing she was dismissing me, ever so nicely, of course. It was just so as to have a chat with such an old friend. She even managed to get in that Sempronia had been abroad for ages and didn't know me – "little tiny Tibbie, my own personal Euterpe and quite a godsend." She couldn't stop chattering so long as I was in the room. But, godsend or not, she never had me back. Next time my aunt took some sewing there, they – well, Gemma can tell you. That's all.'

'But her friend? – Sempronia, I mean.'

'Never said a word to me – didn't get a chance, she saw to that. It would have been too risky. Oh, I knew. I'd heard the voice – and the footsteps. It was a man.'

'Well.' I meant to sound judicial, though momentarily I felt like sharing a giggle with Gemma and wished I could see her. But perhaps my expression was best concealed, though oddly I sensed that the girl was able somehow to detect it.

'A man in her bedroom. And she had that famous reputation for chastity. Not the first either, I'm sure of that.'

'Thank you for telling me what you have. I'm grateful – and I shan't forget,' I added concludingly, groping towards the first step down. 'Come along, Gemma.'

'It was a man,' Tibicina screamed out as we started gingerly descending. 'Don't you understand? Her famous friend Sempronia – perhaps he did it, killed her, when they were in bed together.' A last shriek came from her, almost lost in the rising, half-welcome noise of the families on the lower stairs, where lamps glared fitfully. 'I could smell it was a man!'

'Poor girl,' I said abstractedly when eventually we were outside the tenement.

'Yes, wasn't it awful for her, mum? And all that carrying-on in front of a girl like her. Disgusting, if you ask me, but only too typical of some people. Wanting to have it both ways.'

'Let's hurry back, Gemma,' I said, choosing not to make any comment. 'Before it rains.'

I had no energy to rally her on her sudden access of disapproval. I was not even quite sure I believed Tibicina's story, but Gemma and I certainly, perhaps inevitably, saw her differently.

'It's raining now, mum,' Gemma said.

Tomorrow, I decided, I would go openly to Pontilla Pilata's house and pay my respects as a mourner over her body; it

38

might be a convenient opportunity to speak to some of the servants. Until then I could only ponder the meeting with Tibicina. I ought to feel grateful to Gemma for that, but I kept wondering whether the dead aunt would not have been both calmer and more reliable. She had actually seen Pontilla Pilata, and not merely as the lifeless, tinted image I should find. Then, for a moment, I was tempted to wonder about the two deaths, though they seemed unrelated. Not even the rather twisted nature of Tibicina could have contrived in reality to harm a patrician woman protected by her servants. And those servants themselves I felt ready to dismiss from the case, before I met them. To kill their mistress, and leave her body to be discovered, seemed pointless as well as improbable.

But then, until I knew more about Pontilla Pilata herself, everything seemed improbable or extremely vague. That evening, alone after supper, I tried to think back to the case of the Empress's clothes, when at first the confusion had been no less great. Yet it had been contained within the palace, and part of the achievement lay in that. This time the crime was murder not theft (or supposed theft). This time I had the city to contend with – and more than the city, since I would have wished to visit the Pilatus tomb on the Appian Way, were it not for the law that forbade a Vestal leaving Rome.

Yet something told me I should succeed. If I had been superstitious I might have gone, late as it was, to consult one of the soothsayers; but their increasingly cloudy pronouncements were frequently compared nowadays to those of the unfortunate imperial expertus caeli whose nightly duty was to announce what weather would accompany the Emperor on the subsequent day. And I recollected that when the Empress had consulted soothsayers over the apparent disappearance of her clothes (before she called me in), it had been necessary to send out urgently to a butcher's shop for some entrails. By mistake, these were supplied as a made-up dish and, it was rumoured, were half-consumed before being scrutinised. Hence possibly the information garnered for the Empress that a spotted hind should seek no mate until an eagle alighted on the Esquiline – interpreted as meaning there was nothing to be done.

As I was intending to alight there myself – since it was where Pontilla Pilata had lived – and required no augury of the fact, it seemed a further reason to dispense with divination; and I could hardly hope to be directed by it to the correct hill. No convenient dream came to visit me, but at least I woke still confident. I had something serious to do: that marked the day as different from my usual day.

It showed even in my looks, I thought. To arrive at Pontilla Pilata's house fashionably distraught or dishevelled was the last thing I wished. Curiously, it was as though I anticipated positively meeting her, as I took up a mirror and surveyed my face and hair. Severity was there, it could not be denied. Yet it suited me – 'more your style,' as Gemma would put it – than too many smiles or too much jewellery. I tended to see Pontilla Pilata wreathed in both. She was, she must have looked, younger than I was. But I was not yet forty. And my hair was still flawlessly deep brown and my face almost too youthfully untouched by time or experience: a little blank, to a close critical gaze, and slightly chalky compared with the painted effect of most upper-class women.

Mine, however, had its own distinction, if only for that reason. And then those brown eyes, skilfully enlarged by imperceptible cosmetics, that I encountered in the mirror had an almost passionate intensity: the eyes of a priestess, above all, seeing further than the average person, I hoped, and able to quell or kindle by a glance.

Vesta herself could not ask for better embodiment, though deplorably little was known of her, and even the question of virginity in her case seemed by no means established. Few or no legends had accreted around her. Nothing was recorded of her repulsing a male – god or mortal – who attempted her chastity. Privately one might venture to suspect that she did not sufficiently appeal to them, too care-worn perhaps from constant toil at the original hearth. Diana was a goddess I felt I could better have understood, if I had now to make a choice. In place of the ritual mop, the firewood and the eternal association of ashes amid one's clinging garments, I would have seized a bow and, in something simple and short-skirted, shot like an arrow myself through the open air in pursuit of my quarry.

It was as Vesta that I glanced, not enthusiastically, at the rota lying on the dressing-table, submitted for the following month's temple duties: Valeria, Virgilia, Virginia. . . . They seemed equally interchangeable as girls as well as in their duties. Valeria's eyes bulged more than most, and even dignified full-dress failed to give her the repose essential to our status. But she was, like the others, a good girl – if not a particularly attractive one.

I lifted the rota with a pair of eyebrow tweezers and laid it aside.

'The carriage is here, mum,' Gemma said, coming in rather soberly. She saw the occasion as a formal one, perhaps rightly. I should need all my authority, I guessed, before the morning was over.

'You look good,' she added approvingly.

'Good? I'm not sure that's how I feel.' Or how I am, I might have said.

'That's right,' she said, mishearing. 'Are you taking an extra veil, mum, in case it's chilly?'

'No, Gemma. I'm going to be spartan.'

'If you say so.'

Even half-hidden under the branches of mourning ever-green, the Pontilla Pilata house looked to be large – larger than one might have expected a widow to live in. That reminded me that I knew little or nothing of her husband or how he died. She appeared to have been settled as a widow for many years: 'devoted to his memory', I should probably be told, and perhaps from his death dated her reputation for piety and good works.

On the steps of the house mourners and servants were congregated, despite the chill weather, and I was surprised to see a carriage waiting there. As I alighted from mine, there was an abrupt movement on the steps. The servants roughly pushed at the mourners to create a space, and a major-domo, holding a wreathed wand, began to descend towards me.

It was gratifying to be received so correctly, and again I had the sensation, stronger now than before, that within Pontilla Pilata would be waiting to greet me. What I was not prepared for was the sudden focus of the mourners on a tall, heavily muffled figure reeling almost drunkenly behind the major-domo and at whose emergence I found two dour, black-clad servants linked hands to press even me back. Before I could protest, the figure staggered past, sobbing audibly, and was helped into the other carriage.

'The Empress's brother,' I heard respectful whispers rise around me, while from under their hoods the considerable crowd watched the slow, creaking departure of the carriage as if it carried the corpse itself.

'Came back specially from Spain,' a voice muttered beside me in tones of awe. That would indeed be an achievement, I thought, since the news could hardly have arrived there yet. And was it really the brother of the Empress I had just seen? It must have been a member of the imperial family, it was true, since only they apart from ourselves were allowed to use a carriage in the city.

The Empress's brother was indeed tall. He was seldom seen or spoken of in Rome, since the Emperor strongly disapproved of him. His was a reputation for compulsive womanising of a kind now rarely practised. But only now did it occur to me, as I went forward alone with a stateliness I meant to contrast with the demeanour we had previously witnessed, that his name was Sempronius.

V

'Lord Sempronius,' the major-domo said, masticating each syllable unctuously. 'Representing of course the imperial family in the absence of His Majesty abroad. *Her* Majesty is prostrate, as your ladyship may be aware, and is seeing no one.' He sniffed. 'Quite overcome, Lord Sempronius was. We have been greatly honoured in our grief. If you would kindly step this way, madam. Our beloved mistress's remains are in the atrium.'

'I suppose Lord Sempronius felt it all the more if he knew your mistress well.'

'Never crossed this threshold before. No man ever did. It

42

was our mistress's proudest boast.' He looked rather pitying at me and then sniffed again. 'I thought that was widely known, madam.'

'Her high reputation, naturally . . .' I murmured. 'Though if she ever needed a doctor or a lawyer–. Even members of her family might find it awkward. After all, you yourself. . . .'

'I spoke of guests.'

His narrow, yellow face had sharpened even further. It was almost like squeezing a lemon, but I was doing it too obviously, or he was surprisingly quick to sense any probing.

'She was greatly respected,' I said. 'I share the shock felt in Rome.'

'Been with her twenty years or more, me and my wife.' He sounded somewhat appeased, though he continued to eye me closely while he ran his hand up and down the stiff, dry-seeming foliage of his wand, causing an unpleasant whistling noise. He too was stiff and withered – a stick, but tall and faintly malign. He was not even very old, I saw, as I intentionally moved on, almost brushing him from my path.

With a deep if guilty bow, he recovered and twisted himself ahead of me, walking lugubriously at a pace I was compelled to keep.

There on a bier in the atrium lay propped the body of Pontilla Pilata, heavily veiled in dawn-coloured draperies, giving an oddly headless impression until I realised that the waxen bust placed upright at the far end was of her. Its over-vivid, glassy animation was a horrible contrast to the bundle over which it presided. Reddish blonde hair rose in tiers around a pretty, slightly pouting face, youthful-looking, appealing, I suppose, and yet somehow silly. I had to remember this was not the real woman, only an image.

'The likeness,' I began softly, after allowing a long, ritual-istic pause.

Whatever her silliness, and whatever the truth about her private behaviour, she had until recently been alive – more living, maybe, than I was myself. It was curious to reflect that that living woman would have been unlikely to stir my sympathy, and yet this swathed mound of delicately-tinted silk draperies had some power to affect me.

The major-domo's scrutiny suggested he had hoped for tears, but I intended to offer the greater tribute of gravity.

'Startling is it not? Nobody in the household, I can assure you, madam, has failed to weep on seeing it – even recently acquired slaves. Quite upsetting. The image of our beloved mistress as we knew her – as we last saw her alive. Not, you understand, as she was brought back here after the outrage. Oh, no.'

'Quite. You and your wife in particular will obviously have suffered a lot.'

He nodded complacently.

'It must have been a terrible blow for you both.'

'It is, madam,' he corrected. 'But being manumitted, we feel our position – our duty, you might call it, to protect the house and keep everything properly in order, just as when our mistress was alive, despite our sorrow. That is what she would have wished.'

'Most exemplary,' I said.

The heavy smell of incense, mingled with a resinous scent perhaps partly from the corpse and partly from the heaped-up evergreens, was growing oppressive. Beyond the curtained atrium the house lay unnaturally hushed. I thought of the Pontilla Pilata bedroom and whether I might by any excuse manage to penetrate to it. Yet what would I learn there? Possibly among her personal possessions might be a clue, but I was hardly likely to recognize it as such.

Indeed, it was difficult to know what I had gained by my visit, except perhaps the suspicion of some connection, for all the major-domo's almost brusque denial, between Pontilla Pilata and Sempronius Hispanicus, the Empress's own brother. His grief – unlike that of the major-domo – had certainly not been constrained, still less assumed for public display. And had the Empress spoken merely rhetorically when telling me that she wanted the truth, and would take revenge, even if it involved that brother whom we all knew she loved?

Of course, I might ask to see, though scarcely cross-examine, him. I could anticipate a lightening of his mood – laughter even – as he enquired how he could help me: honoured, naturally, but never before thought of as an authority on Vestal Virgins. Had one of them, by chance, run away? He would have to plead not guilty, though women – curse them – in running anywhere tended to run after him,

44

giving him a reputation that had unduly harmed him in the Emperor's eyes.

Plain bluff soldier though he liked to appear, Sempronius had something of his sister's subtle, slightly devious nature – and perhaps something also, it now appeared, of her adroitly concealed strength of emotion. At least, I need not doubt that he had known Pontilla Pilata. To find out who had killed her, therefore, might also interest him.

I turned to leave, but the major-domo seemed surprised, even slightly alarmed. He indicated, with drooping courtesy, that I should follow him and that I must honour the household by partaking of some refreshment.

Behind the curtain he now raised, I almost expected to see a typical crowd of fashionable mourners, miming profound sorrow while pouring out wine with increasing animation. But the room beyond was apparently deserted, though couches and tables were laid as if for a feast, with sumptuous, well-polished silver. A huge carved bowl, made out of crystal, supported by three fat metal cupids, stood looking like some sort of ostentatious table-fountain, dominating the central area. As I stared, the head of a woman slowly emerged from behind its florid contours, and I saw that she must have been scrutinising it from close to.

'Still not entirely clean,' she muttered angrily, before noticing me and bowing in an impatient, rather sulky manner.

'My wife,' the major-domo said formally, glancing across at her in a way I could not interpret. 'An heirloom,' he added as I still stared at the bowl.

Presumably inherited from Trimalchio, I said to myself, only now noticing the gilt edging round its crinkled rim and the swags of gilded silver amid which the cupids strained, pot-bellied, to support it.

'The upper portion detaches, allowing use as a basin for washing the hands,' he went on. 'It was a prized possession of our mistress's grandfather. And now? It might become the property of anyone – someone, at any rate, with little care for its family associations.'

As he spoke, he moved closer to his wife, and I saw – rather than heard – my title being murmured between them. The woman's face, long like his and as sallow, split into a respectful semi-smile. She was almost as tall as he, but bulky.

45

Her bulkiness increased as she made a fresh, fulsome obeisance, for some reason suggesting the movement of a rusty hinge.

As they stood over me, encircling me with respect, there was a menacing element even in their professed hospitality.

'More wine, my lady?' She poured it without waiting, and some spilt as the cup I had barely put to my lips brimmed over. I looked up into her face but it was fixed, expressionless, a mask of nullity.

'To my regret,' I said, 'I never had the opportunity of knowing your mistress, except by reputation. Now, of course, sadly, it's impossible. Had she a large family here in Rome? You see, I should like to know more about her, and you were both, I feel sure, in her confidence.'

'Hardly any,' he answered. 'She sometimes spoke of an uncle and aunt of hers living in Athens.'

'What sort of things?' The woman asked more slowly, half-caressing the handsome wine jug and seeming to consider the reflection of herself in it.

'She had been married, I know.'

'And widowed, unfortunately,' the man said. 'Madam was left inevitably on her own.'

'Much better that way,' the woman said firmly. 'That husband of hers. . . .'

'I suppose there were no children?'

'She looked on her household as her children, you could say.' The major-domo adjusted his wand, taking a grip on it as though re-asserting his authority. There was no need to ask if he and his wife were also childless. A strangely withered pair they were, physically so similar that they might has passed as brother and sister: withered and yet, I sensed, by no means indifferent figures, very much on their guard, and far from unstirred by my presence.

'I was thinking of her last days – or day. Her piety, of course, was much spoken of. Had she a special purpose in going out to the family tomb on that particular day?'

'She went very regularly,' he replied mournfully. 'Especially in recent months – for anniversaries, I believe.'

'And to see that everything was kept up,' the woman added sharply. 'If she hadn't been so conscientious, she'd be alive today. That's the disgrace of it, my lady. She always liked everything to be neat – of the best, really. She knew good work, when she saw it.

'Of course, getting it's another matter, as I expect you'll be the first to agree. Nothing workmen like more nowadays is there, than putting things over on a woman or a lady? Well, Madam wouldn't have any of that, and I'm the last to blame her. I can picture it all clearly enough – Madam pointing out to that filthy old rogue, drunk as usual, I've no doubt, how he hadn't done what she wanted him to do, then his losing his temper, being in the wrong and with a drop too many in him. Oh, it's the greatest pity he didn't live to be punished.'

'Far too lax behaviour has become.' The major-domo was nodding appreciatively at his wife's increasing animation. 'You hear of households where it's the slaves who virtually have the masters under their thumb, and no real standards like there used to be in the old days. It's hard enough to get good gardeners or a plumber who really knows his job. Even in Rome, of all places. And then something like this happens. There's no justice in it.'

'Justice?' She sounded impatient with his confused lament. 'That's not for us to say. At least, we've done our duty – and shall go on doing so, my lady, never fear.'

'That must bring its own reward,' I said. 'But I'm most interested in your account of the incident – the outrage. As you tell it, it sounds more appalling than I had realised. And with the workman himself dead, what you have to say is bound to be particularly valuable.'

She folded her rather large hands over her stomach, as though digesting my words almost literally. 'Madam told me all about it,' she said. 'The work she was having done to repair and improve the family tomb. She thought nothing of going out there specially on her own, interviewing people and so on. But she always found the workmen so slow – stupid, I suppose – when they weren't lazy or drunk.

'Often she went out in the early afternoon–'

'In her own litter or carriage?' I interrupted.

'That depended,' she said. 'Sometimes she preferred to hire one, as I think she felt–'

She stopped. There was the sound of soft footsteps on the tiles, which she had heard before I did. She and the major-

47

domo stood there, consciously waiting, while a young male servant hurried in, bowing repeatedly and looking frightened.

'Sir, excuse me. Some visitors have arrived – mourners. In mourning,' he added desperately. 'Important visitors, sir, I think.'

'Not, I should assume, more important than the visitors we have had,' the major-domo said severely, glancing at me.

The servant remained standing awkwardly, his eyes cast down but his body tense.

'Please.' I gestured to the major-domo. 'I mustn't hinder you in your duties. But perhaps your wife could spare me a little longer.'

'Certainly,' he said, bowing and backing away, keeping us both in his line of vision. 'Certainly. And if you kindly permit, madam. My obligations at such a time . . . the household on my shoulders. . . .'

The servant raised the curtain respectfully and stood aside. For a moment the major-domo's gaze met mine with an almost greedy glare, as he straightened up, adjusted his tunic and prepared, I felt sure, a suitable phrase or two of welcome. Then he disappeared, and I turned to the wife.

It ought to be easier now. Between us the atmosphere would grow more relaxed, and she might resume her animated, half-gossipy tone. Woman to woman was how it should be, though the prospect grated on me. It was distasteful to think I needed to encourage, virtually woo her. If she were, in some new intimate mood, to offer to take me into Pontilla Pilata's bedroom – and I could see her opening chests and caressing clothes in the near-proprietorial way she had caressed the wine-jug – my instinct was to refuse.

'You were telling me about your mistress,' I resumed, 'and how she so often went out to her family tomb.'

She barely nodded.

'The other day, for instance. Did she, I wonder, go out in her own carriage?'

'I don't know,' she said. 'I didn't see her leave.'

'But I think you were saying before that it varied.'

'What varied, my lady?'

'Whether she used her own vehicle or hired one.'

'Did I? Madam always behaved as she pleased. That was her rule. And she didn't like answering questions, even from me. Very strict in her own way she was – and very much against scandal of any kind.'

I sensed I was losing her, or even to her. It was becoming like a game of dice; and how ever well I threw, her throw beat mine. Or rather, she refused to play, pushing away the dice, untempted, skilfully though I tried to let it roll.

'It was quite cold the other day,' I said. 'I'm impressed that your mistress wasn't deterred. She must have been very anxious about the work. Was it, did you gather, going well?'

'That I can't say. Workmen are workmen all the world over, aren't they? If Madam didn't surprise them, I don't suppose anything would ever have got done.'

'A lesson to us all,' I said.

'Yes, my lady.' She folded her arms with quiet complacency. They were arms a wrestler might have envied.

I paused, as if respecting her mood, letting it harden around her, before I came back more sharply – wishing I had a staff or rod of my own to reinforce with a sharp tap each point I put.

'A pity your mistress never took you out with her on those visits, isn't it? Especially if she thought there would be trouble from one of the workmen. It's surprising, I confess, that she risked being alone with him. A pity also she hadn't kept some servants within call. I don't think she can have done, if your theory's correct, do you?'

'I wasn't there,' she said sullenly.

'Of course not,' I murmured. 'I'm just trying to make out how exactly it happened. It seems as if the only two people who could tell us are dead. But I suppose you knew all about the old man from what your mistress had previously told you.'

'Why do you say that?' She asked slowly, her sallow face darkening.

'Otherwise you wouldn't have been aware of his existence, would you?'

She seemed flustered. 'I never said he was the only one she complained of – an old one, two younger ones, a boy, all much the same, bone-idle and rude. That's what I do know Madam felt. And this one was far too old, past it, she said, and not worth paying. Maybe they did it together. Anyway, it's a terrible thing to have happened. Everyone can see that.'

49

'I suppose there could conceivably have been a plot.' I got up. 'Yes, it's terrible – and it's rather puzzling.'

'But it won't affect things, will it, my lady?' She bulked before me, very much as though she wanted to bar my path. 'Just because it was murder?'

'Well, it can't presumably affect any more lives, if that's what you mean. The case is closed – officially.'

'The case,' she said impatiently, as if it had become irrelevant. 'But Madam's will isn't affected, is it? That's still valid, or whatever they term it?'

'I can't see why not, as long as she made a will.'

As I moved towards the atrium, I could hear hushed voices and a sudden outbreak of sobbing. Then came the deep tones of the major-domo, extolling his mistress's virtues, followed by another bout of sobs. There might be other exits from the villa, I thought, and perhaps Pontilla Pilata herself had had occasion to use them, if she liked to leave unobtrusively, as I somehow surmised.

'Madam's will.' The major-domo's wife had planted herself before me like a highway robber, though she would probably have terrified the average petty thief on the Appian Way.

'What of it?' I asked coldly, moving forward. I decided I must pass through the atrium, though I anticipated it would be full of the White Hen club members in mourning plumage. Any minute now they would flutter distracted into the room and require a feed of more than corn and water.

'Your ladyship has it safe, I'm sure.' She fell back unwillingly as I advanced. 'You'll pardon our natural concern – my husband and I only want what is right, my lady. We've taken care of everything. You can see that. Madam always promised we'd not be forgotten when her will was opened.'

'No doubt. But she lodged no will with us.'

'You haven't got it,' she said half-accusingly. And before I could speak she rushed on. 'Aren't you here this morning to bring Madam's will? My husband told me – do you mean there isn't a will? That we're not getting anything after all these years? I don't believe it. Why, we've served her since she was a girl of seventeen.'

'All I said was, your mistress had lodged no will with the Vestals. That doesn't mean she didn't make a will.'

'Where is it, then?' she said.

50

'That is scarcely for me to answer. However, if your mistress employed a lawyer, he may be able to give an explanation.' Rather unwillingly, I felt I had to add, 'It could be deposited with a friend. There is nothing unusual in that.'

'A friend? Who could that be? Madam's friends are only well-born ladies. Why have they not produced her will? And if there is no will, what becomes of us, my husband and me? Are we to be cheated out of everything because Madam was murdered? Tell me that, my lady.'

'You may be exciting yourself unnecessarily,' I said, noting nevertheless her rising vehemence and wondering what might be the effect if no will was discovered. She obviously found it hard to retain an appearance of courtesy, and even her apparently respectful form of address was almost as threatening as if she had seized my arm with that powerful hand.

'Now I have met you and your husband—'

'You would help us?'

I felt my own temper rising at the interruption. However well Pontilla Pilata believed herself served – guarded, indeed – by this pair, they seemed to behave more like gaolers. Perhaps it was partly to escape the tyranny she had allowed them to develop that she set out so frequently for the tomb on the Appian Way. About that, I suspected they knew only what they had told me: the little she had allowed them to know. And, somehow, it did not make sense. It must be a pretext, though for what was not clear, in a life where everything seemed concealed under attractively-tinted tissues of pretext, wrapped as tightly as those round the corpse.

To unwrap that would tell me nothing. I paused to gaze pointlessly at it again as I passed through the atrium now thronged and noisy with women greeting each other and emitting cries of sorrow under the approving eye of the major-domo.

With his wife I had concluded, in the fewest words, what could only be called a pact. It was uncertain what I could do to help them, and even more uncertain how far they would, quite apart from could, help me. Yet, if no will came to light, they would be aggrieved, angry and possibly eager to reveal all they knew about their mistress. In return, I would, I suppose, be prepared to plead their case with the eventual heirs of Pontilla Pilata, to talk of natural justice and the

51

reward for long service – in the shape perhaps, I thought ironically, of that ornate, gilded crystal bowl. It might suitably come in somewhere; like the pact, it was in doubtful taste.

As she ushered me out, the woman murmured various names in my ear, thinking presumably I would be gratified to have identified at least some of the high-born female figures who were clasping each other and lamenting as they did so. The air seemed heavier than before, and cloudy with incense burning. More evergreens had been heaped around the bier and from somewhere in the crowded space floated the sound of a wailing flute, reminding me of Tibicina. One or two of the women I recognized for myself, including Aurelia Metella, a gruff-spoken, rich widow, nick-named Ferraria Metalla, indicating her iron-like character as well as the source of her wealth. I had not associated her with the White Hen set, and it was surprising to see her stout figure being tearfully embraced, stifled almost, by a writhing, serpentine woman so encumbered with veils that I did not at first see her face. But such shrill-pitched cries of agony could only come from the wife of Quintus Hortensius Hortalus. Her highly charged emotions tended to be vented not in privacy amid her quite numerous family, but on public occasions, often taking the form of supposedly improvised verse. 'Corinna,' as she liked to be addressed, might well have a poem concealed among her voluminous garments or feel the embarrassingly sudden call of the Muse; but there was something quite shrewd about the way she had established herself as Rome's sole female poet, and I might be wise to call on her after the funeral.

The major-domo, after a flickering, almost furtive glance at his wife, came to flank her in escorting me onto the portico. There too, a small crowd was present, lingering in the damp air which struck icy after the house. I looked idly among the press of visitors, with servants and litters arriving, and as one knot formed and another dissolved I thought I caught sight of the unusual fair hair of the Gaùl who had accompanied Publius on the night he came to tell me of Pontilla Pilata's death. For a moment I had the sensation of being watched – examined – and then he, if it was he, had disappeared.

'Julia Maxima mea,' a cheerful voice said, and I felt lips brushing my cheek. Only one man would have dared, and only one man was so smoothly shaved that the contact was almost feminine. 'How unexpected. Have you seen a ghost? I suppose it's rather early for the deceased to manifest herself, but there aren't any rules about such things, are there?'

'You, I feel certain, would break any rule,' I said, trying to concentrate and frown at the appearance on the step beside me of Afranius Dexter, too golden and glamorous for the December weather. 'And it's at least equally unexpected seeing you here. Were you acquainted with Pontilla Pilata? I thought she had the very highest standards of behaviour. Anyway, men weren't, I believe, and aren't admitted.'

'Oh, I don't know,' he said, laughing. 'Not that I'm anxious to go in this morning.' He settled a bracelet on his bare forearm and indicated two good-looking boyish servants who were ascending the steps holding a sheaf of brilliantly-coloured exotic flowers. 'This is going in as as a token of my – well, respect, grief and so on. Aren't they lovely?'

'Very,' I said dryly.

Only he would have managed to obtain such flowers at such a time of year and then chosen to arrive, not even in mourning, with them carried by servants who were admitt-edly younger than he but otherwise almost duplicates in their handsome assured air, as in their jewellery.

'How is your dear wife?' I asked.

'I blush to tell you, but I shall. She's gone on a cruise to Carthage – booked, of course, long before there was any question of advertising to all and sundry. May I see you to your carriage?'

'Thank you. And you have come to condole?'

'I suppose so. Just as you, my dear, have so unexpectedly been doing.'

'Mine was more of a business call,' I said grimly, getting into the carriage.

'I suppose you could say mine is too. Poor little Pontilla and I were partners in a new venture – rather a smart dodge–'

'Selling honey to bees?'

'Not quite but you've got the general idea. Now the sad thing is, I'll have to get a fresh partner, someone no less intensely respectable. ...Why, Julia, this meeting was planned by the gods. Who says they don't exist?

'Hey, careful,' he called in mock-alarm as I wrenched my

hand away from his and gestured imperiously at the driver. 'Or you'll get us publicly linked in the worst possible way: "Vestal Mother's rashness ruptures brilliant young business man's career".'

'We shall not be meeting again,' I said firmly, though it was probably lost in the folds of leather curtain in the carriage.

I lay back, undisturbed by the jolting and feeling it echoed all the jolting that was going on in my mind.

VI

To be greeted, fussed over and bustled up the steps by Gemma was more than usually pleasant. The cloak of welcome she flung round me served to emphasise how exposed and unexpectedly vulnerable I had felt at Pontilla Pilata's house.

In our serene marble vestibule there was no ostentation. It screened no violent or suppressed emotions but simply the plain, white-washed cells of our sisterhood, matching the quiescent, white-robed girls who moved demurely like blanched shadows of my own demure-seeming self. To be taller than all of them was, literally, a distinction. True, no regulation required the Chief Vestal to be of a particular height. One short and swarthy – like, it occurred to me unkindly, the Empress – would not of herself be unworthy to wear the robes. It was merely that she would not have quite the assurance of looking right, of moving in a rhythm of flowing drapery that conveyed dignity without the need of expression or speech.

On this portico, I thought as I paused, I am at home. Instinctively, the household awaits me, welcoming my return even though it gives no outward sign. In Vesta's temple the sacred fire is burning brightly, exuding a faint scent from the

54

pine-cones crushed in the flames. I could even fancy I detected it. Or perhaps the smell drifted out from our kitchen where the cook, with greater imagination than customary, was devising an especially aromatic dish.

Down here, in the centre of the city, it was more misty than it had been on the Esquiline. The day promised to be short, increasing my sense of gladness at being home and ensconced, while the few muffled-up passers-by hurried towards their own homes and the friendly warmth of their hearths.

Then I distinctly saw him again: the Gaul himself, unmistakable this time, wrapped in a deep blue cloak, his head bare, crossing near the temple. He paused, it seemed, to regard me. I looked at and beyond him, blank, unmoving, unconscious (as I hoped) of that scrutiny. It could then hardly have been he at Pontilla Pilata's. To have followed me so speedily would have been difficult and was anyway inexplicable. Was he set by Publius to spy on me? Or was he some hallucination sprung from a fear of my own?

I shook my head to clear my vision; and it made him vanish. He was lost behind a colonnade, had turned grey and insubstantial, absorbed in the greyish, wintry distance. I was left standing there, chill and abruptly forlorn.

'I'm sure nobody did,' Gemma exclaimed emphatically when I asked her, as casually as I could, whether she thought anyone had followed us on the previous day, when we visited Tibicina. 'They wouldn't have dared, mum.'

'Wouldn't they?' I asked. I was by no means certain now of anything.

'Besides,' she added. 'Who'd have guessed where we were going?'

I tried to recall those narrow, dank alleys and faces from the jostling flow of peasants and traders. There had been the indignant old workman I collided with, clutching his paunch and ready to spit. A fat, smiling countrywoman, waddling by, had enjoyed the incident. Amid so much shoving and pushing of so many dark heads had I briefly glimpsed another? Had at one point there passed before me a fair head I had thought nothing of, with hair yellower, it seemed, than Tibicina's and surely worn longer than was customary with us?

It began to seem as if there had, but perhaps only on our return journey. At the corner of some street, while I stopped to adjust my wet cloak, there might have been a gleam – but then the idea became ridiculous. Even though this morning I had undoubtedly seen him, it began to seem less certain that his presence was of any significance. Anyone might have idly stopped to watch my arrival and Gemma's greeting. All the more might a foreigner who had a night or so ago been brought exceptionally to the house not unnaturally pause to look at it by daylight.

'I suppose it'll be a very posh funeral, mum,' Gemma said, once we were inside.

'I suppose so. Gemma, no male visitors – the major-domo told me – ever crossed the threshold of the Pontilla Pilata house. I met Afranius Dexter there – but even he didn't go inside. Sorry as I feel for Tibicina, I can't help wondering if she was mistaken. After all, she couldn't see it was a man. We know Pontilla Pilata's reputation was extremely high, and she seems to have been careful to avoid anything like scandal.'

'Well, I bet it was a man. And I don't mean that Afranius Dexter. Not that I'd trust him an inch. Is he mixed up in it?'

'He's a rogue, I grant you, though a successful and charming one – and perhaps a necessary one too. He's the face of modern commercial Rome, helping to prop up the state even while trying to sell us a scheme for long-burning logs that would do away with the duties of Vestal Virgins.'

'Oh, no, mum.' Gemma sounded genuinely shocked.

'Why not?' I said wearily. 'Though I didn't mean it literally.'

'I wouldn't be surprised. They say his mother came from Syria.'

'Maybe, but it doesn't mean he murdered Pontilla Pilata.' At least, I amended privately, I don't think it does.

Of course, if anything might tempt Publius to reopen the case, it would be the discovery of a political element which flatteringly confirmed the first surmises he had expressed to me. It needed only the addition of something Syrian and underhand to complete the chain which would lead from Pontilla Pilata's grandfather's actions as procurator years ago in Judaea via the Christian sect of today to the recent murder.

The arrest of Afranius Dexter would probably be thought by Publius to be long overdue. And it might be said that, on the face of it, a theory of that kind was rather more plausible than to assume that some wretched aged workman, however goaded by abuse, had attacked and strangled his employer. Could women like Aurelia Metella really believe that? Even if driven by rage or drink to be so foolish as to strike Pontilla Pilata, the old man was more likely to end up strangled himself – and, I should guess, by her.

Perhaps the nature of the death did make one think, though for no very clear reason, of a woman's involvement, something that had fleetingly occurred also, I recollected, to the Empress. Among the White Hen set, if I brought myself to closer study of it, I might possibly find more than one woman intensely jealous of Pontilla Pilata – though killing her seemed less plausible. I almost smiled as I recalled the clinging, constricting embrace Corinna had inflicted on the resistant trunk of Aurelia. Out at the tomb, where Pontilla Pilata happened to be, or to which she had gone conceivably after receiving a message, over the food which might somehow have played its part, had the ostensibly loving embrace of two females ended in the death of one?

Increasingly, I felt the handicap of not seeing that tomb, judging for myself on the spot and perhaps speaking to the other workmen who had laboured for the victim. I even wondered if I might entrust part of the task to Gemma, whose bold, demotic speech would probably draw far more from them than I could hope to do. While her tongue set theirs wagging freely, I might be seen performing some priestess's task, pouring a libation to the aggrieved spirit of the departed, and in fact pondering exactly how she came to die. What more suitable than that I should go out to do both at her ancestors' tomb on the Appian Way?

The question still hung over me the next morning, so strongly that I resolved to visit Publius, in the Emperor's absence, and seek permission to pay my respects at the Pilatus tomb, even though it meant leaving Rome. In the night other less formal solutions had appealed to me: disguised as a man, with Gemma my page, I drove out unnoticed, and back in the city decided to retain my disguise. Even the Blue Toga Club threshold had proved easy of access, though there

Gemma's pert ways led us into rather too risky a popularity . . . and an invitation to strip and enjoy the Club's private baths with other clients – Afranius Dexter and some young friends among them – brought me abruptly to curtail the fantasy.

If Gemma found me more dignified than usual when she came in that morning, she could scarcely know it was in direct response to a sense of shame. Mischievous, wayward thoughts – unsuitable to my position and, I suppose, to my age – seemed to have been creeping like bed-bugs into my mind, to sting me humiliatingly, ever since I had unwrapped the as it seemed fatal piece of linen that advertised the delights of a cruise to Carthage.

'No,' I said, 'I did not sleep well.'

'Not enough blankets, maybe,' Gemma responded chirpily. 'It's getting much colder and you probably felt it.'

'It was nothing to do with the cold. It's these bedclothes, Gemma. Either they need airing, or–'

'Or what, mum?'

'Or through some negligence–' I had not fully thought out my sentence and was still drowsily absorbed in a slow return to reality. 'It may very well be a flea,' I said finally. 'Possibly fleas. And please don't expostulate, Gemma. We've had a mouse and there's no reason why we shouldn't have fleas. It's even conceivable that I've been – er, bitten.'

'Well,' she said. 'Something's got at you – fleas or no fleas.'

I dressed with silent, reproachful decorum, aware that I needed to make an impression on Publius that went beyond anything personal. Gemma, too, was silent. Perhaps she felt excluded by my assumption of an official air or resented our exchange.

We parted coldly. As I got into my litter, I was conscious of how alone I was, but that was perhaps necessary or inevitable; in making a confidante of Gemma, I had been rather impulsive, even possibly unfair to her. She had no reason to bother about the death of Pontilla Pilata, except to see it as a stroke of good if blind fortune. She herself was alive and had every intention of going on living. She would marry one day and have children. That was only right. Gemma would be an admirable mother: I saw that. Less easy to settle was the right sort of husband for her; and perhaps it would have to be that despite all the good qualities I invested him with, he always remained, compared with her, dull.

Marriage seemed the least happy topic to be reflecting on when visiting Publius, though I saw easily enough why it had occurred to me. Still, my meeting with him was to be official. No doubt he would seek for precedents before permitting my short journey; worse, he might decide the timing was inauspicious – better for me to go, if at all, during the February ceremonies when every tomb would have its quota of family mourners, by which date I should have probably lost all urge to go. I might appeal to the Empress, but to her any motive would be too transparent: go, she might say, shrugging, and never speak of it until you are back.

A glance out of the litter as we passed through the Forum and began the steep ascent towards the Capitol showed me the city at its most official, almost as a warning. Temples and public buildings stood like cliffs, dwarfing humanity, each with its sacred, unshakeable idol or relic: the sibylline books, the marble images of the gods, the tablets of bronze recording our history – all seemed as hard, unyielding and inescapable as the Tarpeian rock which looked, however, a deceptively mild expanse in the winter morning sunshine. Yet Tarpeia had been only the first person judged guilty and hurled screaming from it, broken on the stones below.

It might be appropriate that the rock was flanked by the Senate and the Treasury, and certainly that Publius had created what he liked to call 'our civic centre' the Prefect's bureau, in a new building between the two. Here, rather than in his own house, petitioners queued to see him, and here he loved to display charts and plans, regulations for wheeled vehicles, new schemes for taxation of householders or the annual per capita expenditure on drainage.

In light-hearted mood, induced by his latest ingenious scheme, he had once rashly referred in the Senate to putting up an altar to a new deity, Census, god of statistics. Several orders of priesthood had at once complained to the Emperor, and a denial was eventually published in the *Acta diurna*, explaining that the Prefect had spoken jocularly: more worrying than calming was the general verdict. Nevertheless, Publius had thought it prudent to make a round of the most venerated temples – apart from ours – and rather messily despatch a ram, three black chickens and two motherless calves reputed to have been suckled by a mare.

'I am not,' he had told me afterwards, 'a squeamish man, my dear Julia, but even I found I had little stomach for my supper that evening, and my appetite for veal has not yet entirely returned'.

Several passers-by near the entrance to the Prefect's bureau bowed as I climbed out of my litter. I noticed on a pillar a half-effaced graffito of a snarling dog's head, labelled 'Beware of the Census' and a more obscure slogan 'People of the Pontine Marshes–' the rest blotted and over-scribbled with the words '–are frogs'.

A young doorkeeper, occupied in explaining something to a group of angry, rustic-looking citizens, broke off on seeing me approach and seemed glad of the diversion. Perhaps they were a delegation from the Pontine Marshes. Beyond the semi-circle of black and white tessellated floor, presided over by a bust of the Emperor, crowned by a slightly dusty laurel-wreath, archways led off to the various cubicles where a number of secretaries not only worked but created a zone which protected Publius from too easy access.

The doorkeeper must have been prompt to despatch a messenger because I could already see Publius's chief secretary, Calvus, a round euphoric ball of a man, rolling towards me, smiling and rubbing his hands.

'Delightful honour, dear madam, and always a pleasure to have a lady to alleviate our humdrum existence. So much to do – so little time in which to do it. But you're here on business, I'll be bound. Won't you step this way and let's see if some part of our system can meet your wishes? It may be only a matter of a necessary detail, but doesn't one of our poets say something good about the tiny details of life?'

'I can't think of anything,' I said, 'unless there's a poem about a gnat or a flea.'

' "O tiny detail", I think it begins, and then goes on about how essential details are.'

'Perhaps you've a poet on the staff here – or you wrote it yourself, Calvus, in a spare moment.'

'We have all sorts, it's true, but not, alas, I fear, a poet. And I, dear madam, am restricted to prose.'

'You make it sound like doctor's orders. Now, I'm sure

you're busy. I came to see the Prefect, and I hope he can manage to see me.'

'The Prefect?' He stopped rubbing his hands, and though he continued to smile it was clear that my request in some way disturbed the system.

'He's more than a – a detail, I know,' I said. 'But he's why I'm here.'

'Can no one else,' he asked, slightly losing his euphoria, 'be of assistance? I myself would be only too glad – honoured – to provide you with whatever help I could. We have, I believe you will find, a good deal of information at our finger-tips. Not much goes on in the city that we are not aware of.'

'Of course. It's very kind of you, Calvus. This is something, I'm afraid, over which I need to talk to the Prefect. Isn't he here?'

'He leaves for Naples this afternoon – a private trip to see his wife. She is spending the winter there. We felt in all the circumstances it was a propitious moment to leave the city. Nothing of import seems . . . unless your own visit implies some crisis. No bad news has brought you, I trust? You'll pardon my indiscretion, but of course we were badly shaken by the recent event, to which I hardly care to allude.'

'Still,' I said, giving him back some of his own diminished euphoria, 'that's over and done with, I believe. And I have not come here with any news as such, good or bad.'

'No Vestal repenting of her vows?' he asked playfully. 'Ah, dear madam, what Rome owes to examples such as yours. I venture to say as much since I know the Prefect shares that view. He, may I add, is a profound admirer of yours.'

'But, I gather, an absent one?'

'The fact is – strictly between ourselves – that he was urgently summoned to the Palatine, less than an hour ago – orders of the Empress, I think we must infer. Some details – if you'll permit the word – in connection with the Emperor's return.' He gave a modest cough. 'We don't want it generally known as yet, but I'm sure your discretion, your position indeed and the Prefect's known confidence. . . .'

'If it's a state secret, Calvus, I'm probably best left in ignorance.'

I started to move, and he looked disappointed, deprived.

'It must eventually become public knowledge, and

meanwhile I venture to impart it to you. It's the best of news, of course. As anticipated, a major victory for the imperial army but also the imminent return of the Emperor himself. The two events will be announced together at a suitable juncture. We should be grateful. . . .'

'You may rely on me, Calvus.'

'I had no doubt, madam, that we could.'

In intention, my visit to Publius was accomplished. It was as though I had carried out a vow, visited a shrine and learnt only that the god left me to decide my own course of action. There was no point in waiting, now I understood that. Perhaps the absence of Publius was a good omen and itself the god's message. But I was not to leave, I saw, without sampling and admiring some latest 'refinements', as Calvus termed them, to urban progress: a reassuring peep, he would put it, behind the Prefectorial scene.

'To make the streets safer at night,' he explained, as he detained me over a project where a model of the city was set out in a room by itself and two elderly scribes or clerks looked somewhat shamefaced, like children with forbidden toys, as they put down the minute pedestrian dolls with which they had apparently been playing before we entered. 'Men would regularly patrol with torches, in pairs. . . . It would greatly redound to the credit of an enlightened reign. Of course, there will be the question of additional expenditure and I see problems with the praetors. . . .

'But this,' he went on, lowering his voice as he led me away to another, much smaller room, 'is entirely the Prefect's idea and can be achieved without any real outlay. It's a survey of the principal monuments of the city. By a stroke of luck, we managed to devise a task for a youthful guest of ours and give him the opportunity of getting to know Rome. Rather agreeable drawings, don't you think?'

I found myself staring not at them but at the bent fair head of the figure holding the stylus that began to tremble very slightly, so that he was forced to lay it down.

'A little shy,' Calvus was murmuring. 'His command of the language isn't perhaps all that one might expect with his coming from Gaul, but he seems to get on fairly well. Quite a pleasant personality – and some of the ladies, I'm told,

62

have taken him up. And some of the gentlemen too, I fear, if you get my meaning.'

'But surely he hears us?' Or rather you, I might have added, oddly distressed to find we were palpably staring and whispering as though in front of some newly-carved piece of sculpture.

Calvus seemed surprised by my question, taking it perhaps as a criticism not of what he had done but of what he had failed to do. He went quickly across and laid one of his podgy hands on the Gaul's shoulder in the casual gesture of someone settling a disarranged fold of drapery.

'Now, Rufus,' he said briskly, 'the lady Julia Sabina, Virgo Vestalis Maxima, honours you momentarily with her attention. Stand up, my boy – it's as if the Empress herself were to deign to show an interest in you.'

The young man rose awkwardly, flushing and unfolding his thin, rather lanky frame until he seemed to tower over the spherical Calvus and even to overtop me, tall though I considered myself. As if he sensed something indiscreet or challenging in his very height, he bent low and his long hair fell over his face, obscuring it, as he took my hand and bowed with almost exaggerated courtesy.

'Are you really called Rufus?' I spoke to the top of his head, rather displeased to see a reddish tinge which reminded me of the bust of Pontilla Pilata. 'It doesn't sound very Gallic to me.'

'His real name, my dear madam – dear lady–' Calvus intervened, a little flustered, 'is beyond us all, including the Prefect. It seemed convenient to devise one and I, I must confess, hit on this cognomen – not unsuitable, I hope you may feel, given the appearance of our young friend. An alternative might have been Candidus, yet here I hesitated. . . .'

'I answer to Rufus,' the young man said in an unexpectedly resonant voice.

Now he had straightened up, he seemed cool and self-possessed, regarding me out of large, strange-coloured eyes, presumably grey in reality but by a trick of light shining as green and clear as some type of glass. His face was too long to be handsome by our standards and the smooth skin of his beaky, slightly bird-like features was very pale, fringed by

63

those long, girlish plumes of fair hair that added to his unusual appearance.

'We have met before,' I said, not quite addressing him. 'When Publius – the Prefect came to the house.'

Calvus was rubbing his hands and nodding, pleased perhaps to feel that he had produced for me something from the system.

'Scarcely a meeting,' Rufus said. 'I saw your ladyship. I wasn't myself convinced you saw me.'

'Convinced?' Calvus sounded indignant.

'Isn't that the correct word? Or shouldn't you use the reflexive pronoun with a verb like that? It was my – my conviction.'

'That's just what it could be,' Calvus said smartly. 'I'm sure you'll be gracious enough, dear madam, to pardon these manners in a foreigner – a provincial, I should say. It's rather out of character, but then he's young and inexperienced of course, and being over-awed. . . .'

Ignoring him, I asked, 'But didn't I see you yesterday at least once, on the Esquiline?'

'I was there, yes.'

'Many of the villas, you know, madam,' Calvus began, 'and the gardens as well, if not exactly monuments, in the strict sense, are more than worthy of being seen. Some of the best property in Rome. Not the sort of thing to be found in Gaul, I presume.'

'Oh, we have big villas and gardens – and even some big cities. You ought to come and see for yourself.'

'Very good of you, my dear Rufus, but I fear I'm tied down by my duties here.'

'From which,' I said, 'I'm keeping you, Calvus. Please give my greetings to the Prefect. I hope he has a very pleasant stay in Naples with his wife.

'No, your duties call you,' I went on, as he protested he must accompany me to my litter. 'I distinctly hear them. Rome would not forgive me if I delayed you any longer. But as a penalty, this young man may act as escort – with your approval.'

When we were outside I looked around instinctively to see what eyes might be on us, but we seemed unnoticed, silent and still amid the official activity of the Capitol, senators

64

arriving and fulsomely greeting each other, and a cohort of soldiers marching towards the Treasury with a joyful tramp that suggested they were – or expected to be – due for pay bonuses and possibly medals.

'What took you to Pontilla Pilata's house yesterday?' I asked suddenly.

'Took me? I was taken. . . . A lady – Aurelia Metella. She took me.' He seemed to have difficulty in answering or perhaps quite comprehending.

'Was there any reason? I'd be surprised if you knew Pontilla Pilata, or were you just there rather as you are now, in attendance as a sort of lady's escort?'

'No,' he said fiercely. 'No. That is not so.'

'Well, I shall not keep you hanging about as long as dear Aurelia doubtless did.' I signalled towards my litter. The bearers came forward, slapping their arms across their chests as soon as they set it down. 'And I'm pleased you find such good friends in Rome.'

He gave me a frowning, baffled look from those eyes that even in the open air retained their green lustre. I was conscious of his proximity, of his hair ruffled in a gust of wind that blew round the corner, sending some senators' robes skywards in a flurry as they posed on the nearby steps with hands extended like statues of good will.

He came closer still, and I thought he was about to touch me. I was delaying, playing really in no very dignified way. Even Calvus, for all his respectful doubling up and bouncing off contentedly, might privately wonder about my behaviour. At any moment some senior priest or senator would stop to pay grave homage, and then sail away, sniffing a morsel of scandal. It was time to withdraw.

'You,' he said. 'Didn't you understand? It was you I wanted to see again.'

He sounded vehement, half-angry. Something made me pause – if only the awareness that if I moved away his hand would impiously come out to detain me.

'You presume,' I said as lightly as I could. 'Not least on my being stupid. Nobody could possibly guess I would go to Pontilla Pilata's–'

'But you were bound to. We came specially to break the news, so it must have been important to you. I simply had

65

to guess when you'd go. That was chance, I admit, though wasn't yesterday the first day of full mourning, or whatever it's called? Half Rome seemed to be there – those White Hen women, the Empress's brother, Afranius Dexter and you.'

'As a matter of fact, I didn't know her. And it is no part of my duties to attend mourning ceremonies as such.'

'Then,' he said, 'you must have gone for some other reason.'

He seemed undisconcerted by my dry tone, even partly relaxed by it. More confidence than I expected or indeed cared for – impertinence almost, in someone so young – lay below that frank, slightly awkward manner. It was as if he too were playing a game, encouraged by me: at least, it had begun as a game, dictated by our respective positions.

'I must try to guess it,' he said. 'Or will you tell me? Having encountered each other, shall we meet again? I hope I have phrased it right when hoping – expecting – the answer "yes".'

I turned and climbed into the litter, but he remained standing there, a little wan-faced in the chilly air.

'Alone in Rome, I am lonely.' He bowed, as though waiting. 'But at your service.'

'Rome is bound to be rather bewildering,' I said, with a gracious, patient smile, 'after your life somewhere in Gaul. Our laws and society and behaviour – though you don't seem to lack acquaintance. The position of Virgo Vestalis Maxima is unique. She has to be–'

'Like Caesar's wife,' he interrupted. 'Yet not married. I follow. I know a lot about Roman behaviour, but still I can feel alone. And,' he added proudly, 'I am a native of Fréjus – Forum Julii, you would say. Even the Prefect would find the statistics impressive. Our amphitheatre alone seats twelve thousand people. And our weather in winter is better than yours.'

'I expect you've a touch of home-sickness – longing to be under your own roof again.'

I let the litter curtains fall dismissively, too petulantly perhaps, without taking farewell. It seemed impossible that I had heard correctly: that he had dared to say what he appeared to be saying in response, about longing to be under my roof.

66

VII

'My dear,' Aurelia said, re-arranging the striped cushions behind her. 'I would never have made a Vestal Virgin – not in a hundred years. It's a vocation, you must admit.'

'But not a life-sentence, you know,' I said.

'Death sentence – forgive my saying, dear – I've often thought it. You remember that poor foolish woman before you, don't you? Cornelia Claudia something. Perhaps it's as well that her gens has slipped my mind.'

'The statutes permit the Chief Vestal to retire, after all, and even to marry. I think that's often forgotten.'

'Still, rather awkward to find a husband by that time.' She mused, nibbling at one of the honey-soaked cakes that had been served soon after my arrival. 'My dear, how rude and thoughtless I've become. I didn't mean you, of course. And do try one of these. Someone sent them from Sicily, though I believe you can get them perfectly easily at any good pastry-cook's in Rome – and probably fresher too.' She settled herself more comfortably. 'You usually can get what you want in Rome, if you're prepared to pay for it. Now I am, I don't mind telling you.'

'As long as you know what you want,' I said smiling.

'There's that, of course. You, my dear, don't give much impression of being in doubt – any more than I do, I believe. We needn't go on eating these, by the way, if you can't stand them. I can always say I had a divine impulse to offer them in sacrifice. To Plutus, I suppose, if that doesn't seem too dreadfully obvious. I've got something rather more tasty with a chestnut filling, if you'd care to sample it.'

'Even your hospitality is rich, Aurelia.'

'Well, my dear, I hope that's a compliment. And you don't come visiting me every day.'

'I hesitated whether to bother you at all. In fact, I had thought that perhaps Corinna – if she wasn't too preoccupied with the Muses – was the best person to go to.'

She stopped eating and looked doubtful. 'If it's prosody, my dear, then of course I can't pretend to help. Don't even ask me to explain hendecasyllabics. Or are you thinking of having an ode composed to Vesta? I suppose that's a nice, plain, domestic theme for a woman to write about, but Corinna usually prefers something with a little more what you might call–'

'Chestnut filling?'

'Exactly. That reminds me.' She clapped her heavily ringed hands and then lowered them, giving me a rueful, guilty glance. 'Forgive my Eastern ways. I've a new girl who's going to be a real treasure but I got her from Afranius Dexter and she's a darkie, used to extremely oriental goings-on. I feel I ought to be sitting here like a satrap, my dear, with a cushion on my head, while she slobbers over my feet.

'Bring much chestnut filling delicacy, speedy, right-away,' Aurelia commanded as the girl entered. 'And no filthy lick-finger nonsense either. Now, where were we? You were telling me something about our great poetess.'

'Only that I wondered if she, as a member of the White Hen set, could help me a little over Pontilla Pilata. Now she's buried, I don't feel it's quite so awkward to ask questions. But her death still seems to me puzzling. I don't know what you felt. Unfortunately I never knew Pontilla Pilata.'

'Very pretty to look at,' Aurelia said gruffly. 'You couldn't deny that.'

'From her portrait bust I got a feeling she might also be rather silly.'

'Oh, no. Sly perhaps, but not silly – rather shrewd, when you come to think about it. Apart from your Vestals I suppose no woman in Rome was quite so publicly respectable and, my dear, it's absolutely the right thing to be today, as you know.

'Now, where is that dratted child? If she brings in cream cheese when I clearly said chestnut – ah, that's better. You good girl.' She addressed the grinning servant who had swirled in like a dancer, holding a platter on each upturned hand, and then knelt to arrange them before us. 'Mistress all contenty-very. I've had,' she went on confidentially, 'a good deal of trouble in stopping her from balancing plates on her head and virtually giving an acrobatic display when serving guests. Of course, men seem to like it.'

'I found Pontilla Pilata's servants – the major-domo and his wife – rather a suspicious pair, not very agreeable.'

'Well, I've often thought we all get the servants we deserve, and hers, you know, were exactly what she wanted – needed, really. They kept quiet, you see. No gossip and no scandal. But help yourself.' She gestured to the platter piled before me. 'And while we're enjoying our food, do tell me about your interest in the late lamented Pontilla Pilata.'

If I had chosen Corinna, this part would have been much easier.

After some preliminary sighing and adjusting of draperies – still sombre no doubt and hinting at mourning, winding-sheets and poetic grief – Corinna would have happily settled to tell me of the joys of the White Hen Club, with its sewing-parties and exchange of simple tokens among the members, its blameless giggling over trifles and its spotless, even severe, morals.

To talk of how Pontilla Pilata shone at its centre would be only natural to her – was probably, indeed, a stimulus to the verses she was already incubating. My curiosity would seem equally natural. As for the murder, that would probably have been transmuted into a typical act of cruel fate, cutting off in her prime one whose needle had never rusted and whose beauty could not be tarnished by death. Death, in fact, might provide for Corinna the one thing lacking in a life exemplary and admirably conducted but not otherwise an inspiration for her kind of poetry: the glamour of a thread prematurely severed by the savage shears of baleful chance, of a flower trampled on even as it blossomed beside the family tomb.

'Her death,' I said to Aurelia, focusing on her ample, sumptuously-dressed figure and well-coiffed, sensible head, exuding an air which would certainly have banished morbid considerations even from Agamemnon's last bathtime. 'That is what I'm interested in.'

'I confess, my dear, I can't see why. Unless it's to do with her will.'

'Had she made a will, do you know?'

'I don't know – and I now presume your interest goes beyond any will-making. She and I had never been friends, you realise, and in recent years we moved in very different circles. All we had in common was a lawyer. Antique as I'm getting, a party to me hasn't yet come to mean a group of females chattering over plain-stitch or whatever it's called.

I'd rather stay an old grey goose on my own than join Hens of that type.'

'Didn't her death surprise you – its manner, I mean? However it happened, it was murder.'

'Yes,' Aurelia said placidly, 'but something tells me that we're not all going to be strangled in our beds – or our tombs, come to that. And don't think I say that because I read something similar in the *Acta diurna*. Was it our noble Publius giving tongue? Anyway, I shouldn't be worried, if I were you, about your girls.'

'I'm not. But surely you don't believe the Publius version of what happened? Why, I don't believe he does himself.'

'Of course, I don't. Still, it's a convenient solution and causes no trouble. My dear, you've hardly touched your plate. Let me clap for something else for you. Now you've seen me do it, I shan't feel so silly.'

'It's delicious,' I said. 'Truly.'

'Perhaps your appetite is for something more solid – like the truth? That I fear I haven't got.' She gazed thoughtfully at me, unhurried, almost indolent physically, though I was not deceived into supposing that was other than a surface appearance. 'I can't say who killed Pontilla Pilata, or exactly why she was killed. I can think of reasons why some people might wish her dead, which isn't quite the same thing. And I can conceive that there are those – very highly placed indeed perhaps – who would like to get at the real facts. I shouldn't advise it, if only because I suspect they would come as an unpleasant shock and perhaps as something worse.

'I can't think, you'll forgive my saying so bluntly, that you'd be as concerned, my dear, unless you were acting for somebody. Naturally, I don't ask who. But you didn't know the dear deceased, and I'm bound to say that you wouldn't have cared for her, if you had. She wasn't very honest, I'm afraid. She hadn't any of your eagerness to see things come to light. She wanted the imperial respect and so on in our notoriously respectable age, when really she would have been far happier under some earlier regime. I mustn't exaggerate. She wouldn't have cared for Caligula, of course, but perhaps a period when morals were not quite so fashionable and necessary. . . . Personally, I don't mind what people think of me. Never did, and now it doesn't much matter. You'll never

70

find me, I trust, bothering my head about how I'm viewed on the Palatine – not my idea of living well, or dressing well, I might add. There's gossip, naturally, because I've taken up with that young Gaul, Rufus so-called – Rufus Gellidus Pulcher I've dignified him as – but, my dear, the joke is on the gossips. Afranius Dexter took him to the Blue Toga Club one night and auctioned him, in a manner of speaking, to Publius's brother-in-law, the one who's meant to be living under a cloud on the coast near Posidonia. He only crept back, so they say, because the Emperor's abroad. And I believe I'll now have to stop calling my young friend Gellidus. I asked him – are all Gauls divided into three parts? I'm not sure what I meant, of course, but he blushed very prettily. So that's that. Not even Pontilla Pilata, I fear, would ever have managed to get him into bed.'

I felt bewildered, almost bruised, by the forceful, sparkling stream of information she had directed at me. To try and catch fragments while it flowed was pointless, but now I looked down at the rather too smooth-skinned, delicate and oddly useless hands in my lap as though to see what particles of fact had somehow adhered. And it was less of Pontilla Pilata I found I was thinking than of that young Gaul – of Rufus.

Even as gossip, what Aurelia had said displeased me. Silently I denied it, though in his attitude there had been something ambiguous, perhaps teasing. I wanted to say that I knew better – which was absurd, because I knew nothing. But his image was vivid in my mind. The wind rose on the Capitol, and he stood there bareheaded, by no means unbending, half-vulnerable, half-mocking, and very much alone. I wanted to keep that image of him as something personal. It was as I had seen him, and I felt a shameful, unusual pleasure, not least in preserving my silence.

'And so, my dear,' Aurelia was saying comfortably, making me start a little at my inattention, 'there you have it. She was really what my grandmother of blessed memory would have called a harlot – one, however, who didn't have the courage of her own harlotry, if you follow me. Well, perhaps that's harsh. She didn't want to be known as one. Of course, she chose her men cleverly. Patrician class, married as often as not – and usually only too glad to preserve her reputation for their sakes. I'll be surprised if even now they'll want to talk. Why should they? They've everything to gain by showing a decent, not exaggerated sorrow and, above all, by keeping quiet.'

'Yet,' I said, 'you knew, Aurelia. Other people must have.'

'Well, you didn't, for one, did you? I'm not saying it wouldn't have all come out in the end, but she'd managed skilfully so far. Up on the Palatine, I believe, she was the next best thing to a new goddess of respectability. Not that I'm claiming she couldn't have taken me in, only it happened that I got to learn something of the facts and then put two and two together without the aid of any abacus.'

'The servants boasted that no man ever crossed the threshold. I begin to wonder about those visits to the family tomb. Did you know she made a habit of going out there, apparently to supervise some building work?'

'News to me, but I'd hardly say I was her shadow. Still, it makes quite good sense. If you want to know, it was through what you might call the problem of a meeting-place that I learnt what I did.' She looked around her calmly. 'Yes, as you may have guessed, I allowed the use of this villa for a few months when I was out of Rome, a year or two ago. At least, it's fairly well furnished for an assignation. I'm only sorry, my dear, that there's no point in offering it to you.'

'But you lent it to her?' I asked.

'Not exactly,' she said brusquely.

'Oh, but surely you were telling me–'

'Haven't I told you too much already, and without quite understanding, my dear, why you want to know? A friend asked me to do him a particular favour, and do it discreetly. I expect Pontilla Pilata told anyone – if she said anything – that she was dropping in to see my gardens were properly kept up while I was away. Some of the shrubs here are rather rare, as it happens, and there had been a bad drought, so no doubt she was quite a little Juno Pluvia when not otherwise engaged.'

'But the man, Aurelia. He might be the very person who killed her.'

'I find that somehow hard to believe. He idolised her, you see. It was foolish of him, but then you know what men are

72

like. Can you think of one famous love-story from which they don't emerge as utter asses?'

'I suppose perhaps our own Aeneas. . . .'

'My dear, Dido would have lived to regret it if he'd stayed. A prize ass. I always feel the first wife had a lucky escape – Creusa, wasn't she? – just disappearing like that at the fall of Troy.'

I laughed. 'Perhaps things were easier then. Anyway, the man you're talking about is, I take it, no myth. And if he's obviously not guilty, I can't see any harm in my hearing a little more about him. You can trust me.'

'Can I? There, I know that sounds rude – typically rude, some people would say. But I'm very much against meddling with the past, and this murder, or whatever it was, is definitely part of the past. That's where I'd leave it, if I were you. I suspect you won't. Very well. That doesn't, however, mean I have to – to assist you. Besides, my dear, I've a nasty feeling you'll get to the bottom of the matter without any help or hindrance from me.'

'A nasty feeling? Now it sounds as if you aren't so sure your friend is innocent – or, at least, uninvolved. After all, if he idolised her, wouldn't he get a shock if he discovered the truth? Couldn't that have led to his turning violently against her – even perhaps strangling her?'

She frowned so heavily that wrinkles creased her forehead in wavy lines echoing those of her piled, grey coiffure. Everything about her was heavy, opulent and assured. Yet now she was silent, as she twisted the swollen shapes of the rings that splayed her fingers apart – almost as though pondering flinging one away, to be in itself the fortune of anyone lucky enough to seize it.

For some reason, I thought of the Empress, dumpy, drably-dressed yet no less assured. I saw her as waiting for me, not anxiously but with a tenacity far more to be feared. And perhaps Aurelia was thinking of her too, guessing that behind my abrupt interest, my visit, must lie only her.

Something decisive checked the movement of Aurelia's hands. Before she spoke I knew I was not to be the recipient of any carelessly flung-away fresh jewel of information. She smiled, smoothed out her face, and settled herself amid the cushions; and I felt half-angry that by thinking about the

73

Empress I might have reached and affected the current of her thoughts. Although I smiled back, assuming a patient air, I waited knowing that the more Aurelia concealed the more I should try to uncover. In putting me off, if she did, she made me effectively renew, in fiercer terms, my oath to the Empress.

Still placidly smiling, she said, 'You may well be right, my dear. It's not impossible. He's passionate, easily roused and certainly capable of doing stupid things in the way men do. But you must believe me when I state solemnly that he's not a criminal. And no good would come of treating him like one. I'd like you to believe that as well.

'There, I've talked quite enough, but then we don't often meet. I admire you, Julia, you know, even if I can't share your ardour on this occasion or help your case, your cause, or whatever it is.'

'But there was a death – that's undeniable, isn't it? It looks like murder. You said several people might wish her dead – men she'd deceived perhaps? One of them is known to you. If you won't tell me his name–'

'I won't,' she interrupted, almost lazily.

'At least you could question him yourself. You could clear him of suspicion, avoid his being arrested. Why not ask him if he's innocent? Or to explain what happened? Otherwise, somebody else may be accused.'

'I prefer to wait. It's my temperament. Yours, my dear, tells you to find out things, and very admirable that is, in its way. But do take care.'

'Am I in danger?' I asked out of curiosity, smiling more openly as I got up from my couch. 'I feel it might be good for me if I were.'

She looked at me shrewdly, no longer with a smile. She seemed about to say something, stopped, and then clapped her hands. Before we could be interrupted, I crossed towards her, glad to be on my feet again.

'You've been very kind, Aurelia.'

'But not as helpful as I might have been.'

'I've learnt much more about Pontilla Pilata, thanks to you. Yet somehow, I'm not surprised.'

'No,' she agreed. 'I've often thought it all arose because of the grandfather, you know. That need to be so very respectable and respected. Rather a venal and weak person, my

74

family always said, and of course he ended up virtually in disgrace. Not a good type to represent us in the colonies. I believe there was a lot of talk of land-speculation by him in Jordan or Judaea or wherever it was. Now, I'm the last to say a word against money, obviously, but there does seem something fishy about the origin of their wealth.'

'Incidentally, Afranius Dexter told me Pontilla Pilata had been involved in some business deal with him.'

'Oh, my dear, what does that prove? As a matter of fact, I'm considering – mind you, I've said no more than I'll consider – backing one of his schemes myself. You know of course he's behind Celeriter Tours? He sees ways it could expand quite profitably. And that campaign of advertisements was his idea.'

'Afranius Dexter,' I said meditatively, 'is a liar.'

'Julia, Julia, you spend too much time on Vesta's hearth. Rome is full of liars, only most of them aren't either as plausible or shameless as Afranius Dexter.'

'I need help,' I said, aware of uttering the thought aloud.

'Then, my dear, I shouldn't go too near Afranius. Can that wretched girl of mine have fallen asleep or what? Don't tell me I've been sold a darkie with defective hearing.'

'Aurelia, you mentioned a lawyer – yours and Pontilla Pilata's.'

She slowly lowered her hands that had been raised to clap again.

'You persevere,' she said.

'Yes, I do. I must.'

'Well, there's a name I don't mind giving you, if you want it. I've known him most of my life – and while that's not a guarantee of anything, I feel fairly convinced he would not kill one of his clients. He's far too smart, for one thing. Lentulus Trebonius Niger. The family's thoroughly respectable and they've usually had a lawyer or two in every generation. One of them was in partnership with Cicero, I think you'll find. Of course, in those days it was all just talk and more talk, even in a murder trial.'

'Lentulus Trebonius Niger,' I repeated. 'Thank you.'

I bent over to kiss her, feeling oddly desolate at a parting that on the surface was merely social and typical. For all her wealth, her assurance, Aurelia seemed suddenly as alone as

I was myself. I had never thought of her like that before. If I paused much longer, I might begin begging her to join me in my quest.

'What do I wish you?' she asked, putting her hand on my sleeve as though to detain me. 'Good hunting is scarcely appropriate – or is it? That's nearly always dangerous, and I see you don't mind. Perhaps, as you say, it's exactly what you need, my dear.'

'And is there anything you need, Aurelia?'

'Like larks' tongues in aspic, do you mean? I really don't think so. I might take myself off somewhere in the spring, but not to Carthage. Oh, and I'll probably have this villa redecorated while I'm away. If I go as far as Bithynia, I should expect even our Roman workmen to have finished the job before I return. Then I suppose I ought to think about replacing young Rufus, perhaps with somebody rather more exotic. Or is that a mistake? I might do better with a good-looking boy from somewhere in Italy itself, and it could always be said it was a patriotic gesture. I'm not in favour of them, though something tells me they're going to be increasingly fashionable.

'It's no problem, really, when you know you're being loved for your money – rather a relief, in some ways. After all, the money doesn't age or feel tired. With it there's nothing to quarrel about, and that's restful.'

'But the Gaul,' I ventured, not willing yet to leave. 'Your so-called Rufus Gellidus Pulcher. Is it – was it – just a matter of money with him? I'm sorry; I've no right to ask.'

'Bless your innocence, my dear,' she answered cheerfully. 'It's one way to keep young. I suppose you know Publius makes no secret of being in love with you? Better perpetual chastity, I'd say. As far as Rufus goes who can tell? Flattered, I expect, by being taken up – as well as by being knocked down, at auction. A familiar story to most of us, which I'm glad you're spared, Julia.'

But I wasn't fated to be spared hearing his name again before the day finished.

'Bold as brass,' Gemma said, putting her hands indignantly on her hips as though barring the door once more. 'If you please. Had been here some nights ago, brought by the Prefect – not that I'd remember, of course. Wanting to see the Great

Vestal – Chief, you mean, I said, and don't forget it. And be off, I added, before you pollute the place. I can tell you, mum, I gave it to him hot and strong – put, as you might say, a flea in his rear.'

'Did you,' I asked slowly, without a trace of concern, 'gather why he had come?'

I stared down at the fresh rota waiting for me, with its monotonously familiar list of names. Each girl was, I had to remind myself, a person behind the mask of face and regulation dress; but it was easier somehow to recall the days of my childhood, the lively, laughing Oculata sisters and the austere-seeming, tall figure of Cornelia. Never before had I thought of her receiving and glancing at the rota, much as she received our reverential greetings, perhaps telling herself that under our uniform appearance must lurk individualities.

'Oh, him. Some cheeky nonsense about offering his help – his trusty right arm, and thrusting it out for me to see, without any by your leave. Doesn't look up to much, as I said to him. More like a stick of celery, and I've yet to hear the Chief Vestal needs vegetables to protect her, thank you very much.'

'Quite right,' I said regretfully.

'And he's got such a funny accent, mum. I can't tell you how odd. Of course, if he wasn't virtually a foreigner, he'd never have dared turn up here. Anyway, we've seen the last of him, I'd say. What about a bite to eat, now you're back?'

I shook my head.

'It could be useful, Gemma, for me to see him. I'm not sure. There are people I've certainly got to see – Pontilla Pilata's lawyer, for one. I'm learning things about her, and your Tibicina was quite right. Perhaps we'll go and visit her again.'

'She'd come here, if you like, mum.'

Gemma seemed to have grown more relaxed, more like her usual self, with the physical and conversational despatch of Rufus. It was days since we had properly spoken, and I felt guilty. I proffered Tibicina as a token of goodwill restored and because I felt I was going to need that goodwill.

'Never you mind,' she said, watching my face, pondering my silence. 'If he does come back, and you have to see him, I'll be on hand. Any trouble and out he goes. He won't get round me in a hurry.'

'Has working here made you so anti-men, Gemma?'
I tried to put it lightly.

'Me, mum? I'm not thinking of myself. It's you in your position, with the girls and the temple and all.'

'One day,' I said, 'you must marry. We must find a good husband for you.'

'Oh, I'll manage – when the time comes. But not a white-faced foreigner, thanks all the same. I'd never feel comfortable with him in the bed, pardon my saying so. There, mum, I'm just gossiping on, and you'll be wanting to rest.'

She left before I could deny it.

My own private, invisible rota was there to consider, as I went back over all Aurelia had told me: the existence of Pontilla Pilata's lovers, her lawyer, her will, and especially the unidentified man who had borrowed Aurelia's villa. Something told me, as I mentally ran over names, to pause at that of Sempronius. I felt that his was the name Aurelia concealed.

In some way, he was – I had seen for myself – linked to the dead woman. After her death it perhaps no longer mattered, or he no longer cared, but in her lifetime the scandal of their even being known to meet each other must have seemed potentially dangerous. And thinking of their threat to each other brought me to her murder again. Now it could very well have been led to by a lovers' quarrel. They met no longer at Aurelia's but at her family tomb. I saw Sempronius suddenly angry. He was strong, contemptuous, meaning only to frighten her and finding her fallen lifeless as he took his powerful hands from her throat. And perhaps Aurelia too had had such a vision.

I would summon Gemma and seek to speak to him. It was more important to do that, I realised, than waste time with some aged, prosing lawyer. Yet the awareness left me strangely unstirred, oddly unwilling to act.

My conversation with Aurelia, ostensibly concerned with Pontilla Pilata, seemed to have exposed something in me. I could not otherwise explain its after-effect: the shrinking from necessary thought, a distaste from involvement any further in the case of Pontilla Pilata, even a sense of becoming half-inhabited by her. Like hers, my utter respectability began to seem false. I was weary of the burden of it and the tributes paid to it. I wished for other things – but the very vagueness

78

of the words betrayed me. Even as I told myself that I should send a message to Sempronius, as I reflected on the sinister household of Pontilla Pilata and seemed again to enter the atrium and smell the pungently resinous smell around her corpse, I was aware of the persistent, almost mocking image of Rufus. And I saw him, though I covered my eyes as if in real shame, as Pontilla Pilata might have seen him: as a lover.

For three nights he stood in a dream beside my bed. I sent no messages, did not move from the house except to visit the temple. Blankly the statue of Vesta regarded me – while I waited for some expression to cross its face, even if only one of disapproval. Then I could wait no longer.

The business of the house became my occupation. The girls and Gemma, and the doorkeeper himself, old and bowed and ever-respectful, were less capable of hiding their astonishment. I inspected, indeed approved, the blazing hearth, I asked for the inlaid panels of the temple doors to be re-waxed and burnished, and the well-washed steps scoured in the interests of symbolic purity.

The second time Gemma returned from the Palatine with an evasive answer – Lord Sempronius was still indisposed – it seemed a true omen. I had not dreamt that night. I was lingering at the house doorway, watching Rome come noisily to life in the cold bright light of early morning. Behind me the porter snuffled and shuffled, longing to shut the heavy doors but afraid to suggest it.

'Very well,' I said at last, having listened to Gemma. 'Close them.'

It was an effort for him, unaided, but eventually they were shut and the world beyond was excluded. We might have been performing a solemn ceremony, and now I regretted that the calendar offered no excuse for a festival, however minor. It should have been the occasion for a sacrifice, followed by ritual celebration. We might have summoned Tibicina and her flute, if only to break our monotony.

As I gazed at the dark barrier of the doors, I thought of the Emperor's hinted, perhaps imminent, return. A pity that our public role had to be so mute and repressively decorous. On the other hand, a wild cantata of triumph from a band of Vestals turned bacchantes would test their musicianship and almost certainly displease the Emperor. To beg the goddess for the boon of tunefulness for girls like Valeria seemed impractical if not impious, and her failure to respond might merely make proverbial Vesta's deaf ear.

'Stuck-up lot, those servants,' Gemma was grumbling. 'Lord Sempronius this, Lord Sempronius that – and speaking in whispers the whole time. Anyone would have thought he'd passed away instead of just having a hangover or whatever it is. Is he the one who did it, mum?'

'The gods alone know, Gemma. I'm on my way to inspect the kitchens – and there's no need to warn the cook.'

'Very well, mum,' she said resignedly.

It was there she found me shortly afterwards. I was gazing intelligently at the oven while hearing the unexpected number of complaints the cook had to make, not only about its functioning (it seemed quite simple to me) but about the un-Vestal-like behaviour of the girls.

'Stealing food at night?' I asked. 'Aren't they getting all they need during the day?'

'Well, someone's taking it, that I do know. I'm no liar, my lady.'

'Of course not.'

'If anyone thinks I am—'

'I'm sure they don't.'

Gemma's arrival was a welcome diversion, though she looked hardly less grim than the cook.

'A man? Expected?' I broke in excitedly, not waiting for her to finish.

She nodded gloomily.

It was as though the dream had risen from the kitchen floor. He was beside me. I saw the plume of fair hair, his wide green eyes, and I trembled at the proximity.

'What a fug in here,' Gemma said. 'Whew!'

'I shall have to see him,' I said. 'It would look rude otherwise.'

'He thought you'd know the name: Lentulus Trebonius Niger.'

VIII

I felt I should never leave the kitchen. Gemma seemed surprised that I continued to stand there, while the cook looked surly and indifferent beside the open, flaring oven, a female Vulcan, brandishing not a hammer but a ladle.

The longer I remained standing, the more obvious must appear my shock of disappointment. It was intolerably hot there, but still I found it hard to stir. Perhaps I even went on hoping wildly for a mistake; and it was fortunate that when I finally went to the encounter there was a legitimate reason for some emotion to betray itself.

'Quite understandable,' he said rapidly, pleased by what he took to be my reaction and consciously putting me at my ease. 'We often find people get us confused. But my uncle dislikes being known as "the elder". I, on the other hand, have no objection to being called "the younger".'

At first I had even taken him for a boy, so slight and short was he – almost a dwarf. Yet on the exiguous body the large head, with close-cropped black hair had nothing ungainly about it. As he spoke he moved about the room with darting, lizard-like speed, turning to glance at me with hard, glittering eyes that could also have belonged to a lizard: not Lentulus, Aurelia might have said, but Lacertus.

'Nothing for me.' He flickered his tongue as he dismissed the proposal. 'Thank you. A clear brain is the secret of my reputation. I like to think fast. Too many lawyers want to think slow – and act accordingly.'

'At least,' I said, not moving myself, 'you'll sit down?'

'My mind keeps on its toes all the better when my body does the same. Are you wondering why I'm here? My clients tend to be younger than my uncle's – for obvious reasons. But it's a good firm, ours. You'd be surprised perhaps at the number of important or just wealthy figures we act for. Of course, Aurelia's one of my uncle's oldest clients – shrewd old things, both of them. I've often thought they might as well marry. I wouldn't object if they made me their heir.'

'Pontilla Pilata,' I said, after a pause, 'was, I suppose, your client?'

'My client,' he echoed, almost snapping at the words.

'Her sad death . . .' I murmured. It seemed absurd to stand there resenting his presence when I ought really to be grateful. Yet I still felt angry with myself as well as slightly afraid of him. I was determined he should see less a woman than a calm, dignified, conventional high priestess of the state, and be rather more openly impressed than he so far appeared.

'Can I be of some assistance to you?' I asked suavely.

'The very question I've come to ask you,' he said. 'I heard you were puzzled about my client's death. Well, so was I. If you're thinking of investigating it, I am already. And if you suspect she wasn't killed by any odd-job man, old or young, you're perfectly right.'

'You know who killed her?'

'Not yet, but I hope I soon will. I'm working on it, never fear, and I don't mind who I expose in the process. I'm not claiming any great grief, you understand, but I don't like messy situations and I'm not going to see a murderer – or murderess – benefit financially from what's happened. Now, maybe you were friendly with Pontilla Pilata. I don't know. She hadn't been my client long, but of course I'm well aware of her large circle of female friends.'

'And not only female ones, I presume you know?'

'That's right. I'm glad I didn't have to break the news to you.'

'Perhaps there is news you can give me,' I said, watching as he stopped his restless progress, poised only momentarily beside a couch, gripping its sinuous back with hands that looked so tiny they might have been shrunken. When he put one up to his smooth expanse of face it was like a little, shrivelled hairless paw. 'Did Pontilla Pilata leave a will?'

'She did. I have it. Safe.'

'Its contents might provide some clue – some evidence . . .'

'Oh, she wasn't killed for her money exactly. It's a little more ironic and more complicated, I believe. Someone had her killed, that's true enough. Did you see her body after death? Before they got round to embalming it, I mean. No, you probably didn't. It's not exactly a woman's province, this case. So naturally I started wondering when I heard of your interest.'

'Wondering what?' I said coldly, remaining immobile

though tempted physically to retreat from the circle of attraction he created.

I felt like a statue, but one up whose trunk this lizard-like figure might suddenly shoot.

'I have a client,' he said, 'even if a dead one. So should you be concerned about pursuing the matter on her behalf, I'm able to reassure you it's in excellent professional hands. I've not tackled a murder case before, I admit, but you needn't worry. I'll get to the bottom of it and I think you'll enjoy my handling of the trial when I prosecute. It's a long while since there was a murder trial in Rome. This should be it. I hope you'll be able to attend.'

Suddenly he had swerved to come too close to me, and I couldn't help withdrawing my foot at the abrupt, unwelcome proximity.

'You did know her?' he asked. 'You were distressed by her death and impelled to find out what happened? I think it does you great credit. A woman in your position, with your duties. . . . Most would have hesitated, however strongly they felt.'

'How can you think I knew her?' I said impulsively. 'We had nothing in common – nothing. Her death meant absolutely nothing to me.'

He looked up at me ingenuously and dispassionately. The cropped dark hair increased the size of his face and made it seem more boyish, though somehow not youthful. For all its rapidity, the way he spoke was dispassionate too, quiet and neutral, prepared for by occasional flickerings of his tongue over the precise, pouting lines of a minute mouth.

'Curiosity perhaps impelled you,' he said. 'Natural enough in a woman – a lady, I should say. But then it was only something thought about, talked of with other ladies. You probably began to realise the difficulties. I have myself. And of course you could scarcely have carried out any proper investigation. As a Vestal you can't even leave the city, can you, to visit the scene of the crime?'

'It's a very ancient regulation,' I said, smiling, 'but I don't know if it need stop me. We live in a more liberal age.'

'But not a lawless one, I think you'll agree. The same statutes that give you your privileges also lay down the restrictions – and the penalties.'

'Are you' – I tried to make my smile less of a rictus – 'threatening me with the Tarpeian rock?'

'I don't threaten you at all, madam. I was speaking of the law.'

'At least there isn't a law as such against my investigating a crime. And I've gone a little further than you imply.'

'It is a crime that concerns you?'

He was scuttling fast about the room now, circling me and returning to launch each remark. I longed to fix – transfix – him with a glance or even a blow: hold him squirming and compel some sensation to be expressed by that bland face.

I shrugged. 'Not me personally.'

'Let me make myself clear. I have investigated with some care. I have information not known to you – nor ever likely to be, unless I tell you. I think you accept my competence? As the matter nears a solution, I am eager there shall be no blunders – nothing to give an advantage to the guilty party – or guilty parties.'

I felt I was flushing angrily, too irritated to preserve a marble front.

'I'm to throw myself off the case if not the rock? That's your verdict, is it?'

'My advice,' he said softly, gesticulating with those tiny hands as though deprecating violent imagery.

'As a woman I'm too indiscreet, I suppose. And I haven't any legal training. Nevertheless, I don't, I won't, withdraw. And we shall see who wins.'

'You speak as if you had your own client. No – please let me finish. I had already deduced as much. It distresses me, and it certainly surprises me. Your position is unfortunately awkward – grave, in effect – however privately you claim to act. It could cause you considerable embarrassment, I'm afraid. It might jeopardise your status as Chief Vestal. That would be sad.'

'Perhaps it would be, though it's hard to see how my status could be affected.'

'Your client –' he began.

'Whose name I'm under a necessity not to divulge,' I interrupted ponderously. I might manage to crush him better by recovering my temper, assuming vaguely legal-style phraseology and posing as a rival advocate.

He looked shocked – the first emotion I had detected him displaying.

'Of course, I don't ask it,' he said. 'At this stage. But I feel it fair to warn you of something you might have overlooked. Whoever approached you – engaged you – may have done so not to establish the truth but to hush it up. You realise the implication of that? Your client could be the murderer – even, conceivably, an interested party, acting on the murderer's behalf.'

'That's absurd, if not indeed insulting.'

'Not at all. They would be playing on your innate goodness and commonsense – possibly appealing to your civic sense as well. You would undertake to keep them – I say "them" – closely in touch with anything you discovered. As you got nearer to the facts, supposing you did, the more alarmed they would become. You would find the case getting more difficult. Even your client might start to become evasive. To you it would seem very odd, but I should understand it.'

'There's no suggestion of that.'

'Are you certain?'

I hesitated, and he could see I was doing so. Pleased, he went on, 'Now perhaps you realise why it's best you withdraw from the case. Accidentally, I'm sure, you may be making it harder to discover the truth and for justice to be done. The law, excuse my saying, is not really a matter for ladies – however eminent. And neither is crime.'

'But I may have discovered useful evidence – useful, I mean, for your purposes.'

'Permit me, without rudeness, to doubt it. I'm only too happy, of course, to hear any theory you have, should you feel willing to divulge it. Perhaps it's not ethical, I ought to add, if our interests in this case are different.'

'Oh, I want to get at the truth, at least as much as you do. And we start equal: a crime was committed, a woman has been strangled.'

I stopped speaking. He was poised a few feet away, watching me, and nodding his big head at each word.

'You assume that?' He said. 'Very good. And next?'

'At first it seems shocking and incomprehensible.' I refused to seem goaded by his openly indulgent tone. 'A woman of her rank and especially of her repute. The old workman who finds the body is arrested and thrown into prison. Nobody actually believes he strangled her, but when he commits suicide it's a convenient way of closing the matter to assume his guilt. Rome can start to forget the whole tragic affair. Only–'

'Only,' he echoed encouragingly.

I began again, rephrasing my sentence. 'My investigations led me to uncover her real life – her numerous lovers, above all, and her anxiety to conceal them. Going out to inspect the family tomb was probably a pretext for meeting them. Perhaps it was one of them, discovering her behaviour, becoming jealous, who strangled her. In fact,' I added firmly, 'I believe he did.'

'He? You have his identity?'

'Not as such – not yet.'

'A suspicion, though?'

'Didn't you say something about things that were unethical? Even though I'm not a lawyer, I suppose it's hardly right to discuss mere suspicions. Besides, it's premature. I don't mind admitting that. It's all I'm going to admit, and I rather doubt if we have more to say to each other.'

'One moment, madam. Your investigations took you to the Pontilla Pilata villa, didn't they? You met the major-domo and perhaps you also met his wife? A competent person, strong-willed, skilled in various things – quite an expert in, for instance, poisons. You know how country-bred people often are. Homely remedies, household tips, the best thing for cleaning silver – helpful lore of that kind.' He gave a quick, cold smile. 'She usually oversaw the preparation of meals in the villa. If her mistress took food out to the tomb, she almost certainly had a hand, perhaps literally, in it. As soon as I glanced at the corpse, I noticed how bloated it was, and the face was a livid colour. I thought at once of poisoning.'

'But wasn't her scarf–?'

'Tied round her neck afterwards, to suggest strangulation.'

I tried to recall exactly what Publius had told me, that first evening, and realised I was lingering when I ought to walk out of the room, summoning Gemma to take him to the door. I wanted to be away from him and his somehow contaminating presence. Yet perhaps what contaminated me was his

86

knowingness, his patent accumulation of knowledge, secreted in that boy's body and heavy head and now oozing from him as if it could not be contained any longer.

'You want to ask who tied it on and why? It hardly matters who. Why is the important question, isn't it? The one that might really come to concern you, madam, if it doesn't already. The murder was planned, you see. It wasn't any sudden, jealous attack, though it was made to look like one. The real murderer might not even have been in Rome when it happened. I've certainly thought of that.

'The major-domo's wife wouldn't have dared on her own, and why should she? But she was an instrument. Perhaps money tempted her, and the promise of more when her mistress was dead. She probably knew or guessed she and her husband would inherit a lot under Pontilla Pilata's will. And I can tell you that they do. But behind them, if they are both involved, lies the true culprit. A man, I feel sure. Patrician, or could he be of more exalted rank? It doesn't matter. I'll find him.'

'It's ingenious,' I murmured, not attending to his last words. 'But it's only a theory.'

'Think about it,' he urged, darting closer. 'Even let your client know.'

'Oh, my client—'

'The interested party.'

'I—' I began but then checked myself.

'Yes?'

'I don't think all the facts fit. The scarf, for instance. When the workman found her — found the body — it must already have been round her neck. Why otherwise did he assume she had been strangled?'

'Remember neither you nor I spoke to that workman. He found a woman's body in the family tomb, panicked, stopped a carriage on the Appian Way, told his story in a garbled form and was seized. It took no time to alert the Pontilla Pilata household. The major-domo's wife went and identified her mistress and wept a bit, no doubt re-arranging the clothes and so on. Then she was ready with her side of the story — her mistress going out alone on her pious vigil and then to be discovered as a corpse, strangled with one of her favourite scarves. Most affecting. It's a story that would easily impose on the Prefect. If the workman failed to describe a scarf, it was probably further evidence of his guilt. He must be a liar at the very least. Next thing, he'd killed himself. And there I'm delighted to find we agree: *he* did not commit the murder.'

'If all you suggest is true, haven't you given me a lot of valuable information? Mightn't I act on it?'

'You might tell your client, of course. I hope you will. If he's innocent, he'll be greatly relieved. Alternatively – well, it's a risk I'm willing to take. It might make him do something precipitate and thus reveal his identity.'

'And if I prefer to do nothing?'

'The very course I'd commend to you as a lady, and especially one in your position. A most proper conclusion. Admirable restraint, worthy of the best of our ancient traditions.'

'A woman's place, you're saying–'

'Surely the Chief Vestal doesn't need me to urge the claims of the hearth?'

I bowed, dignified and silent. He would have taxed the patience of a goddess – or, rather, a goddess would have been free to express her feelings about him by some instant, gratifying, metamorphosis: changing him into a creature that thereupon met a nasty fate. Hadn't Ceres thrown a bowl of something at the man or boy who mocked her in her quest, transforming him into a spotted reptile?

If Lentulus Trebonius Niger had stayed much longer, I should have been tempted to hurl some object at him, even though no metamorphosis followed. But clearly he felt his task had been achieved, a dilemma posed for me from which he ought somehow to gain advantage, whatever I did. And his ostentatiously respectful farewell suggested that he thought I had resigned myself to the role of inactivity, if not muteness.

As soon as he had gone, I called for my litter. Let him be watching or having me watched, I thought. There was one location which he would find it hard to ascertain my purpose in visiting.

'The Palatine,' I commanded.

Marcus met me as deferentially as ever, detaching me at once from a group of lost-looking petitioners who had arrived at the same moment.

'To see Lord Sempronius?' He made an obeisance and led

me to a carved chair at the end of the vast empty hall. 'Only too gratifying, I feel sure,' he murmured. 'Something was said of his health not being quite . . . though nothing serious, of course, should be assumed. Visits like yours are bound to be appreciated. I think you have been good enough to send earlier messages? Certainly steps should be taken to see that awareness of your kind interest is shown in due course.'

'I have to see him,' I said loudly, 'unless he's seriously ill.'

Marcus remained benevolent-looking, bent a little out of duty and perhaps incipient deafness.

'No cause for alarm has been hinted, I'm glad to assure you. Nothing that could be called grave. Some indisposition was mentioned a morning or two ago, though the recent spell of mild weather will probably have eased it. Agreeable days we've been enjoying, don't you think?'

'My business is urgent, Marcus. Please have my arrival announced. I'm sure Lord Sempronius will see me.'

'I can't doubt it, madam.' He coughed apologetically. 'Always provided that no alteration of plans, for health reasons, has taken place. Medical opinion may have recommended some change of air and possibly of – er, scenery. Will you allow me to make enquiries?'

'Marcus, I positively want you to make them. That's why I'm here.'

He nodded benignly, apparently unperturbed, rippling away from me in a deft, silvery movement that was as elusive as it was polite. Yet he seemed to move with a little more alacrity than usual, perhaps as the result of my deliberately sharp tone. Something of that had communicated itself to him, and I saw him, supposedly out of my sight, gesture with untypical peremptoriness at a page lounging by the staircase that led to the distinguished visitors' suite. Only in the Emperor's absence, I suspected, would the Empress have lodged her brother in the palace.

That the Emperor was indeed out of Rome was indicated by the empty expanse of the reception hall. The group of petitioners only added to its slightly forlorn air, and the weight of silence in such a space had awed them into unnatural stillness. Now and then their heads turned as they glanced half-nervously towards me, causing me to settle into

89

an imperial attitude on my throne-like chair, even while I longed impatiently to pace the floor.

I watched idly as they were escorted into a pillared recess. An official appeared, unsmiling and unhurried. After some fumbling, the petition was handed over. The official bowed, without speaking. Two members of Marcus's staff came forward, their wands unobtrusively steering the subdued yet relieved group, and the tall, double doors opened smoothly for its departure.

An unobtrusive cough recalled me to Marcus, and I got up expectantly, almost as though greeting him. But a glance told me, before he spoke, that he conveyed bad news. Perhaps he wanted me to be aware of that, and prepared, to avoid any violence or breach of decorum.

'No sudden attack of a mysterious illness?' I said graciously. 'Lord Sempronius has always seemed to me wonderfully robust, in every way. It would be too shocking.'

'Fortunately, nothing of the kind.' He matched my tone, with no hint of being disconcerted. 'The mild indisposition has been cured, I gather. I'm sure you will share the general relief. An admirable constitution. . . . Quite a family trait. However, as I had ventured to anticipate, a change of air was recommended – by the imperial physicians no less, I believe. It was felt best to follow their views, especially after a good augury was received from the priests at the temple of Mars Ultor.'

'Just the deity for Sempronius,' I murmured. 'But, anyway, I shan't detain him for long.'

'I very much fear, madam, that it is not possible to do so at all. At the express command of the Empress, Lord Sempronius left the city quietly this very morning.'

'He's gone? Do you know where?'

'Nothing has been said, I regret, of his destination. But it seems possible that he intends to return to Spain. Whether in fact he will do so, I naturally cannot predict. But that you should have been disappointed is to be deplored.'

'Yes,' I said thoughtfully. 'Conveniently banished himself from Rome.'

'Madam?' He spread his hands, drooping apologetically but privately no doubt glad – gratified, as he might put it – to find me taking the news so calmly. And in a moment I

90

should find myself conducted, with almost excessive courtesy, across the highly-polished tessellated floor, departing as inexorably from the palace as had the delegation I somewhat pityingly watched.

'The Empress,' I said, sitting down again and grasping the arms of the chair.

Although he inclined respectfully before me, he seemed to imply by his expression, for all its suavity, that the words were unfamiliar.

'You know who I am, Marcus?'

'Always honoured . . .' he began, looking rather miserable.

'I should like the Empress to know I am here and that I beg her to see me, if only briefly. It's all the more important after what you have told me.'

'Really, I'm not aware, madam, of telling you anything. This is not the easiest of times in the palace, as you'll appreciate. The Emperor's absence . . . pressure of affairs. Her Majesty was, I know, engaged and not available. Normally, of course, your presence would be welcome – warmly welcome. It is deeply distressing for me. . . . In short, my instructions are that Her Majesty is seeing nobody. I regret having to convey as much.'

'Is she indisposed?'

'To some extent there is indisposition, I believe, possibly brought on by fatigue.'

'Worry, perhaps, about her brother?'

'That might, I suppose, be a cause. It is not for me to presume to say. The bearing of heavy responsibilities, madam, often exacts its toll, as you yourself must be aware.'

'At least you can alert a lady-in-waiting that I am here.'

'Of course, madam.' His face had regained its normal composure. 'With the greatest pleasure.'

'You're a loss to the medical profession, Marcus,' I told him.

'I, madam? It's extremely kind of you, but I lay claim to no specialised–'

'Making people swallow your concoctions. Oh, don't protest. It's a compliment. And I don't think I'll trouble you about speaking to a lady-in-waiting. If the Empress is seeing no one–' I broke off.

It had suddenly seemed futile to expose myself to being

91

soothed, nursed almost, by a motherly Marcia, or some such homely figure, interposed as a plump, living cushion between the Empress and the outside world. And, after all, why strive to see the Empress when I had only suspicions – highly charged ones, too – to convey? Perhaps there was nothing, in fact, I could tell her that she did not already know better.

But what checked my speaking was the sight of Publius. He was processing in a stately way across the hall and obviously being escorted from the Empress's apartments. So grave and absorbed did he appear that he would have passed me by if I had not put out my hand – rather patently, I felt as I did so, a petitioner. Or perhaps I was giddy from surprise and uncertainty. The empty hall was abruptly full of lies. The appearance of Publius set oscillating new possibilities, including the possibility of Sempronius never having left the palace.

There was something abstracted in Publius's greeting, or I imagined it. 'You look a little pale,' he said. 'I hope you are quite well, my dear Julia?'

'I didn't expect to see you here,' I said.

'Nor I you.'

'I thought you were in Naples.'

'No,' he said gently, smiling at my mistake and moving on with a dignified tug at his robes.

'But I'm sure Calvus told me you had gone or were going. And I thought the dear Empress was seeing no one. I've just heard as much when I had hoped to see her myself.'

'Sadly indisposed,' he murmured obliquely. 'Bearing up wonderfully, of course.'

'Of course.'

'Somehow I never thought of the two of you as close, but your womanly sympathy does you the greatest credit, Julia. I'm touched you should have come. At the same time, I trust news of the Empress's indisposition – temporary, I feel confident – has gone no further than your own walls. We don't want rumours spreading in the city.'

'The truth, however–' I started to say.

'The truth?' He paused, courteously enough but with just a hint of masculine impatience masked without being entirely hidden: he was called by duty or by a need to escape questions, and today not even a promise to marry him would win me more attention.

I looked at the imposing head of hair which he seemed offering a last valedictory sight of. Without it, he would certainly be rather different, and as I gazed at its healthy, washed luxuriance, I felt convinced the Empress had been right: it was a wig.

'Do we want the truth spreading?' I asked. 'Anyway, it's often quite difficult to know what it is.'

'Simple truths, my dear, are best. You and I know that much. The old Roman virtues – but I must not detain you with a speech.'

Marcus had slid noiselessly up, as though tacitly summoned by Publius, parting us in a show of reluctant duty. The Prefect was going, like a middle-aged Hector, to the strife of public affairs, and I should take the conventional, sorrowing, domestic role of the woman, the wife. My tasks were not so different from those of Homer's Andromache, substituting the sacred flame for her loom; and scarcely more exciting. Yet Andromache had not, whatever she suffered, had to suffer a bruising sense of deceit.

It almost resounded, I thought, from the Palatine walls. It was enshrined in the neat-jointed automaton that was Marcus, speaking as he was told to speak. The Empress, Sempronius, Publius were all guilty – shared their guilt perhaps – even though I could not quite grasp the exact nature of the crime.

Tears of anger, it must be, pricked my eyes as I stood outside the palace. My bearers hurried up with my litter. How white and impractical it looked: ostentatiously unsullied, a fragile, half-repellent cage of silk.

Before I could get in, I heard a commotion behind me. A coarse, half-whistled shout accompanied the jangle of mule-harness. I turned and my eyes cleared. There, just driven up, was one of the imperial carriages. I had only to wait to see revealed something of Marcus's lying. Any moment Sempronius would surely rush from the palace, disguised doubtless as a woman.

Then the curtains parted. A man jumped down, and to my amazement I found I was being greeted by Afranius Dexter. He gleamed with oil and jewels and mischief. A scarlet cloak

93

was draped about him, and he extended a fold of it invitingly in a gesture that wafted heavy scent towards me.

'At your service,' he said cheerfully.

IX

'You can trust the driver,' he said, laughing, seeing me scrutinising the back of the hunched, hooded figure who seemed to have considerable difficulty in controlling the mules and who swore every so often at them in some obscure tongue.

'But can I trust you?'

Putting the question was its own answer, of course. He laughed again, probably aware that I no longer cared.

If I had I would hardly have allowed my litter to go back empty to the house and accepted his offer of a ride down the hill. As it was, we or at least he had already broken the law by being in a carriage reserved for members of the imperial family. But I was sufficiently interested to know how he had obtained one and what he had been doing with it.

'Helping to confuse the issue,' he said. 'Acting under orders, though – for once. In fact, I was returning this vehicle when I happened to see you, my dear, and rather cross and upset you appeared. A frustrating visit, I can guess, yours must have been. And so I thought I would do something to cheer you up. This is a sort of polite, social rape, if you like.'

'You're impossible. I ought to get out at once. It's obviously madness to accept anything from you.'

'Afraid?'

He lay back lazily, his hands busy preening himself, twisting into place a lock of gilded hair that anyway was barely disarranged. Even his slanted eyelids looked to be gilded this morning, and his golden-brown eyes sparkled with self-appreciation. I was in no danger from his proximity. If I

94

could recover my equilibrium, I might share in his own appreciation and also perhaps exploit his vanity.

'They say you have a mirror in your carriage,' I remarked severely.

'They will say anything. Besides, it's only when I lend the carriage to other people. For you, Julia my dear, it simply wouldn't be necessary, any more than for me. We don't need mirrors.'

'And so,' I said thoughtfully, 'you were told to borrow this carriage – to drive around the city perhaps and be conspicuous. Somebody else, I suppose, was meanwhile leaving the palace inconspicuously? That's what happened, isn't it? Of course it was the Empress's idea. Perhaps she actually left with him.'

'Him?' He raised an eyebrow.

'Him,' I repeated. 'Have you sworn not to reveal the name? It doesn't matter. I'm beginning to understand it all.'

'Happy you in that case, but what is there to understand?'

'From the first, they all thought of one man. As soon as they heard of Pontilla Pilata's murder.' I felt excited now. 'I was to investigate it only to see how close I could get to the truth. If I never got near, all was well. No wonder my refusing caused a problem – and then wondering what I would find out on my own. And, on top of that, her lawyer's suspicions. He'll know the truth by now, just as I do. I expect he meant me to go up to the Palatine – it told him something he'd half-guessed.

'Thank you, Afranius. If I hadn't met you and this carriage, I might have gone on stupidly being baffled, hovering on the brink of the truth. And while I thought myself quite shrewd, they must have been laughing quietly at me. I suppose you were in it too, laughing away. You probably knew already that morning at Pontilla Pilata's villa. And Aurelia knew. Only I, like a fool . . .'

'I'm fascinated,' he said. 'But this is so unlike you, Julia. Rome would be amazed to hear these weird recriminations. And I'm not sure they suit you. It's a shock – rather like seeing a pillar struck by lightning.'

'For Pluto's sake,' I said angrily. 'I am not a pillar. I'm a person – a woman. And please don't start saying something insincere about my being a charming one.'

'Oh, I shan't. I wouldn't consider you had charm exactly. You're too tall, for one thing. Dignity – yes. More than enough, though given your status it suits, I admit. Probity – definitely. Now that's a useful quality.'

'Not one of yours, anyway.'

'No, I've got charm instead. But you have maturity.'

'And you, I suppose, eternal youth.'

'So far,' he agreed.

'Eternal cleverness I'll grant you,' I said. 'And at present I simply feel very obtuse. Tell me all about it. Now he's left the city there's nothing I can do – nothing any of us can do. It's over.'

'I hate to think this, never mind say it, Julia most dear, but whatever's gone on has been happening without my knowledge. But then my business interests don't include murder. I neither killed Pontilla Pilata nor know who killed her. You, if I follow correctly, have been trying to find out. And now you have. Felicitations. I was always sure you couldn't remain content with your – not pillar but pedestal. I'd have been prepared to show you some good commercial openings, had I realised you were looking for an occupation. Perhaps investigating crimes could be it. That's an idea. Problems solved. Enquiries undertaken. Fees moderate – I'd handle that side of things.'

'Don't be absurd – or cruel. Whom were you helping this morning?'

'Sempronius, of course.'

'On whose orders?'

'Not many people can order me around. Well, I suppose the Emperor can, when he's here.'

'And in his absence?'

'It's obvious, isn't it?'

'And when Aurelia lent her villa to someone?'

'Sempronius. Hadn't you guessed that?'

'So, logically, he's the person who killed Pontilla Pilata. Or had her killed. Yes, that possibility had crossed my mind, but still I don't think it's in his character. Do you?'

'You should have been an augur, my dear. You're wasted as a mere Vestal, even Chief one. But reading the entrails is child's play, you know, compared to reading character. After all, one liver's much like another. With people – well, they're

96

enjoyably various. I shouldn't care to say that Sempronius wouldn't or couldn't strangle a woman who was deceiving him, perhaps even teasing him. There's quite a lot of the savage in Sempronius – as in most of us men.

'Brutes,' he added complacently, after a pause, pushing a wide band of gold bracelet higher up his plump, hairless brown arm, 'when we're roused.'

'But if she wasn't strangled at all? If the crime was no sudden, angry impulse but carefully thought out and achieved by other means? Supposing she was actually killed by poison?'

'That might be interesting – very. Traditionally, it's something preferred by women, isn't it? I suppose there may even be imperial precedents–'

'Careful,' I whispered, indicating the driver.

'Oh, I'm talking about ancient history. It won't bother him to hear about the Empress Livia, for example. She was a splendid wife to Augustus, and nobody can be sure she did poison her grandsons. As you know, Julia, people can say the most awful things about any of us. But my loyalty's not in doubt. I deeply admire the Empress's devotion – not only to her husband, of course, but also to her brother. I really am impressed by that, especially after what you've just told me.'

I sat up, with a cry.

'Oh, come,' he said. 'You're flattering me – not that I object. But I can't believe that you didn't want me to reach that conclusion, having got there first yourself.'

'Stop,' I said. 'Where on earth are we?'

In talking to Afranius, I had paid no attention to the time. And I suddenly realised we must long ago have reached the house, were perhaps circling it if the driver dimly understood we were pre-occupied or did not dare break in on our conversation.

As I reached out to pull back the curtain, Afranius seized my hand. 'Wait. Don't show yourself and remember this is an imperial carriage. Just reflect.'

'Where are we?' I asked angrily, but somehow I let the curtain fall from my fingers, though still glaring at him. The carriage, I noticed, had stopped.

'Probably not very far from the Appian Gate,' he said indolently.

'What!'

'That's where I meant us to be. Yes, it looks as if we're there. Do you want to turn back?'

'Of course,' I said. 'At once. You know I can't play games like this with you. I'm–'

'A pillar, after all, my dear. I'm not altogether surprised, though I had wondered. . . . I am very good-natured and I like to be helpful.'

'Helpful?'

'Five milestones from here – on the left, I think – is the Pilatus tomb. Rather ostentatious, as you'd expect, but personally that doesn't worry me. Only the easier to distinguish. Spacious, too, I believe. It's quite a mild morning for a drive, and in this carriage nobody is going to stop you. They won't even dare think of it.

'Do you fear you'll feel the cold? You're welcome to borrow my cloak – keep it, if you like, as a souvenir of the adventure. It's good quality wool. And the secret? What you feed the sheep on. I'm intending to have them imported next year in quantity.'

'The sheep?' I had not meant to smile. I felt confused, savage at heart but strangely reckless.

'How's that for soft?' he said. 'Just stroke that pile. It's the perfect cloak for you, Julia. It really is.'

'My household, for one thing, expect my return. In fact, they'll already be wondering what's happened. And for another thing, I'm breaking the law – or would be breaking it if I went out of Rome with you. You know that as well as I do. It's a terrible risk.'

'But what isn't? Anyway, this good old creature is discreet.' He prodded the driver's thin back. 'You'll find he can keep his mouth shut on the matter – as on most others. As for breaking the law, I can't help thinking it's been broken by several people recently. But then laws don't mean a great deal to me somehow. I don't know why.'

'You intended this,' I stated.

Perhaps it was the way I had been reclining, but I felt my body tremble and I hoped he did not see it. He unclasped his scarlet cloak and half-threw it at me. Its barbaric-looking ruby brooch glinted. The jewel hung like fruit on a golden branch, supported in its setting by the beaks of twin pecking birds.

98

I thought of Pontilla Pilata's jewellery. Hadn't Publius said something that first evening about its eastern origin? I seemed to hear again the boom of his voice, hiding perhaps near-panic; today, both had subsided, like his ardour. And underneath that first evening, I had been pleased at the disruption of the norm caused by his visit. I welcomed, even if I declined, the challenge of the puzzle: the dead body in the tomb, the scarf, the unstolen jewellery – acquired in the very part of the world from which Afranius Dexter came. Publius's visit had been followed by my summons to the Empress. She had been forceful enough but probably not frank. Nobody had been prepared to tell the whole truth. Perhaps nobody minded, for various reasons, that Pontilla Pilata was dead.

'What an expensive-looking clasp,' I said. 'Where did you get it?'

'It's nothing.' He shrugged his partly bare shoulders. 'My mother gave it to me when I was a boy. You may keep it, of course.'

'Thank you. I wouldn't rob you of your mother's gift. Besides, the Vestals are not permitted to wear jewellery.'

'It wasn't really a gift from my mother.'

'I thought not.'

'So please keep it, after the expedition. You can wear it in private.'

'Are you importing them in quantity?'

'But it was a gift – from Pontilla Pilata, as a matter of fact. Absurd, you know, when really I can put my hands on far better stuff. This is the kind of thing made for foreign visitors. The jewel's glass.'

'Very well.' My body was no longer trembling, though I was oddly glad to have the cloak to wrap round me. 'I'm ready. I want to see the tomb. I don't know why, but I do.'

'Wise woman. May it bring you your heart's desire.'

'My downfall, more likely.'

He began to move, uncoiling himself as the carriage slowly creaked into motion. 'And,' he said, 'your household will relax, relieved to hear from my own lips that you're spending the day with the Lady Aurelia. Yes. Some god's just suggested the one thing I'd overlooked.'

'What do you mean, you'll tell them?'

'Ah, Julia.' He brought his face caressingly close to mine,

so that I could see the gleam of its cosmetics and smell the scent, on his breath, it seemed, as well as on his skin. 'How I'd have enjoyed accompanying you, but business compels me to stay in the city. Surely you realise I'm truly torn, though I can at least be the bearer of your message. So I play my part, after all. Farewell.'

He had slipped away as he spoke, and the carriage, lightened, was now gathering speed. The driver seemed determined to whip up the wretched mules. Harness jangled and the carriage swayed perilously, but I lay there exhilarated by its movement, uncaring whether we trotted on day and night until we reached Capua. Through the flapping curtains I caught glimpses of the tree-lined road. Now and then vehicles met or passed us. Let them see, I thought, as they slackened pace out of respect. At most there might be a flash of scarlet from our interior: some member of the imperial family on a mysterious mission, they would assure each other, perhaps reminded of the Emperor's absence and feeling that great events had brushed their lives.

Although I thought of the Vestals, the effect was to make me nearly smile. I had broken the law, but the words lacked meaning. In my own mind, I had committed no impiety, no crime. Generations of Vestals might line the route, open-eyed; and astonishment would turn them into pine trees, whispering in their stiff, dusty foliage of the scandal, as if I had fled Rome with a lover. Yet I should go back, once I had visited the tomb, throw off Afranius's cloak, resume my status and treasure this moment of liberty even as I once more led a dignified procession through thronging, silent crowds to the temple of Vesta.

We stopped, and another sort of silence surrounded me. I felt queasy with apprehension. It was as though I had become naked. After all, I was stripped of everything at this moment and conscious of the world outside the carriage waiting – almost holding its breath – for me to appear. It was very quiet now, stiflingly so. Yet before me must lie, however unfamiliar, no crowds, no people, but only a winter country scene of some cypresses clustering around the façade of a tomb.

'Are we there?' I called, to hide any hesitation, in a loud, commanding tone.

The failure to respond gave me impetus. Perhaps the old fool, huddled up in his coarse, sacking hood, was deaf.

As I jumped onto the grass, I found he too had got down and I confronted Rufus, holding out his arm to assist me.

The daylight seemed too harshly bright but I moved firmly away to where the high white portico of the tomb shone lividly against a guardian ring of black trees. The vast expanse of open air washed around me with dizzying effect, and I might almost have been swimming as I laboured through the heavy waves.

I could not even tell if I was surprised. Had I suspected some trick of Afranius's – though not exactly this one – from the time I accepted his invitation? No doubt they had planned it together, perhaps not daring to hope it would succeed so well. At some point, as indeed had happened, the driver would stop; and I, as I took his proffered arm, would become his willing victim. It came too late. Anyway, the arm didn't look strong enough, I thought, recollecting wryly Gemma's comment on its celery-like nature.

He ran up behind me and actually caught at a trailing fold of Afranius's cloak. Nervousness was what I expected rather than the grinning impudence with which he stood there, confident of my response.

For a moment I was afraid. He loomed half-threateningly against the intensely pale expanse of sky, arched like a shield of steel, and the mass of distant hills that seemed closing in, thunderously dark, glimpsed between the tall spears of the cypresses.

'Don't you recognize me?' He said it furiously, while I continued to gaze at the hand that had dared grasp the fold of cloak.

'As my driver? Of course. Not that you seemed to drive particularly well.'

'I'm not a mule driver,' he answered sullenly, flushing. 'And your Roman traffic–'

'Would you please release my cloak?' I interrupted. 'Wait for me by the carriage until I have visited the tomb.'

'I'm not a slave either. I did this to see you, you must understand that. How else could I have managed? And now you behave in this haughty way, as if you didn't care a straw for me.'

'A straw? I'm not familiar with the idiom, but perhaps they teach you to speak like that in Gaul. Or I suppose it may be in use among the mule-drivers and such people.'

'Don't pretend,' he said. 'You already know – you must – what I feel. I'm in earnest. It's obvious. I'm in love and I don't mind saying so. Why pretend you don't follow? A woman like you can't be as obtuse as that. And why would I go to all this trouble? Because I feel what I do. You've got to believe that and stop humiliating me.'

'It's humiliating for me – listening to your words. And hopeless for you.'

'You feel nothing yourself – is that what you're telling me?'

He took a step nearer, pushing back the hood that hid his fair hair. His patched, ragged tunic gave him a forlorn air and yet seemed partly disguise, as though an actor was playing a servant. It was all a game, for Afranius and for him, however much I might wish it weren't.

'Do you know who I am?' I found myself saying for the second time that morning. 'If you do, you'll understand perfectly well. Your – your advances are dangerous for you and impossible as far as I'm concerned. I'd be mad to believe you but even madder to be swayed by what you say. Why,' I exclaimed, tugging the cloak from his hand, 'you're sufficiently in demand, aren't you, at the Blue Toga Club? That should serve. And be glad I don't have you arrested for insulting the Chief Vestal.'

'Listen to me, please. I don't mind your being angry, but listen. I mean all I've said – and I don't think you're indifferent either. The other day on the Capitol, when we met–'

'I took notice, briefly, of a young Gaul under the Prefect's aegis. Was that you, so often auctioned and today's menial? Don't presume too far on it, anyway. Be my slave – my servant – if that's what you wish. And wait here until I'm ready to return.'

'You care for me,' he said boldly.

'I care, as you put it, for no one. I do not. I cannot. Your successes elsewhere have turned your head. Next you'll be saying the Empress is in love with you, or possibly the Prefect. Perhaps nobody in the city is safe from the contagion? Well, my status is notoriously unique. Move aside.'

'Julia.'

At that word, I stared up at him. For uttering it a goddess might have slain him; Diana had, for less, had Actaeon's hounds tear their master's body to bloody shreds. And Rufus looked vulnerable enough, despite the baffled, feral gleam in his green eyes. Goddesses, of course, did not always repulse youthful mortal lovers. But then, being goddesses, they believed – I suppose – that they were loved.

I pushed him gently aside, or he fell back as I gestured automatically. How could he have resisted? The aura of inviolability around me was too strong. He could only watch, defeated, as at solemn, processional pace I walked towards the grandiose portico of the tomb, very much a solitary mourner.

It seemed to be growing oppressively dark, or I was still confused. Once I stumbled and momentarily I wondered foolishly if it would bring him back beside me. He watched, I felt sure, but he did not stir.

Inside the tomb, I should find nothing. It was no longer apparent why I had been so eager to visit it. Indeed, I had difficulty in bringing my mind back to what had once been the case of Pontilla Pilata. Yet it was here, I had to recall, as I passed through the bronze doors into the chill penumbra of the domed chamber, lit by a high oculus, that a woman had been murdered. Poisoned or strangled, she had fallen here, in agony, alone. In niches round the wall were placed the urns of her ancestors' ashes, and I could just see the unlit lamps and the mouldering garlands suspended before them.

There was a tang of death about this dim space. In the damp air it was almost palpable. A brazen clang might signify that the doors had slammed behind me and that I was sealed into a shadowy grave. As I advanced cautiously, having glanced back to the faint slit of light showing where the entrance was, my foot encountered a broken glass vessel, implements, a table overturned, it seemed, or tools dropped by the workman who had discovered the body.

The smell now was pungent. Some food had slowly decayed, eaten away perhaps by the poison it contained. I poked at the remains, futile and suddenly more pitiful than any corpse would have been. From outside came the low reverberation of distant thunder.

If in some after-life I were to meet Rufus, might I then appease his shade and tell him how, had existence been different, we would have been able to come together and embrace? But when in that underworld we met each other, it would be only I who remembered. His life would have been full and rich. Children and grandchildren would have grieved at his bier. Shades would cluster about to greet him, while I passed, close enough to see the plumes of his hair turned grey, veiled and unnoticed, in death as in life slipping into oblivion.

A flash of lightning illumined the tomb's interior, and the crack of thunder overhead might have been the roof splitting, so savage was it. It rolled away in echoes as I ran to the doorway. Already I could hear the rising hiss of rain. Before I could reach the doors themselves, I felt myself seized. Another flash of lightning lit up the pale face of Rufus, and I struggled all the more in the momentary, suffocating blackness that followed.

'You disobeyed my orders,' I panted as I fought myself free.

'There's a storm outside, if you hadn't noticed, and we can hardly go back until it's over.'

I moved away, retreating into the recesses of the chamber. 'Your place is with the mules.'

'Yours may be, if you like. I'm staying here.'

'Do Gauls melt in the rain? A Roman would do as I bid and remain at his post.'

'And get soaking wet for his stupidity. Yes, we aren't like that in Gaul.'

'Don't shout,' I said. 'This is a sacred – well, nearly sacred – spot. It's the Pilatus family tomb, and it's also where Pontilla Pilata was killed. Her body may have fallen just here, where I'm standing. Some utensils were broken as she fell. There are traces of food too, and you probably overheard what I told Afranius about her being poisoned.'

'No, I didn't hear,' he said. 'Poisoned, was she?'

'You doubt it?'

'It's an interesting theory. Was her body found here, then?'

'Yes, it was.'

'On the threshold?'

'Yes, on the threshold. It was discovered by a wretched workman. He's now dead. What happened was, he saw the corpse straight away, dropped his tools and fled. The next thing that occurred, according to Pontilla Pilata's lawyer–'

'Who cares?' He interrupted. 'She's dead, and it's all over and done with. But we're alive. Alive and alone here. Think of that.'

'In a tomb,' I murmured, after a pause.

'Well, it keeps the rain off, to some extent. Give me your hand and let's see if we can find our way down to the room below.'

'Don't touch me.'

'Because it's a crime?' He sounded mocking and much closer than I had realised. I could sense his physical proximity, exuding a warmth that was somehow tempting in the damp greyish obscurity where I stood. I hoped he would not ask me if I was afraid.

'I don't mind about the so-called crime,' he went on. 'About anything, as you must know, except you yourself. Surely you understand that, don't you? I'm in love with you, Julia. People in Rome seem much the same in that way as we are at home. You've even had poets who wrote about being in love – I could quote from some of them, if you like.'

'I'm glad you're so well educated.'

'You're teasing,' he said. 'But this time I'm not going to be annoyed. In fact, it tells me you do feel something. You're not the superior, indifferent creature you're trying to seem. And I'm hardly your first lover, am I? Roman women are notorious among us, I can tell you. So I don't see what makes all the confusion – the fuss – between us. Is that put rightly? To make a fuss: is that the correct idiom? Or do you have a verb, to fuss?'

'Are you in love with me so as to get advanced Latin lessons?'

'Having been admirably taught, I speak well, on the whole, and probably I know more of the grammar rules than you.'

'Gemma – my maid – thinks you've got a funny accent. She's quite right.'

'Oh, I'm not Roman, I grant. I don't wish to be. I have my own native country. But what do you know of factitive verbs in the passive tense? They become copulative. Shall I give you an example?'

105

'If that's a Gallic way of threatening rape, I don't advise you to.'

'Here, I think is a good example. You are considered by me the most desirable woman in Rome.'

He spoke boastfully, so that I might have twitted him – had I felt like it – with intending a compliment for himself. But I had nothing to say.

Instead, as we stood there silently, hearing the slackening pace of the rain on the roof (the storm would soon subside), I reached out and softly took his hand. How hot and palpable it was – and strange. It was flesh other than my own that I had actually sought in contact, that I clasped as though some communication would pass from it to me.

I held his hand and tried to join it on, as it were, to the arm, the shoulder, torso and head of a living other person. As an invocation, I said his name to myself, but he remained a phantom. Away in Gaul he had been born. He had been a child, grown up, taken this shape, become a particular individual, with tastes and habits and thoughts of which I knew nothing. He had parents, siblings probably, a home to which he would return. He stood free and uncapturable by my imagination, however tightly I might hold his hand and think I grasped reality. Soon I must let it fall, much as one might let fall the hand of a corpse.

Let me love him, I prayed. I would forget, ignore, indeed leap with one bound all the barriers of birth and age and custom that fenced us from each other. I longed for clouds of cupids to descend amid roses with lighted torches and with fiery arrows, laughing as they pricked and wreathed and chained our unprotesting bodies, to leave us in the darkness of intimacy. And then let death perhaps come. It would not be unwelcome as I lay in his arms, if it took us both, myrtle-crowned, to wander in some ghostly grove by the Stygian lake, together and for ever.

As though he had heard my prayer, he stirred. I felt his body embracing, almost absorbing mine, and yet it hung about me like an encumbrance. I wrestled with it clumsily as I struggled to respond. Desired or hated, this was he. I wished for the sensation of his weight, and to feel with more than physical awareness the sliding muscles of his upper arm, the form of his throat, the hair at the nape of his neck. No longer could I claim that he was not alive. And then I understood that it was I who was the encumbrance, I who hung heavily about him: the corpse was myself.

X

The darkness was a shroud I was glad of, but I could feel it dissolving even as I stood there, willing it to last and vainly trying to hold it around myself. Soon I should be exposed. Perhaps Rufus already saw me for what I was. I did not raise my eyes to look at him.

The air had grown less stifling, though I found it no easier to breathe. I sensed rather than saw him come closer.

'Kiss me,' he said.

Unable to speak, I shook my head.

'Still unsure of me? Or frightened perhaps? I won't harm you – believe me.'

'More likely – more likely I'll harm you,' I said sadly, after a pause.

He laughed. 'Not a chance. But do you want to try?'

He took me in his arms and kissed my closed lips.

No peel of thunder shook the domed roof of the tomb.

I felt the continuing stiffness of my own body and the resistance in my mind, and yet I could have leant my head on his shoulder and wept. Had I not dreamt of such a moment? And now its reality was joyless, sterile and inert.

'I love you,' he murmured, but there was something plaintive, even bewildered, in his tone.

'Thank you,' I said.

'Julia, I'm talking about love – not an invitation to a supper-party. You know what I feel, don't you? And you share that feeling.'

'Whatever it is, it's meaningless between us. Meaningless and impossible. The storm must be over by now. We'll go back to Rome. I've committed enough crimes for one day, for a lifetime really.'

'Look at me,' he said.

'You're very confident,' I said. 'But I shan't look at you. I don't need to. And instead, you listen to me.

'There can be nothing between us – nothing. Oh, you're young, charming no doubt, possibly loving in your way. But it's too late, as far as I'm concerned. I'm not Aurelia, you've got to realise, still less some pathetic old man in the Blue Toga Club. I don't possess the very feelings you're trying to appeal to. It's flattering of you to presume otherwise, I suppose, but I am a woman without lovers.'

'You mean, as Chief Vestal . . .? It's incredible. In fact, I don't believe it. No one could put up with such a life, and in Rome of all places.'

'I've disappointed you, I see, by my rectitude. But whatever you were brought up to believe in the provinces, Rome today is ruled by rectitude, quite literally. The Emperor himself is famous for his virtues. And the Empress too, of course.'

'And Pontilla Pilata? Wasn't she thought to be notoriously virtuous until the truth came out?'

'She and I are – were – very different women indeed, if that's what you're trying to imply.'

'Do you hate men? Is that it? No, I can't think that. And I can't be the first man to admire you. There's pompous old Publius for one. Now, just listen to me for a moment. Are you happy?'

'Happy?' I struggled not to raise my eyes to his.

It was strange that I had not moved away, that we remained so close without touching. Or perhaps that was the heart of the situation. I was so conscious of his closeness that I seemed the possessor of all the externals that made up Rufus as a physical presence. His sacking tunic itself seemed to breathe. It hung awry, leaving bared below the knee one thin leg, paler in its flesh than any Roman man's. In clumsy, coarse sandals his bony feet looked vulnerable, almost absurd. It was displeasing to think how easily they could be crushed: displeasing or, more truly, part of the charm he held for me, even though I had no idea of the personality hidden beneath the skin and bone.

108

'Happy,' he repeated. 'Contented. Do you have some other word?'

'There are such words but they don't apply to the Chief Vestal. She exists and does her duty. That's all.'

'No, it's not all. You've met me. I've entered your life, regardless of what it was like before. You're no longer just on your own – and neither am I.'

'Oh, your position is rather different, in so far as you have a position. You seem to have made yourself quite popular enough in the city. You shouldn't be lonely. Besides, you don't live here. Quite soon, I suppose, you'll be going home, to Forjus, or Forjum, wherever it is.'

'Fréjus.'

'Anyway, back to Gaul. If I did feel anything for you – came to feel anything – I should scarcely make myself happy, as you put it. And can one fall in love with a shadow? I know nothing about you, except you're young and foreign. You know nothing – absolutely nothing – of me and my life. You haven't entered it at all. You've seen me and presumed, dangerously so, to speak intimately to me, touch me even. I pardon you, though perhaps I shouldn't. But don't presume any further, unless you want to spend the rest of your days in the Tullianum. It's a prison.'

'You don't have to tell me,' he said sullenly. 'I lodge near there.'

'Lodging in it might be rather different.'

'My lodging's fairly squalid, as it is. I don't mind. I'm used to a hard life. We're a tougher lot in Fréjus than the sort of people I've met in Rome. Tougher, poorer and more honest. I don't like what I've seen of them here. I don't trust them, for one thing. But I do trust you. I want you to love me. And I think you do, or you would if you weren't so proud. We could be happy, even if only for a short time. Is that so terrible? Isn't it better than nothing?'

'Alas,' I said, feeling an unaccustomed weakness. The knowledge that I might reach out and hold him made me tense to the point of shivering.

Darkness lingered now only in the furthest recess of the tomb. The stillness after the storm was strongly palpable and far more disturbing. Outside, the light would be harshly bright, and the hills beyond the dripping cypresses closing round like giant spectators, when finally we emerged.

'Look,' he said urgently. 'If not at me, at least at how things are. We're here alone, unknown to anyone except Afranius Dexter. I begged him to help me. I had all sorts of ideas about getting to see you – dressing up, disguising myself. Being asked to take the imperial carriage gave him the best idea really. We went first to your house – or he did, rather. I sat tight. I didn't let your maid catch sight of me.

'And now we're together. You wanted to come here. Here we are. The gods have meant it to be so. Don't defy them.'

'This has nothing to do with the gods. It's true, though no concern of yours, that I wanted to come out here, but hardly to meet you. Pontilla Pilata's murder–'

'Haven't we something more important to talk about, if we must talk? I'm tired of hearing about her. We're alive, after all. Time may be short for us, but there's no need to make it shorter. Besides, why so much talk? Trust your sensations, if nothing else. I want you, Julia, and that's all I have to say. Must I go on saying it to convince you?'

He put his arms about me roughly and forced me to look up.

For the first time I reached out and touched him gladly: his neck, his cheek, his lips that slightly quivered into a smile under my touch. How frail his face seemed, but perhaps every face was frail when explored as I was exploring. The skin under his eyes was very faintly wrinkled, freckled, oddly dis-coloured as though stained by the colour of those brilliant, green glass pupils that glowed as they gazed at me.

'No,' I said, as he began moving his hands over my body. 'No. If this is to be anything, it must be Pygmalion and Galatea in reverse. And you needn't speak. You're too sure, too quick – too conceited as a man to understand. Be careful of coming alive for me. Nobody has done for so long, perhaps never before. And perhaps you've never encountered an actual woman before. Not just a sensation of two bodies together – in love, or whatever it's called – but meeting, mixing with a complete human being.'

'I've had plenty of women, I can tell you,' he said proudly, frowning at me and uneasily stirring. 'Don't worry about that. I can play my part as a lover. You'll see if you give me

110

the chance. It's you who don't respond properly. You're afraid. I'm not.'

'Of course I'm afraid. There's every reason to be. And it's bound to take me time to conceive of anyone existing beyond myself. I've had no urge to do so.'

'But I'm here in front of you. You can feel I'm alive, can't you? Flesh and blood, all right.'

'There's flesh and blood in a calf going to be sacrificed. Or even in Publius. It's nothing to do with that – or with your successes as a lover. Rome is full of young men boasting of their conquests. Gaul, I gather, is no different.

'Understand that whatever I do, I won't be just another of your conquests – I, of all people. And I don't trust my sensations. How can I? They tell me nothing about who you are, what you're really like, your character, your family, your career – in a word, you. As long as you're a stranger – a non-person – it all means nothing to me.'

'I'm a man.'

'Do you expect me to reply "I'm a woman"?'

'Well.' He grinned. 'You are.'

'Now perhaps I'm learning what you're like – what men so often are like.'

'There's more to me than meets the eye.'

'So I should hope. Ah, that wounds your vanity.'

He took my hand that still rested on his shoulder and impatiently shifted it.

'You're better at wounding than loving,' he said.

'More practised, I admit. And I'd ask a lot of you, as a woman – as this particular woman, whom you don't yet know. It was a mistake to approach me, to interest me. You aimed too high or chose very badly. I'm like someone who's been blind and deaf most of their adult life – by choice, in my case. I don't see and hear, still less understand, everything straight away. How could I?

'I don't understand love, to start with. Oh, it's not just my own chastity that's the trouble. I can understand lust – I think. Isn't that much commoner, even in Gaul? I'm not certain what my feelings are yet about you, whoever you are. And it's no good my being offered a bundle of statistics, of the kind Calvus enjoys so much: Gallic male, fair-haired, presentable, speaking reasonable Latin. . . . You might as

111

well be a slave or a household pet. I'm not in want of either. But another human being aspiring to make me – what was it? – happy. How? By pressing his body against mine until I feel some equivalent heat, and we grapple with each other in a paroxysm of passion. Afterwards I should lie there wondering who washed your clothes, if your mother was still alive and whether you had siblings.

'And by then I should want you to be curious about me – to learn things I've told no one. What it was like living with my father when I was very young – how proud he was of me. I might almost have been an Empress. When I first joined the Vestals I was very shy. Shy and desperately ignorant. Some of the girls had lovers. It was more like the Rome of your imagination. I never sought a lover. Now I'm old and honoured and it's too late – impossible, really – and a young foreigner presumes to say he loves me. Is it any wonder I can't believe it?

'I'm dead, my dear Rufus. I haven't got the power to bring myself back to life – let alone you. You'll have to remain an idol for me – a dream. It's much better like that. You were quite right. I don't want the risk. Oh, I don't mean to my position so much as the responsibility of another person. I couldn't respond to anything you felt. I should remain cold, just as I have been – cruel also perhaps, because of it. Yours too has been a dream, I'm afraid. A flattering one, for me. It will keep me warm as I lie in bed alone on chilly nights. You will forget me, I know. But, if it's any consolation, I shall always remember you.'

'As a dream, I suppose?'

'As a dream from the gate of ivory.'

'Why think of me as so false?'

'Because you can have no existence for me. You may not be false but certainly you aren't real or true. And now we must go back to the city. We shan't meet again.'

I went towards the doorway, strangely buoyed up by my own despairing resolve. It was painful, but even amid the pain I felt my dominance. It was not nothing to keep on my way, advancing towards the porch as if confident the bronze doors would fly open at my approach and the carriage, miraculously dry, be found waiting there for me to enter. Perhaps I was not quite clear what I had done – wounded

112

myself irreparably, it might be – but it was inevitable and wise and for the best.

It was true, though, that I should often dream of Rufus. I saw no need to banish that image and make myself yet lonelier.

'Julia.' His voice rang out, echoing rather nasally across the tomb, a thin cry lacking Roman authority and yet it made me pause. To hesitate was weakness. To turn was madness, or the final test of my resolve. Before me lay the closed doors which no will-power by itself would ever open.

I prayed for a renewed outbreak of the storm, with lightning that should strike stone, melt bronze and fuse our bodies even as it incinerated them. So I should not grow old – and solitary and more stately because my body could no longer move in any other way. The cycle of feast days and games, and all the blank domestic days too that stretched before me, would be annihilated in one searing flash. Mercifully I should be extinguished, my last consciousness my lips eagerly pressed against his as total blackness engulfed us.

I turned.

He stood quite naked, illuminated by no lightning bolt but in a shaft of sun that momentarily burnished his body into chryselephantine tones. He gestured unselfconsciously, smiling, drawing me back towards the shadowy recess, half-indicating the room that lay below. Like Hermes Psychopompus, he would conduct me down to subterranean regions – except that he was no god but mortal, with the same body I had tentatively caressed, of flesh not ivory, its skin freckled, with tufts of reddish gold that gleamed like metal but were merely human hair.

And I was no shade. I was weak, foolish even, but abruptly human and swept by sheer human longing. No supernatural aids were necessary – no cupids, thunderclaps or sudden death. I wanted nothing but him, but above all it was the intoxication of experiencing emotion that thrilled me.

I scarcely realised how rapidly I had crossed the room. I was standing in the same shaft of sunlight as I too threw off my heavy tunic, having let Afranius's cloak slide to the floor. Under his gaze I moved without haste now, prolonging the sweetness I felt at the stirring of my own blood, confident that I had only to touch his body to make it tingle into comparable life.

He is beautiful, I thought without surprise. I had known it already but it had not seemed more than outward envelope. Now it meant something different; I felt as if I were its possessor, its owner. He was mine, and it was the knowledge of that possession that excited me. Because I wished it, he would make love to me. Beyond that, I could see nothing.

'I love you,' he said huskily.

'You may.'

'What does that mean?'

'You have my permission.'

He laughed as he drew me closer. It was strange. He was unfamiliar, almost indifferent, it seemed, to quite who I was, and if I protested verbally it was only half-heartedly as I sensed my personality gliding away from me.

'I've never met a woman before exactly like you,' he said.

'The Chief Vestal is unique.'

'Not quite, if she's a woman – and I'll remind her that she is. It's something you've forgotten for too long, Julia.'

He spread out Afranius's cloak, making a scarlet patch on the sunlit floor.

'Isn't there an underground room?' I asked, shying away from the glowing pool of colour. 'Here, I mean, under this one. I thought you said–'

'Forget what I said. Forget everything but us. Forget Rome and your rank and your dreadful existence.'

'Dreadful because it lacked you?'

'That's right.'

'And what,' I started asking as he gently pulled me down to lie beside him, 'have you to forget? Both Rome and Gaul, and your funnily-named home town, where I suppose some girl is waiting for you? Do you go home to be a magistrate? Perhaps you're the son of the Prefect.'

'Me? I haven't even got a father.' He lay partly on me, pushing aside my hair and looking into my eyes. 'And if you want to know, it's my mother who works. She sells vegetables in the local market. Isn't that shocking? You'd never speak to such a woman, would you, in Rome? So, yes, let's forget all about our antecedents, if you call them that. You have nice eyes, Julia. I like brown eyes.'

114

'Nothing shocks me,' I said. 'But in fact I admire a woman who does something. I don't approve of idleness — in men or women.'

'Everything shocks you, beginning with me. But it doesn't matter. It's good for you to have a man. A real man and not some stuffy middle-aged Roman who's probably impotent most of the time. I'll be a lover you'll always remember, however long you live.'

'And am I good for you?' I took his narrow face in my hands. I wanted to study it all over again, and scrutinising it so closely I saw how easily his pale complexion marked and how fine were the long, unexpectedly dark-grey eyelashes he lowered as I traced with my thumbs the shape of his features. A reddish pimple on his jawline, rising amid the slightest hint of bristles, was almost wonderful in reminding me by a flaw of his imperfect, intense humanity.

'Of course you are,' he said carelessly. 'You'll see.'

'Who are you anyway? A stranger — a presumptuous foreigner whose Latin isn't as good as he thinks it is. Listen—'

'Why should I?' And he kissed me hotly.

As he drew away, I pulled his face down again, kissing his lips, that pimple and then his chin.

'When you use the ablative absolute . . .' I whispered.

He shook himself impatiently at the words, and the heat and weight of his body made me languorous.

'Remember,' I said, fighting my own sensations. 'You shouldn't use it when the noun with which the participle agrees forms part of the principal sentence. When you spoke earlier of having been well taught, you were the subject, you see—'

But his hand came over my mouth, so roughly that I was tempted to bite it. I did nothing. I was silenced, silent, absorbed, as he made love to me.

115

XI

'In what way help you, mum?' Gemma asked sharply. 'Isn't the case over? Everyone's sick and tired of hearing about *her*, from what I can gather. One of her lovers did it, and that's no surprise now we know how she carried on.'

'Nevertheless, he may be able to help,' I said, aware it sounded feeble.

I was more than half-indifferent, lulled by memories and the warm milky water of the bath where I lay, not much disturbed by Gemma's deliberate throwing in of so many awkward conversational pebbles.

'You mean he'll be coming here, do you?'

'Oh, I expect so,' I said idly. 'We must consider how best to avoid scandal, of course. You'll have some bright idea, Gemma, I'm sure.'

'I'm sure I don't know I shall,' she said, squinting down at me. 'I don't like it, mum, I can tell you. What's he got to do with it, anyway? One of her lovers, was he? She took up with all sorts, she did, and a thoroughly nasty lot they were. Tib was right, wasn't she, after all? Take my advice and let the whole thing go hang.'

Lacking the energy to laugh, I smiled; and perhaps she thought I was convinced, or soon would be. The case would serve, I hoped, to cover at least one or two of Rufus's visits – and after that what happened was unclear. Like so much that had occupied me, it did not matter. I had been conscious of that when I left the Palatine, only that morning, though it seemed now so long ago. In abandoning my litter, I had declared as much to myself. I rather doubted if I should ever see the Empress again, except on state occasions. And our house would certainly be barred to Publius, supposing that he sought to see me.

It was not the case that had changed my existence, as possibly it had at first seemed it might. It was Rufus. And instead of his incursion being abrupt, it had come – I felt – with marvellous inevitability, as I looked back, lying there contentedly, uncaring of the distinctly cooling water. Without the case would I even have met him? And without the gradual disillusionment it had brought me, I should never have first stood, then lain beside him, in a tomb on the Appian Way.

But it had all seemed present from the first: my sense of being followed by him, and then dreaming of him, so that he was far more familiar than he realised. From a dream he had sprung into life and made me live also. Already we shared something. We had our past, whatever might be waiting for us in the future.

The truth too about Pontilla Pilata was oddly relevant, however vehemently I might deny that she and I had anything in common. She had taken lovers and concealed the fact for the sake of her reputation. I was hardly different. Excited though I still was, I knew quite well that I was not about to give up my position because Rufus was my lover. Indeed, I was expecting Gemma to help me hide exactly that – and was meanwhile hoping to hide it from her. Yet I was not ashamed or boastful. Others may have written or spoken of the pleasure of telling you are loved, or of naming the lover's name. To me, it was the secret knowledge that I possessed that thrilled me.

Naked, bathed and alone at last (Gemma I had sent away for some scissors as a pretext), I was conscious of Rufus as intensely as if I still enjoyed the luxury of his body hung heavily against mine. I was with him again in that tomb, sprawled shamelessly on the floor, willing his hand's progress over my stiffening breast as positively as though guiding it myself. It was the re-creation of those sensations that I indulged. Water and oil and scent were no threat to them, because I felt my flesh would never cease to carry the marks of its contact with him.

I wanted nothing else, except for him to be close beside me again: a living, throbbing being, as I was, yet both wonderfully stripped of individuality, drowned in the anonymity of love. All my nagging urge to know about him had gone, along with fear – that fear I had clung to, like a last, pathetic veil – that I could never respond. I was too conscious, too old, and also too little experienced, I had dreaded, to yield as I longed to yield. Not garments, but personality was what I needed to discard.

To be rid of it, to feel it going, melting under his warm, urgent contact had been marvellously sweet. And though I knew that I must eventually stir myself, dress, assume again the outward shape of the Chief Vestal, it would all now be unreal: a disguise I should eagerly cast off as soon as he bent and touched me again. What he had violated was my image of myself, and in that destruction I was no passive partner but the instigator. His glance would be enough to halt me, even if I stood fully robed and veiled at the altar. Far from fearing it, I realised it was what I positively longed for.

I am ill, I should say, to explain how little I was going in future to appear publicly; I am seeing no-one. The winter and the Emperor's absence would seem to foster decorous retreat. Vesta, dear goddess, demanded domesticity. The hearth should blaze, even if in doing so it illuminated Rufus's naked limbs entwined with mine.

'Well, Gemma,' I began the next morning. 'What have you thought up?'

'About what, mum?' she said stubbornly.

Even now, I was displeased to find, I could not quite speak with the ease I had imagined.

'You remember. What we were talking about – finding a way for that young Gaul to come here unobtrusively, should it turn out to be necessary.'

'Why can't he come like anyone else?'

'More than one visit might start tongues wagging, you know. We don't want that.'

'Don't want him at all, if you ask me.'

'Why, Gemma,' I said lightly, 'I'm surprised at you. Just because he's foreign, we shouldn't be prejudiced. Perhaps he seems a little odd to you. His skin is very fair, and of course he speaks with a rather funny accent. But in a way he's a guest of Rome's. He's on his own here, too.'

'On the make, more like.'

'Perhaps that's how you talk in Butunti, but I don't care for the tone.' I forgot to sound casual. 'It's enough that I think it useful to see him, Gemma – and I've explained why. That really settles the matter.'

'Very well, mum.'

'And please don't take it out, as you might say, on the silver basin. It isn't improved by being banged around like that. Why,' I went on, more quietly, smiling in her direction, 'we may as well get the case cleared up between us. For

Tibicina's sake, you'd surely be glad to know who the murderer was.'

But she was not to be cajoled.

I thought of Aurelia's villa as a possible place to meet, before I recalled that she knew Rufus. Wildly, I even wondered momentarily if I could go to his lodgings. Then having wandered half-angrily through the house, feeling in its very spaces bars, I came back to my own quarters. There lay the answer. Beyond my bedroom was a short passage that led to the storeroom piled with unwanted furniture and the blocked doorway opening on to the alley outside.

Gemma would understand, of course, my sudden orders to have the furniture shifted, but I was too impetuous to care. Dusty as it was, the room was transfigured for me as I stood there, gazing at the heavy beam – too heavy for me to move myself – that obstructed the slightly warped panels of the wooden door through which showed chinks of daylight.

Soon there was dust on my hands and clothes, and that seemed no taint but right, delightful even, and part of the mark of Rufus. Here I should wait for him. Gemma should take a message this very day – she would never dare fail to deliver it – and in her absence I would have the beam removed. This evening, I would be at the door, listening for his knock, to guide him through the Hades of lumber where were piled broken couches and tables, cracked, discarded oil lamps and even a damaged candelabrum that I seemed to recall had decorated the apartments of Cornelia as Chief Vestal when I first came to the house.

'It's all disgracefully untidy,' I said to the two indifferent servants I had summoned who panted as they heaved the beam aside. 'But you can leave the rest. We'll attend to it on another day.'

Immediately they had gone, I tried the door. It was flimsy but stiff to open. Outside the alleyway looked narrow, black and empty, with a stench of drains I had not been prepared for. I shut it abruptly, feeling my exhilaration slowly dwindling.

It was difficult, suddenly, to believe in the continued existence of Rufus. His very image would fade – perhaps was already fading – while I waited and waited in the semi-darkness, amid the jumbled, useless furniture, beside the frail door on which I should never hear the signal of his knock.

The dawn would find me as alone as before, located suitably among those dusty, discarded objects in by-gone style. I should not think of him as betraying me. Rather, it would be I who had failed, though through no fault of my own. I was, I recognized, a foolish, infatuated woman, awoken too late. That was what the night would surely teach me, as the cold crept into my aching bones and reminded me also that I was no longer young. My expectation, like my cramped, exhausted posture, proved ridiculous. It was making me ridiculous in the eyes of the sole person who mattered: myself.

From the day I had entered this house, had been received by Cornelia, probably in a room where that now tarnished candelabrum had stood displayed, a place in life had been allotted to me: privileged and safeguarded, but a spectator's. I had wanted that, taken pleasure in that – needed it, I could calmly admit. In myself I had felt for so long wonderfully free, uncluttered by distracting emotions. I had been confident of exuding a healing, medicinal aura that would always lower any threatened fever of passion, leaving only a residue of admiration as I passed on. Such was the proper role of a priestess woman in Rome.

The respect itself nowadays was probably thought, here and there, to be excessive and antiquated. In our male-oriented society it gave a place to a woman not otherwise paralleled and might make men somewhat uneasy if tactlessly demonstrated. To women it was, only now did it occur to me, perhaps even less acceptable, for in many ways the respect arose from self-suppression, from being unlike a normal woman.

To withdraw, as the Vestals withdrew from the Lupercalia, had never been any hardship for me. Seldom indeed had the quietness of the house and its female flavour been more welcome than on all those occasions when we left, or could leave, public spectacles that had turned bloody, savage and frightening in their unbridled licence. I had never seen the Empress blench at men hacking each other's bodies into stumps or driving on a host of half-disembowelled maddened animals in the arena. As for Aurelia, her tastes were notoriously robust; it was not perhaps too gross a caricature that a satirist had penned of her lamenting that only age prevented her from volunteering for a bout herself as a gladiator.

Yet in our world's eyes they were real women, as I had never been. They took their places in the amphitheatre, as they might anywhere else, as part of society, and joined in all the shouts of joy, the jeers, groans and sighs that expressed a basic pleasure in the always bloody spectacle that always ended with death. It was one of Rome's boasts that we had invented gladiatorial combats, even female ones, and the regular, public slaughter of hundreds of animals. To witness creatures struggling for life, but doomed to lose it, was our way of taking joy in great and trivial events.

That it was real, raw and actual was why it appealed. It was exciting to see other people die and go on living oneself – far more exciting than the most savage scene on the stage that lacked actuality. Life, my dear, I could hear Aurelia gruffly assuring me, is full of disgusting things: men will fight, whether we encourage them or not, and so will beasts. It's an instinct just as strong as love: quite natural, you see, and we may as well sit back and enjoy it. The Lupercalia says it all, I did not need her to remind me. Blood splatters the half-naked young men chosen to run, and their thongs of torn goatskin promise fertility to any girl they strike: the boon of becoming the vessel for another life which must be the greatest blessing for a woman.

Far better it had seemed to me to wear the unsullied robes of a Vestal, and to play at the harmless domestic tasks Vesta's worship required, though it produced a glut of corn and sacred cakes of a doughy simplicity that not even Afranius Dexter could have successfully marketed. It was all a retreat: I saw that, of course, but it was calm, ordered and safe. I had been true to my nature in opting for an existence as much as possible unlike that of a female gladiator.

Only now did it trouble me that in turning away from the blood, the noise, the rank dust that rose metaphorically if not literally to blot out the cool, white lines of colonnades, I had shut myself off from any real relationship with Rufus. He, somehow, was part of the bigger arena I shunned. His flesh, which I longed to embrace again, was of the same substance as Publius's – and yet at that contact I had felt near-nausea. The openly sexual rites of the Lupercalia frightened me not from any supposed obscenity but because they were in their crude way an incitement to life, to couple as I had positively done with Rufus.

Yet life meant not merely our two bodies lying at last in contented languor but bodies fighting each other, locked in hatred as well as love, or forced into stale intimacy by time, while affection dwindled and the bodies themselves sagged or swelled, grew wrinkled, withered, putrid even, under the blows of the years. It was flesh that one saw at the games, horribly ripped and mutilated – an arm hacked from a shoulder and hung on a fearful shred of skin – with every reminder of its frailty. Mine would be no different, but it was mine. I had never taken on the responsibility for loving flesh in another person – an actual, breathing, thinking, suffering creature who was not myself but who must look to me, as I perhaps to him, for some reason to live.

Perhaps there lay an element submerged of hope under my fear that Rufus would not come that evening. Let him fade as a reality, a responsibility, and remain a dream. The dream would have no awkward physical palpability. No blood or bowels would spill from it. In no arena would it ever sweat and struggle, grow weary or old, lose its faculties or suffer indignity. Behind its handsome blond head no mind would start to wonder about me, doubt me or demand whatever it was that love was meant to give.

And this new feeling helped me suppress any eagerness on Gemma's return. Almost coldly I heard her message that Rufus would come, as arranged. However shrewdly she scrutinised me, suspecting something and disliking it all, she would find it difficult to detect any emotion.

'You explained, of course, about the door?' I said. 'The one in the alleyway?'

'I did.'

'He understood about knocking three times, didn't he? I wouldn't want to risk opening it to some beggar or drunken lout.'

'He said he understood.'

'Very well. It's not important, Gemma.'

'Isn't it, mum?'

'No reason why you should stay up, and we don't want the

whole house disturbed. It's rather fortunate I recollected about that disused doorway, isn't it?'

'Yes, mum.'

'I'm slightly surprised something didn't occur to you about it. I've not forgotten how you gave me the first clue really – over the murder, I mean – when you suggested we should go and see Tibicina. That helped a great deal.'

She stood before me, looking almost aggressively squat and mute.

'Yes,' I went on. 'We ought to do something about Tibicina. It seems awful to think of her on her own. Perhaps on a future occasion . . . or, you know, Gemma, you could always ask her here one evening yourself. I'd be glad to feel she wasn't neglected.'

She nodded, but I was not sure it was in agreement.

I had never been capricious about servants, unlike many Roman ladies, and oddly it seemed disloyal to realise, as Gemma left the room, that I had begun to consider dispensing with her. She ought to be married: that was really the truth. And as I grew older, I needed perhaps a mature woman, not too elderly, pleasant-tempered, experienced too, possibly a widow. No doubt, after Gemma, she might seem dull and prosy but maybe soothing. If I decided my health meant I had to live more quietly, it would not irk her or cause pointed questioning.

My thoughts were still on the subject when eventually I crept to the lumber-room to wait for Rufus. It was chill and grew more chill as I sat in the dark on some broken couch, waiting and listening. I could not quite explain why I had brought no light, unless it was that I wanted us to meet – if we were to meet – in total, comforting darkness. And if he never came, the darkness would be only the more comforting.

A nurse-like figure was what I could really do with: a sort of Eurycleia, combined with one of those convenient creatures who console the heroine in Greek tragedy and seem otherwise without purpose. Such a person would certainly have followed me from my bedroom, not to spy but to be ready with a rug to put round me if I were doomed to sit through the night.

The sudden rapping on the door, repeated three times, roused me from what I suppose was dozing. I did not pause to consider or to fear. Stumbling as I ran, I tugged at the iron handle of the door and virtually catapulted myself into the arms I knew were Rufus's.

'Hey,' he said, slightly falling back. 'And I was wondering about my welcome. I wasn't even sure you'd let me in.'

'And I wasn't sure you'd come,' I said. 'I wasn't even sure you existed.'

He laughed. 'Now you know.'

'I don't know anything.'

'Well, you ought at least to know how cold it is. I'm freezing. Aren't you going to let me enter now I'm here.'

'Nobody followed you, did they? You were careful about that?' I drew him in as I spoke, still hanging on him like an impediment but happy to be one.

'To this smelly lane – or whatever you call it – at this time of night? No one. Most of Rome seems to be in bed, and I hope we shall soon be there too. Are we in your bedroom, or where are we? I can't see anything.'

'Keep quiet,' I said, though I felt an urge to burst out laughing. 'Let me guide you. It's not far.'

'Like Orpheus and Eurydice – in reverse – except neither of us can see the other. You couldn't tell whose arms you'd tumbled into. Even now, I might be a strange man you shouldn't by your standards encourage in this way. Or should you? You'll have to warm me up anyway, now I'm here.'

'There's mulled wine,' I said primly. 'And this is my room.'

'Not very luxurious,' he said, looking round, 'but at least you keep it hot. Deliciously so. It's an invitation to undress, which I'll accept.'

I remained studiedly occupied with pouring the wine, conscious that I must be blushing and that in my sudden embarrassment I was about to spill it.

'Mulled Falernian, I suppose,' he said, when at last I straightened up and passed him his glass. 'Last time I wasn't so lucky as to have it served by you personally – least of all in your bedroom. Remember? And now here I am, with it made.'

'With what made? The wine? I don't understand.'

He laughed. 'It's a phrase – an idiom – at home. Something I'll have to teach you. Julia, come here.'

'Why?'

'For a lesson, of course.'

124

'It's too late for lessons, Rufus,' I said, standing immobile and awkward, though it was my own room and his presence in it was meant to be the culmination of so many hopes and fears.

'Isn't that rather ungrateful? I've crept across Rome on a chilly night to be here – at your request. Don't I get my reward? And I don't mean another glass of wine.'

'I shouldn't have asked you. I'm sorry. It's no good.' I sat down where I was, consciously keeping my distance from him. He filled the room, as he filled my mind, effortlessly; but in the familiar surroundings his presence was unsettling, too much for me to absorb and treat naturally. I felt like a callow girl: a girl more callow even than I had once been, less innocent also, ashamed of my awareness of every movement his body made.

I fingered the wine flask and thought of the sleeping household. Why now should the image of that lumpy girl Valeria recur, I could not say. She would be lying peacefully, dreamlessly, in the narrow white bed which was probably a little too narrow for her, in that dormitory I knew so well. If I cared, I could take a lamp and go like a tutelary spirit through the house, past the crouched, dozing doorman, by the bolted doors, muttering a little drowsily, and find the recumbent figure of the cook, not far from her oven, and Gemma, tucked up and curled up, as abandoned in sleep as an animal. The building breathed of harmlessness and security. In its way, it – not the Palatine and not the Prefect's office – was the heart of Rome, and I was its custodian. That was what I had vowed to be.

A faint rustle made me look up from my reverie. Rufus was kneeling before me, and as I looked he placed his hands solemnly on mine. I smiled at the pleading in his beautiful, scarcely glinting, shadowed eyes, but I knew it was a smile of utter sadness.

'I've come to teach you,' he said softly, 'since you wouldn't come to me. I'm a good teacher, Julia. You ought to trust me by now.'

'Ought I?' I spoke as softly, staring at him.

'Of course. Didn't you feel that yesterday when I was making love to you? Your body hasn't any doubts, has it?

125

You responded all right on the Appian Way. You want that sensation again. That's why I'm here and ready. You'll see.'

I shook my head. 'I don't want even to talk of such things, Rufus. I can't. It's impossible you should understand. I don't understand myself. All I can say is, I'm sorry if I've hurt you, if I've behaved badly to you.'

'You asked me–'

'I did. I know I did. And you came.' I stopped at his changing expression. 'Why does that amuse you?'

'Your verb and its sexual innuendo, in the context. Oh, you're shy of such things – of everything, really, that happens between us. I'm not used to Romans behaving like you. You're odd, Julia, but don't worry. I think it's part of your appeal for me. Here I am, actually in the bedroom of the Chief Vestal, by invitation, what's more.'

'Let's talk of other things – for a few moments before you go. Yes,' I went on, checking his protest. 'You have to go, Rufus, I'm afraid. I had no right to send the message I did. It was weakness – if not stupidity. Not that I don't feel fond of you.'

'You feel too much. And it bewilders you because you've never met anyone before who gave you such sensations. That's what it's all about.'

'Possibly. But it's no use discussing it. Nor do you have to kneel to me, Rufus. I'm not worth your worshipping. Tell me – oh, tell me how you like Rome. It must seem very overwhelming to you as a city.'

I got up as I spoke, and he rose too, keeping my hands clasped in his. We stood there as though caught in some ceremony, and then he guided me slowly towards the bed.

'We may at least recline while we talk,' he said. 'As for Rome, it's big, I grant you, but it doesn't really impress me. I prefer a city with a breath of sea air, as we have at home. And there's more liveliness with us, perhaps just because we're a port. Something always seems happening.'

'But,' I said, concentrating on his words and only rather stiffly submitting to lying beside him, 'we have Ostia. Surely you've seen it? It's the finest port in the world, and it's recently been much improved by the Emperor. Why, it's a complete town in itself.'

126

'You're all alike, you Romans.' He laughed. 'Male or female.'

'Indeed,' I said coldly.

'Always convinced nowhere can be better than Rome but always asking for reassurance on the point.'

'Still, I presume you wanted to come and see it or you wouldn't be here.'

'I had the chance to travel. A rich man – the usual story. Only, he happened to have good contacts, you might say, and I'm meant to be improving myself before going home and getting a real job in something similar to the Prefect's department.'

'Like Calvus,' I said, with a yawn.

'Quite unlike Calvus,' he answered putting an arm round my neck. 'I could become someone important in the years ahead – responsible for public order, solving crimes, things of that kind.'

'You mean, a magistrate.'

'But that's a sort of judge, sitting in court. This is more practical. And much more clever, Julia. I might be on the street myself – only just to start with. After that, I'll have people under me carrying out my wishes when I investigate and catch criminals. You don't understand. There isn't a word for it with you.'

'Public order here is the admiration of the world, you know. So is our legal system. Roman law is one of our greatest gifts to mankind.'

As he went on lying there silent, I added after a pause, 'It's a great opportunity for someone like you, Rufus, being in Rome.'

'Oh, I've enjoyed it. Am enjoying it,' he said. 'And going, I think, to enjoy it even more. I hope you are too.'

He stretched out a hand half-lazily and turned my face towards his. How casually he sprawled there, barely clad, in my bed, while I lay rigid along the edge, apprehensive and obscurely ashamed. An affectionate smile touched his lips, and I found it hard not to respond.

'I understand,' he said gently.

'About Rome,' I said, rather desperately. 'For a stranger it's bound at first to seem almost too impressive – too grand. I can see that. After living in Gaul, the contrast must be

127

striking. People coming from abroad always feel the scale, I think. It's not just the architecture. It's what Rome stands for, isn't it?'

'You love it because you have always lived here.'

'Of course. And because—'

'It's the capital of everything. You've just said as much. Julia, I love my home town, and I certainly prefer my fellow-countrymen to yours. We're far less stolid and prosaic – much brighter in the head altogether than your average citizen. If you want to know, we're the future. Rome is the past. Now, I'm off, just as you said I should be.'

'But wait,' I expostulated, uncertain whether it was he or his observations that prompted my sudden eagerness. 'Remarks like that—'

'Look. If we're not making love, we're definitely not making conversation at this hour of the night.'

'You're leaving?'

'I'm leaving. Isn't that what you said you wanted? All right. It's too soon to see me again. You're still in a state of shock. I get it. I even accept it – something I wouldn't do for every woman, let me tell you.'

He swung off the bed, dangling his feet momentarily before he stood up. In that moment I had meant to touch him, detain him; my hand tautened and started to move to clutch his bony knee, but then it failed.

He threw his clothes around his body as carelessly as he had discarded them, indifferent, it seemed, to my imploring gaze.

'When shall I see you again?' I asked as calmly as I could. 'Tomorrow?'

'No, that's no good.'

'The following day?'

'I doubt it. I'm going to a supper-party of Afranius Dexter's. I shan't be in a fit state for much after that, and anyway I can't be sure whose bed I might end up in.'

'You don't mean it,' I said at last, feeling the words like a blow that only gradually grew into insistent, throbbing pain.

Now cloaked and muffled, he looked at me in a way that seemed almost pitying.

'I'm not a Vestal Virgin, you know,' he said.

I slowly bowed my head.

128

'We'll meet,' he said. 'So cheer up.'

'Should I – should I perhaps come to you?' I murmured the words more to myself than him.

'That really would be a scandal. I can just picture your stepping out of your litter and my landlady's face when she saw who you were.'

'I could come disguised, I suppose.'

'As a member of the Praetorian Guard? No, if anybody dresses up it'll be me. And not in armour.'

'But Rufus, quite seriously, how shall we be in contact? Shall I send Gemma with a message in two days' time?'

'So as to have another midnight discussion about Roman justice? No, my dear, you wait to hear from me. That way I can be fairly sure you won't have time to wonder and worry so much beforehand about what you're doing. And it keeps that slave-girl of yours out of it. I shouldn't trust her too much, if I were you.'

'Slave-girl? Gemma isn't a slave. She's my personal maid, very devoted – and I've always trusted her. Oh, I know what it is. You think she doesn't admire you as she ought to. You're quite right. To start with, she thinks your arms are like sticks of celery.'

He stood there unmoving, and I had to peer to see the expression on his face as the lamp burned low. I felt almost as exhausted as it was, stricken by the storm of conflicting emotions which seemed to have swept in when I opened the door to admit Rufus, though I knew they were already there before he arrived. And though I might rally a little, try and banter with him, I recognized his domination over me. I waited for his response as I should wait for a signal when he was prepared to visit me again. In some ways, he was wiser – I could acknowledge that to myself – for all his youth.

His arms suddenly flashed out from under his cloak, and his fingers pressed painfully as they tightened round my throat.

'Celery?' He muttered it playfully and slowly slackened the grip of his hand. 'Nobody better than you to tell her otherwise.' His voice grew louder. 'Only, don't tell her anything.'

My cheek brushed against the coarse wool of his cloak, and its washed, faintly soapy smell was in my nostrils. I sensed he bent to kiss my head.

'Don't move,' he said. 'May your gods let you sleep well.'

129

'The door . . . It won't be barred if I don't get up.'

'I'll pull it to. No one will notice.'

I felt too drowsy to demur, though I made an effort to stir before sinking back on the bed.

'You won't forget?'

'The door?'

'To send . . . send a message, so that I know. Don't leave me—'

But he had gone. The lamp still flickered and went on flickering as I gazed across the room once more, and then my eyelids fell.

Not for three days did I hear from him. On the first I stayed in, determined to miss no messenger, wondering at each appearance of Gemma's, however trivial, if she brought news of him. She, like me, seemed tired. She was respectful but unusually subdued, without exactly sulking. When I looked at her, I realised how worn her grey dress had become and how unsuitable its neutral colour was.

'You must have a new dress, Gemma,' I said decisively as she brought in the lamps at the end of the day.

'Is it for some special feast, mum?'

'No, of course not. Just for everyday wear. We must choose something bright for you.'

'I'd rather stick to this for ordinary days, thank you, mum. There's plenty of wear in it yet.'

'Nonsense. It's looking extremely shabby and far too dull. It reflects badly on the whole household. People will suppose me as economical as the Empress.'

'Very well, mum. Is that all for now?'

The next day I thought how foolish it was to remain in the house. After all, it might be that some breathless messenger would approach me as I climbed into my litter, or Rufus himself might draw near, without causing comment, virtually as a petitioner, if I visited the Capitoline. Or perhaps a child would run artlessly up to me at some juncture of two streets and thrust at me a sealed tablet with the words I wanted.

And so I gave orders for a visit to the Prefect, though when we drew near I countermanded them. I even thought of going to the Palatine, or setting out to see Aurelia; but the associations of both had become somehow dangerous, I felt, as well as distasteful.

'Messages?' Gemma made my enquiry on my return from an idle, wearisome day seem so unexpected as to be in itself scandalous. 'No, mum. Nice and quiet, it's all been.'

When it came, I was unprepared. I had temporarily forgotten, or tried to forget, Rufus. The following morning was cold, and I woke chilled, aching, uneager to do anything and almost glad of an excuse to play at being an invalid.

The small box Gemma brought in and placed on the table beside me was like something from a jeweller's, though less elaborate. My cold made me dull, slow to investigate it. No jewel but a miniature wax apple, lightly gilded, lay inside, with a scroll: 'For the fairest.' It made me smile in its extravagance; I was a mortal, conscious of watering eyes and an increasingly sore, probably reddening nose.

Yet I knew enough to take a knife from the plate of food I had failed to eat and slice it open. 'Tomorrow night, without fail,' were the words skilfully embedded in the wax.

I pressed it closed again in my hot palms, moulding the wax as I brooded, until the apple itself seemed to be shrinking and dissolving, leaving me only with my skin powdered by tiny flecks of gilt.

XII

'But you got the message – both messages – didn't you?'

'Yes, and they banished the cold I was suffering from, my lord Paris,' I said. 'Or perhaps you prefer to be just a shepherd. Either way, the legend tells us he was wonderfully good-looking.'

We lay in the dark, and if we whispered it was no precaution but part of our intimacy. Indeed, Rufus had arrived noisily enough, blundering among the lumber and calling out my name so loudly that I had almost feared he would rouse the whole household.

He it was who had put out the lamp beside the bed, as soon as he entered the room. Rather like Cupid visiting Psyche, I thought wryly, though mine was the body that needed, or wanted, to be hidden. Only in darkness could I feel entirely at ease with him and his love-making. I gladly surrendered sight for an ecstasy of the other senses, smell and taste among them. The taste of his skin – somehow tasting pale, like thin wine – and the pungent smell I seemed to crush, like garlic, out of the crevices of his trunk made me half-delirious in my greed.

I threw myself on his warm, exhausted body to savour once more its heat and weight, to realise all over again the sheer fact of that male flesh stretched out unashamedly as the occupant of my bed.

'Rufus or Paris – it's all the same. I love you. Do you hear?' I whispered softly, bringing my lips close enough tenderly to graze his ear. 'I love you for ever.'

'I won't last long if I don't breathe,' he said fondly. 'And I can't if you lie on me quite so heavily. I take it you're not anxious to have a corpse to dispose of in your bedroom.'

I shifted reluctantly and only slightly, leaving one arm extended across his torso. 'Don't talk like that, please,' I said.

'Would I be a problem? You could probably hush the whole thing up very convincingly, in a typically Roman way. And since you're so thoroughly respectable as the Chief Vestal or Great Mother, or something, I don't suppose you'd come under suspicion even if you left my body outside to be collected by the rubbish-cart. At home we have an excellent public system for dealing with rubbish – regardless of corpses, I mean. Here, as far as I can gather from Calvus, it's nothing like so well organised.'

'I fear I don't know. You must pursue your enquiries with Calvus if it interests you so much.'

'You sound quite jealous, Julia.'

'No. Just irritated.'

'By mention of dust-carts and rubbish? Oh, such things exist all right, in some form, though they may not have come to your notice. So, after all, do corpses. You may not have encountered many of them.'

'Have you?'

'Perhaps not, but my mother often helps wash and lay

132

them out. You see, that's the sort of stratum of society I come from: poor, humble, you might say squalid.'

I pressed myself more urgently against him. 'Does it matter? Does any of it matter to us? I love you.'

'But who am I? You don't know. I'm not really a Trojan prince, Julia, disguised as a shepherd. I'm not even a shepherd, Trojan or otherwise.'

'I feel I shall soon know all about you, Rufus.'

He muttered something I could not follow, and then was silent. His breathing deepened as he slipped into sleep. I lay there content, sharing as it were in his sleep while conscious of staying awake, keeping watch over him.

Day would come, but we would lie on. Perhaps I would persuade him not to leave the house. I would hide him in these rooms – or not so much hide as proclaim him, I thought drowsily, and defy Rome to do its worst. There was nothing to hide.

When he woke me, accidentally it seemed, I longed for us to go back to oblivion: to recover the dream I had had of standing before the Emperor, declaring my love. It was not at the Palatine but in the amphitheatre, positively in the arena, and I faced a crowd of heads blurring as I gazed round, even as I addressed the Emperor, vainly seeking to see the head of Rufus. But of course he was with me, was joining me in front of the assembled citizens, stepping into the sunlight, smiling self-confidently and garlanded as a Roman bridegroom.

'I dreamt of you,' I said, as though in obscure reproach.

'Glad to hear it. What was I up to? Nothing too horrific, I hope. Well? Was it so awful?'

'You were my bridegroom.'

He laughed. 'I thought I was that already.'

'No, this was in the sight of everybody. I was explaining to the Emperor. . . . At first I couldn't find you, and then you appeared in the arena.'

'The arena? That seems a funny place to be making love to you – just the sort of thing a dream would suggest. Inconvenient, too, with all that sand. I prefer here.'

'You'll stay?'

'Here, do you mean? Of course I'll stay a bit longer, if I'm wanted.'

133

'Stay on, Rufus, don't go. You can remain here. Gemma will help us – I'm sure she will. Nobody else need know. We can be together, properly, for days. I'll say I'm ill if any visitors call. We'll have time to live our lives, talk to each other, really know each other if you like. And we'll be safe. It can all be kept secret.'

'It's a charming idea. It shows just how much you're in love, Julia, but where does it get us?'

'Aren't you in love, then?' I asked as coldly as I dared, dreading his answer.

'Of course I am.' He kissed me on the cheek. 'But scarcely for the first time in my life.'

'Is that a reproach to me? Because I haven't lived the kind of life you imagined a Roman lady leads, had countless lovers, created scandal, am I somehow at fault? I should have thought a man would be pleased – pleased and relieved.'

'Tell you what I think I do love about you,' he said, lightly stroking my shoulder as he spoke. 'And that's something very Roman – your lack of humour.'

'My lack–' I began, perplexed.

'Perhaps there isn't a proper word for it with you people, at least for what I mean. For obvious reasons. I'm sure you're very good-tempered, Julia, in your way, but there's a sort of solemnity which in the case of you is rather touching. Like a child who has never quite grown up. Now I'm very much the opposite.'

'And you think love is funny?'

'Well, certainly not to be taken too solemnly. Oh, maybe it's only your delightful lack of experience but I think your character tends to take everything very seriously. Must be admirable and useful, of course, when you're on parade as Chief Vestal. I can see that. But then, frankly, the institution would strike most people as fairly ludicrous in today's world. We don't have Vestal Virgins in Gaul, you know.'

'Indeed not; but this is Rome.'

'Capital of the empire and so on, founded whenever it was, occupying seven hills. Yes, we get taught all that. And about Romulus and Remus – not much brotherly love with them, was there?'

'I admit Romulus never seems quite what the founder of

134

the greatest city should be. Of course, he was provoked by Remus . . .'

'He couldn't see a joke, that was his trouble. No sense of humour, Julia, my darling. But with you it's different.'

'Thank you.'

'No, I mean it. I mean it too when I say it's part of what I love about you. You have very solemn eyes, for one thing, and they have a beautiful solemnity. And you always look very grave. I prefer that to some silly giggling girl's face. Being dark suits you in every way. You're dark temperamentally. Blondes often turn out to have thoroughly trivial, fickle natures, but you're faithfully serious and seriously faithful. That's what I feel about you.'

'Ah,' I said, sighing yet taking pleasure in doing so, letting my head rest against his. 'I can't help it, Rufus. I love you.'

'I know, and it's very delightful.'

'No novelty, of course,' I said severely.

'No novelty.' He agreed calmly. 'Except that I don't usually feel the older partner, in the way I do with you. Isn't it odd? Here you are, Great Mother of the Vestals, ever so dignified and mature, and I almost feel I've seduced some chicken.'

'I'm not a chicken, as you call it. Nor am I someone to be seduced. I don't really like that word in our case. We love each other, Rufus.'

'Still, you must admit I seduced you.'

'Mayn't I feel I seduced you?'

'But you didn't. You were frosty and off-putting – and anybody less versed than I am might have stopped trying and gone away. As a matter of fact, I must do exactly that now, though I'll be back.'

'I can't even seduce you into staying?'

As I spoke I reached towards him and almost gingerly wreathed my arms around his torso. That it was there in the darkness, solid yet slight, more sinewy than muscular, seemed still amazing. I shaped it out with my finger-tips: enjoying, as I passed over the bony hollow at the base of his neck and the flat, low contour of his stomach, my own blindness – until the stray thought of Tibicina came abruptly to displease me.

'We about to leave, salute you,' he said.

'Why must you go? And where?'

135

'It's almost dawn. You don't want me to be found in your bed.'

'I do, Rufus. I do.'

He laughed contentedly. 'My turn to say you're mad – splendidly so. But you'd only be sorry if I stayed; and I'd look rather foolish, wouldn't I, mooning about here, keeping away from your Vestals? No. I'll be back, with due warning. I must think of another gift to send you.'

'Why should I be sorry if you stayed? Anyway, it's not madness but sheer sense, prudence really. We run fewer risks that way. It's far better for you to stay.'

'I won't light the lamp,' he said, as he ducked and shifted away from my embrace.

'If I beg you, Rufus–'

'It's for both our sakes. We'd only bore each other, or worse, if I stayed. You must learn to sleep the days away and come awake at night for me. Then there's something to look forward to. Without it, there'd be no uncertainty and no excitement.'

'If you stayed, we would get to know each other.'

'Exactly.'

'Is that your much-vaunted experience? I'm less ignorant than you think, as well as more trusting, or faithful, as you might put it. People who love each other, Rufus, want to be together, to know about each other. That's part of being properly in love. You may say I've had no feelings to go on – that I've missed adventures like yours – but at least I believe men and women can live and love each other, for years. Not every marriage is a cynical bargain or a yoking of two people who become bored with each other.' I paused, tense myself, almost breathless, expecting some cynical retort from him but he said nothing. 'I know my father loved my mother, Rufus, even though they lived together only a few years. When she died, giving birth to me, it nearly killed him. He might have hated me. He loved me for her sake, because I reminded him of her. What about your parents? Don't they love each other? Is that it?'

'I never had a father – practically speaking. I suppose some man, several I'd guess, made love to my mother, and then she had me. I've a younger brother and sister at home, and they're not bad-looking. We get our looks from my mother.'

136

'But about us,' I said desperately.

It was only by an effort that I did not reach out and grab his arm, his clothes – anything, to detain him. I felt he was melting away, eluding me, even as I struggled to prolong the moment.

'Listen, Rufus, did you understand what I was saying, what I meant? Think who I am and how easily I can control what goes on here. We could stay in these rooms. They're quite private. We'll be together undisturbed. Even Gemma needn't know . . . Besides, it's my life. I'm not answerable to anyone except the Emperor.'

'About us, my dear Julia, sweet, simple, naive Julia, the truth is that our happiness consists of not being too close to each other for too long.'

'Oh, no,' I moaned.

'Of course it does. You couldn't do with a man really living with you – not even me. Maybe me least of all. We're totally different people, out of bed, as it were. We don't even speak the same language, as at first you were fond of pointing out.'

'Rufus–'

'And that isn't even my name – just a convenient, condescending nickname. The sort of thing upper-class Romans allot to a favourite slave. Do you want to be called Brownie?'

'Anything you like – anything. I don't mind being humiliated by you.' I knew I was close to weeping.

'No humiliation intended. Just a dose of the plain facts. Don't let's spoil everything that works well by too much talk or exaggerated claims. If I go now, it's not to hurt you – as you probably think. It's to remind you, for your own good, not to become obsessed, besotted–'

'Besotted?'

'Can't one say that? Infatuated, then, if that's clearer. What a poor vocabulary yours is where passion is concerned. In a word, don't love me too much. We've got to part sooner or later. Your life and my life are two different things. They're bound to be. No one can alter that – not the gods or fate. Don't you try.'

I felt utterly beaten, battered almost physically by the force behind his sentences, though he had been speaking with deadly calmness. Anger should have come to my rescue – anger and pride – but for some reason my only emotion was fear rising like a fever until I was panting. Under my shudders, the bed shook. As he stood somewhere in the shadows, he must hear it, just as I heard it; and it seemed horribly to mock our love-making.

'Remember,' he said. 'You're still the fairest, for me.'

Until the next one, I thought. Yet the words refused to be spoken. I heard his soft, affectionate farewell, but even then I did not speak, rigid, unstirring except for the spasms that continued at intervals to contort my limbs. Yet, even in my suffering there was not pleasure but a sort of wonder: that I could be affected so much by another human being. Whatever happened, I would never hate Rufus. I had told him only the truth: I knew I should love him for ever, on earth or among the shadows below, as long as I existed as a consciousness.

Let Gemma be as inquisitive as she liked. I should resist her, conceivably dismiss her. I was ready for her by the morning, and it seemed strange when she did not appear. Instead, a nervous, red-haired servant-girl I barely knew tiptoed in, obviously uncertain whether her duty was to wake me or leave me undisturbed.

'Where's Gemma?' I asked so brusquely that she nearly dropped the brimming earthenware cup she was bringing to the bedside. Unfortunately it did not spill. Its contents of half-warmed goats-milk were something I never drank, though ritual required the Chief Vestal to start the day, and finish it as well, by taking the simple beverage in honour of Vesta. Gemma had ingeniously reduced the amount involved to a drop which she flavoured in ways I deliberately ignored but which certainly made it more palatable.

'Well?' I asked again, looking with distaste at the frothy surface of the liquid. It would have to be poured away, of course, as an oblation to the goddess, I should tell myself.

'She's sick, mum – my lady,' the girl replied at last. 'Sends her apologies and hopes you'll pardon her. Taken bad in the night. She's all shivery, poor thing. Not fit for you to have in here, my lady.'

'I've never known her ill before,' I said rather peevishly.

'No, mum?' She sounded quite envious. 'We always say she's wonderful – so cheerful, you know. Makes a joke of everything.'

'Indeed. Perhaps I had better visit her after I get up.'

138

Very kind of you, I'm sure,' she said without enthusiasm. 'I know she was trying to get some sleep. . . .'

'Oh, very well.'

I still felt feverish myself. In many ways it was a relief not to have to see Gemma, to know that I was free. Suddenly it came to me how free I was. The day need not pass in thinking uselessly of Rufus in the very space he had so recently occupied.

'I shall go out,' I told the girl, summoning her back as she was leaving the room.

'Out?' She stared dully at me. 'My lady,' she added as an afterthought. Her pinched, high-coloured face seemed to be made smaller by the mass of untidy red hair bunched behind in curls. She stood there stick-like and tall, with a puzzled frown suggesting she had difficulty in understanding. Tall enough to be a soldier, she might almost have been set to be my guard.

'There's a grey cloak I shall want. And ask them to get my litter ready.'

It was a risk I took, and more than the risk was the ridiculousness, coldly considered, of what I intended doing.

Yet on a busy morning in a crowded, public part of Rome, I might hope to pass unnoticed as I wandered in the streets near the Tullianum prison. Somehow I should discover where Rufus lodged. Unperceived by him, I might even watch while he came or went, and enjoy a secret sense of more than knowledge – of possession.

If I found nothing, missed seeing him, I would at least be mingling briefly in that elusive fluid, life, where he swam. A few drops of it might sprinkle themselves on me, and I now knew enough not to withdraw at the contact. Indeed, in this mood of recklessness, I might have borrowed a basket and some simple wares Afranius Dexter happened to have left on his hands, and tried my skill as a street-vendor.

The splash of reality was as abrupt as a jet of water in the face. Momentarily it was frightening. When I actually poised there, as if on a brink, and saw my empty litter disappearing among the crowd, it seemed an act of folly to have ventured out alone. With no Gemma at my side I felt how unequipped I was for drifting in the streets around the foot of the Capitoline, just as I was for climbing the hill itself.

139

The low bulk of the prison, set into the slope and looking more like hewn rock than a building, was no place to linger. Even in the glittering winter sunlight it failed to gleam. It lay darkly squat, unimportant-seeming but somehow obtrusive, barred and silent. Its existence had never troubled me before; I could not be sure I had ever consciously gazed at it, and I was glad to turn away.

As I moved, something stopped me. A man's fingers were gripping my arm through the voluminous cloak, and I felt almost an interior smile, a rush of relief and delight at his presence beside me. Confidently, I let myself be led into a shallow porch, apart from the throng. Only then did I find I was looking down on the tiny hairless hand of Lentulus Trebonius Niger.

The shock was more than he could realise.

'You're here looking for someone?' He asked eagerly. Not you, I wanted to answer, but I was still too disconcerted to do more than stammer. I flicked away his profaning contact with a gesture I knew was hardly justified by my appearance. He found me stripped of moral authority and already half a victim. 'I understand,' he went on, hardly noticing my confusion, or hoping to add to it. 'My investigations have gone well – very well. As I presume you have heard. Did you come to see for yourself? Or for your client?'

'Do I have a client?'

I looked round, over his head – anywhere but at him and his narrow black eyes that I knew must be fixed on my face.

'Your remarkable persistence.' He almost hissed the word. 'Even after all I told you. It deserves to be gratified. I shall place no obstacles in your way. On the contrary, I should like you to be kept abreast of developments.'

'I scarcely understand,' I said absently. Though I shifted restlessly, implying I must go, it was not clear what I should do.

'But you're not here by accident, Madam? Alone. And dressed as you are? The prison is nearby. I invite you to visit it.'

'My maid is sick–' I could explain that much at least. 'And I have no wish to enter the prison.'

'You might be interested in a prisoner.'

'I doubt it.'

140

'Madam, you think me more stupid than I am. Two days ago I had a certain Beroe, the wife of Pontilla Pilata's major-domo, taken there. I thought it would, if you follow me, help loosen her tongue. It has.'

'You've had her tortured – and that's not the law.' In my surprise, I turned on him with real vehemence.

Now he was looking up at me with an expression of partly mocking admiration. Could this dangerous little creature, whose very features repelled me and whom I feared as much as he seemed to enjoy threatening me, harbour some other feelings for me? A few months earlier I should not have had such a thought; but then a few months earlier I should never have encountered him at a disadvantage.

'You may see for yourself,' he replied with an insinuating smile. 'As I feel sure you hoped to. And I feel even more sure you will be interested in what she has to say. I shall be happy to escort you.'

'Can't I go alone?'

'In order to see her, I fear my presence will be necessary. Fortunately, I happened to be at hand. I saw your arrival, which – allow me to say – was handled most discreetly. I shouldn't like you to go away disappointed, as you would otherwise do. Ah, let's pause for one moment.'

'Why?'

Then I drew back, as he had done, though carefully keeping our bodies apart.

'The Prefect is passing.'

And there was Publius walking solemnly and slowly, on his way to the Capitol, stopping now and then to greet a friend, creating a respectful space as he advanced, smiling on all sides. Each tread of his heavy foot seemed a re-assurance to the crowd. Like Publius, Rome would go on.

I glanced at the boyish, quick-moving figure beside me.

'It's your cleverness I'm to admire,' I told him abruptly when we had crossed to stand in the shadow of the prison gateway. 'But have you found the culprit, the murderer?'

'A leading question. As you have taken such a very close interest in the case, remarkably close, I think I shall leave you to judge the evidence for yourself. That may be best – and safest also.'

'Tainted evidence, if she's in some filthy, damp cell,' I said

141

angrily. 'Put you in the same conditions and you'd accuse anyone, even your own uncle.'

'His involvement had, I confess, occurred to me,' he answered promptly. 'One must consider everyone as a possible suspect. But you will, I believe, find Beroe in excellent health. Hers is an interesting character, you may also agree. She comes from Thessaly and seems to have had some repute among the other servants as a witch.'

The gate opened as he spoke. At the sight of the narrow court-yard beyond, I hesitated. It was quite ordinary, but being ushered in by him was somehow sinister. Despite what he had said, I was still afraid of finding the major-domo's wife not as I remembered her but broken, perhaps even dying, her previous shield of aggressive muteness torn away to reveal a babbling, demented being, no longer human.

How easily that could happen here to anyone, I felt as we followed a gaoler down sheer stone corridors and into a bare, cell-like room. I had listened for dreadful cries, rattle of chains, the scraping back of bolts, for sounds of some kind; but far more terrifying was the heavy silence, itself like stone, and a coldness that made me think the walls were carved from ice.

Already I was bewildered about why I had come, what I was doing in this prison and how I should escape. Under pressure of the stone and the cold and the total silence, my mind would be unable to resist: my personality would collapse. I too would start to babble, admit my guilt, accuse anyone, so as to recover the sensations of being an individual.

'You may leave her with us,' Lentulus Trebonius Niger was saying, and it might have been me he was speaking of. 'Wait outside.'

The woman who stood before us seemed at first unchanged. The wretched, scanty prison shift showed her powerful physique, unbowed, unbruised, though I saw her wrists were manacled. Her hair was matted – in need of washing, I noticed with distaste, but still dark and thick, and she looked at us proudly. If she knew me, she gave no sign. I decided to keep the hood of my cloak over my face.

'You are Beroe, the wife of the major-domo of the late Lady Pontilla Pilata?' he asked with a formal gravity I had not expected.

She nodded.

'Answer,' he said.

'I am.'

I stood there impatiently while he seemed to enjoy going through the ritual of interrogation, establishing and displaying, as if for my benefit, his mastery over the woman. Looking at her more closely, I could detect under the brave, almost arrogant front a deep weariness, perhaps dread.

'Your mistress had lovers, hadn't she, despite her chaste reputation?'

'Yes.'

'They came to the house, didn't they? Didn't they?'

I waited for her response.

'I have told all this before–' Beroe began, looking for the first time towards me.

'And you will tell it as many times as are necessary. The lovers came to the house?'

'They did, and then suddenly it stopped. Madam stopped it.'

'How did they manage to be admitted?' As he put the question, he could not help his gaze swerving towards me, with a glint of triumph.

'They were dressed up – disguised – as women.'

'You knew that. Did you know their names?'

'No.'

'Did you ever see one of these men in the house – possibly in your mistress's bedroom?'

'Once, by accident.'

'And who was he?'

'Lord Sempronius.' She whispered the words, still looking at me.

'The brother of the Empress?'

'Yes.'

'Now, the idea of the men being disguised. Was that your idea?'

'Never,' she said, with a shake of the head.

'Your mistress's, perhaps?'

'No. You know that.'

'I wish to hear it again from your lips. Whose idea was it to begin with? Did it come from one of the men himself?'

'It was Afranius Dexter. It was his being clever . . . a joke, I think he called it.'

143

'A joke . . . a useful one, especially for her when they ceased to be lovers. And he would always be able to guess what was going on. Then, you say, the practice ceased. When was that?'

'Recently.'

'How recently?'

'I can't tell. One month ago, perhaps more. I don't know. All I know is that Madam stopped having such visitors – so-called ladies to see her in her bedroom.'

'About the same time as she started, didn't she, to take an interest in work on her family tomb? That meant she had the opportunity and the excuse to go out to it on the Appian Way. Did you ever go with her?'

'Not once.'

'But you did prepare food for her on such expeditions.'

'Food was prepared of course, if Madam wished it.'

Without bothering to lower his voice, he turned to address me.

'She supervised the kitchens. Other servants confirm that. Some of them probably guessed too about the female visitors, even though they won't admit it. Quite a few familiar names, I think we can assume, dressed themselves up for the pleasure of climbing into Pontilla Pilata's bed, and one at least she's prepared to testify to – as you noted, I'm sure.'

'Of course.' I spoke frigidly.

'And, of course, you are not surprised. Neither am I. And I'm delighted that we can, as you see, prove it.'

'In itself it proves nothing.'

'There, madam, I fear you show your inexperience.'

I made a sudden decision.

'Whatever I show, I should like to question her myself. Do you object?'

'Naturally, I don't. It's an admirable proposal, one I thought you might suggest. I can withdraw, if you prefer. She can't escape, and you are in no danger from her.'

He made a great show of vanishing from the room, and I was glad when he had gone. Nevertheless, it had been too easy. I felt sure that somewhere within the solidity of the well-built walls he was watching and listening. I wondered if Beroe also sensed it.

Alone with her in these circumstances, I realised the false-ness of my position. Yet it was true that I had questions for

144

her. Almost as if I were a doctor about to examine or operate, I threw off my hood decisively and stepped up to her upright, passive figure.

'You know me,' I said. And it was obvious she did. 'About Lord Sempronius—'

'He loved her – loved Madam.' Suddenly it was as though my words had acted like an instrument. She writhed and fell at my feet. Her voice was not muffled but vehement, a far from incoherent flood. 'He loved my mistress. He was the only one who really ever did. She sent him away after their first – first affair, but he came back and made him meet her, found somewhere. . . .'

'Aurelia's villa,' I said softly.

'What he hated was the way she lived. She laughed when she, madam, told me about it, but I think she felt something for him too. She might have done what he said – urged – about their going away together to live in Spain. He was the only one of them who really grieved at her death. I know that. My husband said he wept – wept when he saw Madam's body laid out, and her image looked lovely and no one could say it wasn't like her. You saw it, didn't you, my lady? She attracted men of all kinds, but then she tired of them. She was so lovely to look at – that was it. Too lovely, I suppose you might say, to last.'

'Please get up.' I tried to speak not unsympathetically but the sudden dissolving of her strong personality was repellent, and as if aware of this she reached out and caught at my skirt in her powerful hands.

'Don't let them harm my husband,' she begged. 'He knows nothing really – nothing of all this. Madam never confided in him, but he worshipped her. Let him live, my lady, whatever happens to me.'

She let go my skirt and sat there on the floor, huddled and wrapping herself round with those muscular arms bared to the shoulder.

'Nothing need happen to you, if you tell the truth. Describe finding your mistress's body.'

'It was late in the day, early evening really, and they came to tell us at home that something awful had happened. An official – from the Prefect's office, I think he said. I didn't listen properly. I couldn't. They thought it must be her body in the family tomb. I went out there.'

'Not alone?'

'Oh, no, I took my husband and three of the household girls – women more, but I call them girls. And the official came. It was getting dark, so we lit torches. And there on the threshold, Madam was lying. . . . The men went up first, before they let me near. I saw one of her favourite scarves, crocus-coloured – suited her fairness, it always did. It was tight round her neck and I wanted to loosen it. But it didn't matter, it wasn't any use by then.'

'So the men distinctly saw the body before you did, and well before you got close to it?'

'Oh yes, my lady.'

'I suppose they would swear to that. Now, tell me, did you prepare any food for your mistress on that day for her to take out?'

'None. I swear I didn't.'

'There was food in the tomb.'

She shrugged, calmer now, though she remained squatting on the floor, perhaps glad to rest there.

'Is it true you're skilled in concocting herbs, making potions and so on?'

'I have some skill in such things – for healing purposes.'

'Could your mistress have been poisoned?'

'Poisoned? She was strangled, strangled by some man. That is the truth and you know it.'

'You speak rather disrespectfully to someone like myself, prepared to help you.'

She said nothing.

'Don't you believe me?' I asked at last, staring down at her. 'If you have committed no crime, you have nothing to fear.' Roman law, I meant to go on, will protect the innocent. Whether it would protect her against a lawyer, I was increasingly unsure.

'I have committed no crime,' she said in a slow, deep voice.

'And nobody ever approached you to help them commit a crime?'

It was as if she had not heard.

'If you are innocent,' I began again.

'I shall never leave here,' she said, becoming agitated.

'Never. You know that too. There are cells very deep down – they've shown them to me – where you stand in water, chained to the wall. That's where I'm to go. But don't let them take my husband. I love him. You can't understand that, can you? The likes of us being in love. . . . But I'll say I'm guilty of anything, if they let him live.' The jangle of her manacled wrists startled me as she tried to push her hair from her wild face. I ought to have bent and lifted it for her, touched that matted, dark mass, coarse-textured no doubt, like the mane of a beast.

'Oh, madam, my lady – you're a woman, after all. It's not me, it's for his sake. Let him live.'

She screamed the last words at me, and it seemed she was still screaming when I closed the door, though the corridor was silent.

'You must release her,' I said as soon as Trebonius Niger darted forward. 'She's guilty of nothing, and your theory of poisoning is absurd – wrong. Pontilla Pilata was strangled in some quarrel, long before she got there.'

'Who did it then, in your view – or don't you care to say?'

'I think I know who didn't. Anyway, you must let her go, and do nothing to harm her husband.'

'So that they can benefit from the will? You've forgotten that.'

'But I'm sure they're innocent, she as much as he.'

'And all this is based on a woman's – pardon, a lady's – intuition?'

He was virtually sneering as he spoke.

'No worse basis than a lawyer's,' I answered hotly. 'If she isn't freed, I shall appeal to the Empress.'

'In the circumstances–' He stressed each word meaning-fully. 'Would you be wise, I wonder, to involve the Palatine?'

'Oh, I'm not afraid,' I said, with a confidence I did not possess. 'Justice must be done – but I mean real justice.'

'I concur.' He paused.

Facing him in that cold stone corridor was more oppressive than standing in the cell with Beroe at my feet.

'Men dressed up as women,' he mused. 'An interesting new fact, wasn't it? Quite like something at the Blue Toga Club . . . Afranius Dexter, too, with his enviable reputation for

147

being involved in every form of shady deal. Could he have gone so far as to murder someone?'

'I suspect everyone I meet,' I said satirically. 'Every man, that is.'

'Excellent. My practice entirely.'

'Ah, but with a difference, I think. My own suspects include you.'

It was something to have left him with, wriggling a little, if only scratched by the prick of a pin – a lady's weapon, he might have said – when I should have preferred to see him transfixed by a javelin.

Still, I should solve it before he does, I reassured myself. At least I believed Beroe, though I could not feel any emotion for her; and something told me she had, without knowing it, provided a clue.

To find the lanky, ginger-haired girl protruding anxiously from the porch of the house – like a ritual mop left out – was both distracting and annoying. At the sight of me she ran down the steps.

'It's Gemma, mum,' she said breathlessly. 'She's took worse, I think, and she's asking every minute for you.'

XIII

'Why, Gemma,' I said, entering with emphatic cheerfulness. 'This isn't like you.'

The white husk propped in the bed was certainly unrecognisable enough to give unfortunate resonance to my greeting.

One of the older servants who had been sitting on the bed, apparently soothing her, got up and left the cubicle respectfully. Although I approached and took the thin hand that lay on the coverlet, I hesitated to sit down. But when she spoke, her voice was so hoarse that I had to bend to catch it, and eventually I found myself occupying the still warm place that had been vacated.

'Have I what?' I said, even then missing part of her question.

'Been out investigating, mum?'

'Well, it hardly matters, Gemma, now I'm back. The main thing is for us to get you better. I expect it's only a severe cold, a chill, but if you're not better soon, we must have the doctor.'

'I don't want any doctor. I wanted to see you, mum. That's what I wanted.'

'Well,' I said, feeling half ashamed of my sense at that moment of health, beneficence, buoyancy almost: I had alighted at her bedside like a goddess radiantly prepared to grant a boon, totally sure of being able to do so. 'Here I am.'

Her pallor was frightening, now I was close, and there was a shrunkenness, a loss of vitality, that might be no more than fatigue but which seemed deathly. I felt I was starting to look at her with eyes as dark and wide as her own, though scarcely so huge. No divine radiance of mine illumined her; and my own faltered at the thought of her being gravely ill, of her dying here, far away from her native Butunti, and while still so young.

With an effort I recovered and smiled. 'Here I am, Gemma,' I repeated. For her I should become a healing presence.

'Mum,' she said hoarsely. 'That foreigner helping you – the one who's working with you, you told me, on your case. That's all it is, isn't it? He doesn't . . . doesn't mean anything to you, does he?'

'Mean anything?' I kept smiling. 'My poor little Gemma, has that been worrying you in some way? Perhaps it would hardly be your concern, though I don't intend to speak harshly. And I mustn't burden you with problems, least of all just now – any problems of my position. I've trusted you a great deal, Gemma, of course, very gladly. I depend on you, so you must get well quickly.'

'You've been ever so good to me, mum,' she muttered, shivering. 'You are good, I know. Please say you'll forgive me. I had no right – no right to ask, but I had to. I've done wrong, in every way, and you've every right to be angry. But

149

it doesn't matter now I know about him.' She gave me a weak smile. 'It was all wrong, mum, and I'm to blame. Not Tib, though it was she who heard him – spotted him, you might say, quick as a flash. So it's what you were looking for, mum, in a way. A clue, wasn't that it?'

I felt unable to say anything. She was rallying, growing visibly less white and shrivelled, nervous though she might still be, while I sat rigid with apprehension. It seemed important not to move, though the blood was draining from my veins and I was locked into a frozen posture at odds with the quivering, internal sensation of waiting for her next words.

When she continued to look at me, with fresh, rising alarm, I tried to speak calmly: that too was important. Surely there was something yet to save.

'What–' I could only bring the words out with great effort. 'What have you done?'

'It's all right, mum,' she said. 'It really is. Now I can talk to you I don't feel so rotten. I've been awfully worried, though, turning things over in my mind and so on. I thought I might die, and I know that's silly. Supposing you'd refused to see me, in case I had an infection and you'd catch it? Some ladies would, I bet.'

'Just tell me, Gemma – please.'

'You said how Tib might come one evening – Tibicina, the girl whose aunt–'

'Yes, yes. I remember.'

'Well, you said she could visit me, so I asked her. She was coming late, you see, because she plays first at that Club for nancy-boys and I don't know what. And as I was sitting up last night waiting for her, I heard *him* arrive, and you'd told me before he might be helping you – on the case, you said. So I told her, so as she shouldn't think we'd forgotten.

'If he hadn't been so noisy arriving, I suppose I mightn't have thought of it. I wouldn't have told anyone else, mum. You know that. But Tib's different. She'd never blab, and after all it was her business too – in a way – if you think about it. Still, maybe some people would say I shouldn't have told her.'

'You told her, anyway.'

'I didn't see any harm in it, mum, and as things turned out, you won't be sorry either. What was wrong was our

150

hiding in the storeroom, waiting for him to leave. And I'm punished for that, with this fearful sore throat and all. It was creepy in the dark – not that Tib minded – and really nippy. We both had the idea at the same time.'

'Were you eavesdropping? Was that the idea?'

'Not on you, mum. I promise. It was just that Tib said she wanted to hear his voice, and perhaps I thought I'd give him a fright, pretend to be a ghost, you know. I got the fright, all right. As soon as she heard it, she knew it was the same – the same voice. She'd heard it before. And guess where? In the bedroom of Lady Poison-pot on that very day they forgot she was there and got all lovey-dovey. So he's the man, mum, isn't he? That foreigner.'

She lay back, half-exhausted and yet exhilarated, glancing at me with timid expectation. 'I'm not sure, Gemma,' I said at last, when the silence had become unbearable. I got up from the bed. 'I find it all rather shocking, I'm bound to tell you – your behaviour and that girl's. I'm disappointed in you particularly. But we'll discuss that when you've recovered. Of course, even your illness, now I learn what you were doing . . . yes, I expect it was sent by the gods to punish you.'

'But, mum, at least we found him out, didn't we? The gods didn't do that.'

'That sounds boastful if not impious. Besides . . .' I turned on her more fiercely than I meant to. She looked up at me, shaken and white again, and somewhat puzzled. I could have shaken her, literally, and yet I felt her hurt almost as much as my own. 'I'm by no means convinced you've established anything by what you chose to do – either of you. A blind girl's supposition over someone's voice isn't exactly evidence. She could have been, probably was, mistaken. As for you, Gemma, you've been hostile from the first towards – that foreigner.

'Oh, I suppose you thought you were acting for the best. I'll assume so, anyway. But I don't need the protection of my maid, you know, in dealing with a man. My position, Gemma, protects me. All you were asked to be was discreet and devoted. I'm sorry to find you've been neither. Now, I mustn't upset you. You have told me what you did, and that is some reparation.'

'Don't you think it was him, then?' She asked, with a note

of disappointment. 'Tib's got ever such sharp ears, and his voice does sound funny – unusual. She's sure it's the same one. . . . It could have been him too, couldn't it, who did her in – choked her? Then he might well want to find out what was happening and if you were investigating and–'

'Gemma.' I hesitated between speaking severely and adopting a mild, dismissive tone suited to someone ill, a little confused and prey to fancies. 'You're not feeling your best–'

'But I'm feeling better, mum, now I've told you,' she interrupted.

'I'm glad to hear it. I think we should both forget about the whole incident, at least for the moment. If there is anything to do I shall of course do it. When you are up again, I'll talk to you seriously, and now I must let you get some rest.'

'Yes, mum.' She sounded subdued, slipping and shrinking back under the coverlet but with eyes wide open, staring up at the ceiling. 'Would you like to see Tib?' she asked with a last flicker of spirit. 'She'd be able to tell you exactly. You'd believe her, if you talked to her, you really would.'

Murmuring what I hoped sounded soothing words, I got out of the cubicle at last, walking with head erect and almost hoping to encounter some tittering, ill-dressed Vestal or a squabble between servants – anything at which I could discharge the weight of emotion under which I was bending. The only Vestal I passed shyly made a demure reverence and hastily scurried, without actually running, behind a pillar: a pretty girl, Crispinia something, someone's niece (could it be Calvus's?), who always seemed smiling and content. It might be that one day she would become Chief Vestal, and I could see her quite easily assuming the role, privately and publicly, welcoming a novice, moving gracefully to take her place at the front in the amphitheatre or alighting from her litter in the Forum, to pardon some criminal she had met on the way to execution. And for all her air of contentment, it was perhaps the same future that she was formulating, even as she fluttered away from me like a white butterfly, for herself.

Never before had I thought in such personal terms of being succeeded, relegated, retired. Extinction was different, soothing even, compared with the awareness of living on while another woman occupied my place and my rooms, smiled over what I had chosen to be my surroundings and probably commanded changes so as to avoid breathing too patently the atmosphere of her predecessor.

Sometimes I had felt weary – certainly that was true. But weariness was nothing – nothing – to the pain I was now suffering. It made the cycle of Vestal existence irrelevant and useless. Let Crispinia assume the status of Chief Vestal tomorrow, as long as it ceased to throb and burn like a venom on the skin or percolating through the veins. Dressed as I was, I threw myself on the bed to blot out all sensation. Then it suddenly seemed as though some poisoned garment clung to me and I tore open my clothes for relief and once more flung myself down. But, after a moment's respite, it began coursing again within me, corroding as it ran, leaving me powerless to check its progress.

It was Rufus I flung myself on, no longer in a paroxysm of love but of agony. Yet what did the wretched blind girl's identification establish, even if she were correct? Only that he had been Pontilla Pilata's lover on one occasion, and surely I understood – I could hear him almost loftily pointing out, in schoolmaster fashion, teaching me one more lesson – he was a lover, and beloved, of many people in Rome. Aurelia, for instance, had taken him up, petted him, parted from him; and she had definitely not ended strangled in a tomb on the Appian Way.

If he had told me . . . whereas, I seemed to recollect, he had at some point – hadn't he? – denied even knowing Pontilla Pilata. Yet that deceit was not by any means at the core. Something more fearful and fatal lay underneath. Gemma, by her meddling and her chatter, had only uncovered what I myself had buried, had forgotten and been happy to forget.

I thrust my face into the bedclothes for oblivion – or, rather, to go back to the time before I had this pain far worse than any earlier loneliness, for it was the loss of what I had thought I grasped, had in fact grasped, as I lay close to Rufus and absorbed in him. Now it was as though I had wasted that precious time in coyness or trivial conversation. I had lost him, it seemed momentarily, because my love was not great enough. I had not even got up to cross the corridor and let him out of the lumber-room, when I should undoubtedly have discovered Gemma and Tibicina, and somehow have silenced them at once.

There would have been no talk of evidence, of proof; and the very fears roused in me this morning would have lain dormant, gradually withering away as time passed and only Rufus filled my mind. I had been too proud to tell him – show him – how utterly I loved him. He thought of it as affection of the kind he was used to evoking, transient, however fervent or lustful. But my love for him was rooted in my being: to be alive meant to be loving Rufus. I had been too shy or ashamed, even when I had learnt at last and abandoned my naked body across his a mere night ago in a coupling more significant than sex, to confess my lingering dream: of our being together like that for ever. Transported to his Gaul, I was, would become, his wife. Secretly, beyond any admitting, I had seen myself in some foreign market-place stoutly at my stall, in a plain, patched gown, sleeves rolled up, my hair gone grey perhaps, my hands calloused – much as any stall-holder could daily be seen in Rome – bawling my wares. Then it would be for my tongue to get round another language, shout, argue, cajole – and be laughed at for my clumsy speech and uncouth accent. But as I trudged home at the close of day, sweaty and stained, my stall possibly part of my burden, with only a few pence to show for the hard hours of labour, I should know that waiting for me was Rufus.

This bed still held him, I swore, as I pressed my cheek deeper into it. It need not be too late to whisper my dream and let him, if he wished, fondly mock me. His dreams too, I ought to ask about, as I had never done. Yet there had been a reason for that, I was aware, as I lay there, half curled in misery. My dreams were so many veils to mask the real future: my future. But for him there need not be such flimsy, hopeless hiding of reality. Whatever he dreamt of, it was – I knew, for all my conjuring up of his physical presence – not of an existence with me. To have tenderly sought his thoughts as we lay pressed close together would have been to set a spark to that wispy drapery and destroy it utterly. Life, he would have asserted, is what waits for me; and there it is, to be grasped by my hands, to be shaped as I want, for my satisfaction.

And if I had foolishly (woman-like, most men would say) tracked on along the pathway of his thoughts as I idly, gladly, tracked the hard outline of his pelvis, I should have come face to face with the stubborn truth of things. It was exactly as he had warned me. He was no more one of Priam's sons than I a goddess; we had never trod Mount Ida, but walked as two mortals today, ill-assorted and doomed to take diverging roads. I had moaned at the thought, but whatever the pain of it, it had been almost assuaging compared to my present torment.

Better if he had lied totally from the first and never set up to be honest, realistic, and a breaker of female fantasy and dreams. All would have been false. Or, more probably, it had been. Gemma's shrewd, peasant-cynical concept saw him ingratiating himself with me – though she knew little of the facts – for only one reason: to ascertain whether I would pursue the question of Pontilla Pilata's death. She did not, obviously, even to herself, wonder if I 'meant' anything to Rufus, just as she accepted, as I had wanted her to accept, that he was nothing to me.

He had seen me, followed me, aimed to intrigue me, felt confident of sufficient physical allure to beguile me – me, the incarnation of chastity – and been prudent enough not to disguise much of his real nature. After all, I myself was not entirely stupid, even in love. Would I have believed him had he sworn eternal devotion or posed as chaste or promised to carry me back with him to Gaul? Then it would have been I who laughed and mocked. And even as I felt that, I had a poignant vision of his pale, narrow face and the careless, falling plumes of fair hair and those green eyes, as though washed in their luminosity and set off by fringed grey lashes, gleaming as he gazed at me with what had seemed affection as well as mockery.

Now it seemed better, far, if he had from the first been honest, thrown himself with all his youth and charm, on my mercy. At least, once he knew the intensity of my love, he must have realised I could never betray him, whatever he had done. To have been loved by Pontilla Pilata was no crime, though hardly, it appeared, a distinction. And had he to confess having loved her, that too was not a crime. Judging by Sempronius, it was not even unique. I would not have been called on to understand – merely to forgive. Rufus found me callow, unversed in the ways of women of the world; but, no Aurelia as I was, I knew enough by instinct to know that I had only to cradle his head briefly, smooth his disordered hair and raise him from where he knelt, thus miming pardon.

But over a crime, over murder (if murder it was), I would not have been able so lightly to play-act. Still, there would have been the flattering appeal to my aid and my power: to shelter him, as I should have felt urged to do, disguising him, it might be, as some female attendant, brought from the Northern provinces and unhappily a mute. . . . Above all, I should have known what happened. I could have judged the circumstances and considered what I believed justice to require. The death of Pontilla Pilata, however he had been involved in it, would be no wanton, simple act. To that extent, at least, I felt sure of Rufus.

Yet any lifting of the spirit, as I seemed partly to detect in myself as I sat up and looked round the familiar room, was an illusion. None of these things had happened. Rufus had not knelt lover-like at my feet for forgiveness, nor wept as he confessed an appalling accident, a crime. That was no more so than that my frantic clutching at the bed-clothes had conjured up his body in my bed.

He had deceived me: that was the sole truth. Or so it was if I accepted what Tibicina claimed – a faint, inconclusive, hasty supposition, based on a bare few words overheard, and yet somehow made almost sacred by her blindness. After all, I had only to ask him, though in doing so I would test both him and myself. I feared – not putting the question but his reply. And beyond that answer, under it, other questions lay coiled, more fearful in their implications and heavy in my own mind, whether I uttered them or not.

I rang the bell loudly for the red-haired girl. I must bathe, change my dress, eat some food, resume the routine of what was left of the day. She came in awkwardly and kept her distance as though expecting me to be hostile.

'Well?' I said, seeing she lingered dully, even after I had given my commands. At least while she served me I should have no temptation to confide. I felt no eagerness even to ask her name. 'Is it about Gemma? How is she?'

'Sleeping,' she answered in a mechanical way.

'Good. And now will you–'

'Something came, mum – my lady – for you. I didn't think

156

it proper to disturb you. A boy brought it, so the porter says. It's very small – a little parcel, I'd call it.'

'Well, where is it?'

Her slowness angered me, but so too did my own immediate reaction. To cast off all dread at the very mention of something delivered, to be ready to recover before I even glimpsed the medicine, showed how little decided I was. It was hope he sent, though that too might prove false.

'Fetch it,' I told her.

'Now, my lady, do you mean? Before you take your bath? It's nothing much by the look of it.'

'Bring it here – at once. And then you can go.'

Certainly it was small. I saw that instantly. It was nut-like in its hardness, as I could feel through the minute leather pouch that held it. No words accompanied this gift: a pair of ivory dice, marked unusually with pips on all sides.

I held them for a moment in my palm before rolling them. How harmless they looked, and insignificant: very much a toy. I threw, threw again, and then yet a third time. They were loaded, I realised. However often shaken, at each throw they showed a pair of 2s.

Rufus would be with me on the second night. Suddenly it seemed nothing to smile over, not though I thought to twit him with perhaps purchasing his gifts from Afranius Dexter (nobody better to handle a consignment of loaded dice, quite apart from wax fruit).

It all ran a little too smoothly for Rufus, choosing his time, sure he would be welcome. With me however lay the decision whether that door should be unbarred or whether he would beat on it in vain. And perhaps that would be the safest course: silence, while I let myself listen to the knocking gradually dying away; and for the last time I would send the dice clattering across the table, to fall on the floor and be left to lie in a dark corner until they were swept away.

But I knew that when the night came, I should not behave in that fashion. However safe, it was not brave but cowardly. Besides, it assumed Rufus's guilt and gave him no opportunity to prove otherwise.

As I began more calmly to reflect, as the hours passed, as I lay alone, as the very smells of the house asserted themselves, homely and slightly fragrant, my instant acceptance of

Gemma's story seemed shameful, even monstrous. I was a traitor to love who, like one of those stupid, jealous women of legend, believed whatever some ill-omened crow or crone repeated, always with disastrous effect.

Chattering like mischievous birds, partly playing a spiteful prank, Gemma and the blind girl I had disliked from the first delighted to peck accusingly at Rufus – the foreigner and the intruder, guilty above all of being male. I recollected Tibicina shrieking down on me from her tenement the words 'it was a man', as though she herself had been the victim of rape. And Gemma, too, now I thought of it, had more than once – indeed, on the actual evening when Publius brought Rufus to the house – implied a virginal repugnance which I had carelessly supposed she assumed for my benefit or just characteristic irreverence about people generally.

These were the witnesses with whom I had been prepared to confront, if not condemn, Rufus, whose girlish indiscretions and impertinences I should have punished when I heard them, instead of imbibing them so greedily that I might have wanted him to be the culprit. Mine was the guilt, though he should never know it. I, who claimed deep, eternal love, defying the world, allowed the slightest whisper of menials' ill-natured gossip to tarnish that affection, bending and reeling under what amounted to no more than a sour breath from inquisitive, excluded servants. I felt ashamed now that Crispinia should have witnessed, though probably not comprehended, my agonised tottering to my rooms, trailing my supposedly envenomed robes. And all the time there was no need to be a tragedy-queen. I had only to keep my faith in Rufus. Far from indulging insane suspicions and barring doors against him, I ought to stand like Hero watching for my lover as he navigated Rome: myself a beacon, glowing in prayers for his safety and burning for the moment of being reunited with him.

Impatience with myself made the waiting harder than it had ever been before. It was apparent, I knew, as, too early in the evening, I rearranged the room once again, giving prominence on a dish to the two cubes of ivory dice – only to regret my action.

'My dear,' Aurelia said, almost as soon as she was ushered in, 'I never associated you with games of chance. It shows how little we know of each other. And I feel I'm imposing on you, dropping in or popping in, whatever the phrase is nowadays, when I'm really on my way to a poetic supper-party at Corinna's. Odes are on the menu, I'm afraid, though nothing else may be. But I haven't come for sympathy, or even for a bite of something, and perhaps I've come at the wrong moment.'

'Not at all,' I had to murmur. 'You very kindly received me. I'm only sorry that everything must seem so plain. . . .'

'Nicely kept up, though,' she said approvingly. 'I like things well polished, whatever they are. Your doors are quite a treat, my dear – positively gleaming. I can see you've no problem with servants. Have you had that old doorkeeper for years? He looked thoroughly dependable and respectable, quite safe with girls. Still, I'm not here to gabble about servants, or we'd be sitting up half the night. That darkie of mine – you remember? – she's a good girl, I must say, but she's started to see things, if you know what I mean. One day it's an omen of three cranes flying south, the next it's the Tiber running blue. Blue. I ask you. Whatever next?

'All rubbish, of course. But the odd thing is that there does seem to have been a spate of rumour recently, and I felt I ought just to give you a friendly word of warning–'

'Of warning?'

I had been trying to suppress my nervous irritation while she went amiably on. Not for an hour or so, at the very earliest, would Rufus arrive.

Over-alert, I sat up, rather too jerkily. Aurelia seemed startled, though she settled herself and continued calmly enough. She looked splendidly impregnable tonight, armoured by her metallic-textured dress and bristling with layers of knobbly emerald necklace that hid most of the inter-vening bare skin. Her coiffure, piled higher than by day, curved greyly above her heavy face like a helmet.

'Well, advice call it. Apology too, if it comes to that. For one thing, I gather you never managed to see my lawyer but ended up with that young sprig, his nephew, whom I can't abide. Clever, no doubt, in his smarmy way, but can you believe it? He's had the effrontery to insinuate scandal everywhere over that Pontilla Pilata business – and all

159

because she was his client. His mistress, I suppose we'll hear next.

'Somehow he's got wind of my having lent my villa to – an important person. Oh, he dreams of a really dramatic court case, citing half Rome. He's not, my dear, very well disposed towards you, and he's bullied servants, interviewed all sorts of riff-raff, carriage-drivers and such like. One wretched woman he's actually had thrown into prison. Now, I know you were taking an interest in the affair. I'm going to assume an old woman's privilege – I don't mind putting it like that – and urge you, for all our sakes, to let it be, leave it alone.'

'I'm sorry he dared approach you, Aurelia. It's my fault. He must have overheard something I said when he took me to see Beroe – the woman in prison, the major-domo's wife. I told him she was innocent, though he keeps on claiming she poisoned her mistress. I'm sure she had nothing to do with it.'

I realised I was glaring at her and I apologised.

'Oh, my dear, I shan't be offended, though I'm not a judge and we're not – the gods be praised – in court. Anyway, I think you managed to convince him it wasn't a case of poisoning. Now he's sniffed out some poor creature who plies for hire with a carriage and a broken-down mule, and he admits it was he who ferried Pontilla Pilata out to the tomb in the late morning. What's more he says he brought her back.'

'What? How could–?'

'Don't ask me. As I said, there are rumours everywhere. We'll all be spattered with mud at this rate. Our conceited young friend's theory is that the poor fool brought back the murderer disguised – anyway wearing her cloak. Apparently, and this somehow implicates that woman, what's-her-name, all over again, Pontilla Pilata went out wearing a drab, greenish cloak. It wasn't found with her body, but nobody bothered to remark on that. All the driver keeps reiterating is that he brought back to the city someone who left the tomb in the same cloak, hooded of course, but looked similar, fair complexion from what he thinks he glimpsed. She didn't speak. Well, he thought nothing of that. She'd paid him before the journey. When I say she, of course, it couldn't have been Pontilla – oh, it's too confusing to bother with.'

'I suppose he believes Beroe went out somehow and hid in the tomb, then killed her, put on the cloak. . . . But she's almost swarthy. It's absurd – and wrong.'

'I'm very much inclined to agree. As a matter of fact, though I'm not setting myself up as an oracle, I've got a pet theory of my own. I told young master Trebonius Niger as much.'

'Please tell me,' I said anxiously.

'Well, it's no more crazy than some of the things people are saying, and frankly it takes the whole unpleasant business out of our circle. You know about that Christian sect, with their hymn-singing and so on, don't you? It occurred to me that Pontilla Pilata's grandfather made an administrative blunder out East over some native leader of theirs – lost his nerve or sentenced the wrong man. Now, could they be at the bottom of this? Taking some sort of revenge. Of course, nowadays you're told they're as meek as milk, but I just wonder. All that liking to live underground and singing hymns doesn't sound healthy, does it?'

'I only wish it was the answer, Aurelia; it would solve so much.'

'That jumped-up young lawyer had the cheek to tell me he'd never heard anything so improbable.'

'The Prefect – Publius – did suggest it when he first heard the news. I remember his coming here. . . . He too thought it could have been the Christians.'

'H'm. That's the worst I've learnt about it,' she said gruffly. 'Still, it would be nice and political, and then let him go dabbling in the murky waters. You'd have no cause to be involved. Talking of public affairs, I've heard that the Emperor's about to return – or perhaps you knew that already? You don't have to answer. The Palatine's in a terrible state, they say. Nobody thought he'd return so soon to Italy. It's victoriously, of course. *She* can't make up her mind whether to go out to the Flaminian Gate or wait for him in the palace. It all depends on the augurs, my dear, and I hope you won't mind my saying I prefer to put my faith in my dressmaker. At least she foretells the future of fashion without any messy entrails and never mistakes a seam for a gusset.

161

I'm a living tribute to that, or I shouldn't be reclining here tonight so comfortably. But I'm boring you, my dear. You've things on your mind, I can tell.'

'It's only that I expect someone . . . later. Please don't go yet; I'm grateful to you for coming.'

'I've done my duty, Julia. I'll be off. Now, are you going to take my advice or not? There, that's a bossy way of putting it.'

'It was Sempronius, wasn't it,' I said slowly, 'to whom you lent your villa? Beroe told me she thought he really loved Pontilla Pilata. I tried to see him. I went specially to the Palatine. What's more, I went out to the tomb, their family tomb, Aurelia, on the Appian Way.'

'Very thorough,' she said. 'Did you discover much?'

'About the murder? Nothing. Yes, perhaps I did – I'm not sure. I'm not sure of anything at the moment. I'm beginning to wonder why I was born, what my life is meant to mean, where it's going. . . .'

We were both standing now, and her sturdy, armoured figure was like a glittering trophy of good omen, which I felt an impulse to embrace. In response she put an arm affectionately round me, and I welcomed its steely pressure, increased by the broad gold bangles which plated it.

'Start examining life, my dear, and you'll only get in a muddle – forgive my saying. Best leave that sort of thing to philosophers and other impractical people. It's no surprise to me we haven't had any female philosophers: to our credit, really. Nothing to do with life, you know, but get on with it – or give it up. If that's stoicism, I'm a stoic, my dear. I'm sure you are too.

'And now, talking of female this and that, our famous poetess will be asking where I am and devising all sorts of catastrophes that must have overwhelmed me. I'm waited for, and you're waiting. Let's hope each of us has an agreeable evening. But you must drop in on me another day. And don't forget what I've said.'

'Of course I shan't. I want to think about it. And thank you again.'

'Nonsense.' She kissed me and paused before leaving the room, glancing towards the dice. 'I wish you good luck,' she said meaningly.

'Aurelia Metella came to see me,' I told Rufus almost as soon as he arrived. I knew if I did not mention it straight away, I should find reasons not to do so and regret it. Yet it was an effort to say her name, and I noticed he frowned as I spoke.

Like me, he seemed not totally at ease. He was unusually quiet, almost abstracted, though he had greeted me in a gentle, wistful way, just clinging silently as if the contact of our bodies was its own reassurance.

'Ferraria Metalla,' I said. 'As they tend to call her. You know her, don't you?'

'Of course I know her,' he said impatiently.' Then he looked ashamed. 'She was about the first person here – first woman, anyway – to take me up, as you must be perfectly aware.

'Look, can I have some wine and something to eat? I'm starving. Yes, old Ferraria Metalla was very decent to me, rather funny in her no-nonsense way, and fond but undemanding. Quite an experienced old bird, too.'

'Not besotted?' I said with a smile, approaching him with one of Vesta's thimbles brimming and a plate of cold guinea fowl.

'What? Oh no, never that. I was hardly the first boy in her bed, was I? Business-like, sensible, but surprisingly kind, I'd say. She just enjoyed having me around. You don't want the intimate details, but obviously not much went on. . . . So you needn't look depressed, and you definitely don't need to be jealous. It, such as it was, was over, finished, before you and I met. And Julia, for Vesta's sake, or whatever you say, don't think it was in any way like our – our relationship. For one thing, I didn't love her.'

'But you love me?'

'Do you need convincing?' He sounded exasperated, yet I went on staring at him, watching him eat, noticing how dispirited he appeared and how his face in the lamplight seemed thinner than usual. Fatigue, perhaps, made him look younger than ever; even his rather clumsy way of eating enhanced his youthfulness. As I watched, I felt welling up a fondness so intense and pervasive that it made my eyes mist over.

'It's marvellous seeing you,' he continued, munching on.

163

His glass was empty and I left it unrefilled, determined not to be deflected from my scrutiny. 'And being here. I know I sent the dice for tonight – I wanted to see you – but I'm not sure if I'm in the mood . . . you know, for making love. I'm sorry. It seems an awful thing to say, put like that.'

'Did you think it was the only way of convincing me?'

'No, of course not. I just want you to realise that being in love, love altogether, if you come to that, isn't only a matter of going to bed. What I'm saying I'm saying badly, but I feel fairly tired. It's an emotion, not just a physical thing. I love you, Julia – that's all, and I certainly didn't love Aurelia.'

'Oh, I'm not jealous. You must believe that. But I am curious. When you first came here, with the Prefect, did you come specially to see me? Did you even know I existed? Indeed, why did you come at all? There had been Pontilla Pilata's murder, if you remember. That brought Publius; but why you?'

'May I?' He asked, holding up his glass. By an effort of will I remained where I was, seated, nodding that he should get up and refill it for himself. As he sauntered over, he seemed more relaxed. In the proximity of pouring out the wine he bent his fair head to brush mine and let his hand lightly clasp my shoulder. I too relaxed at that contact.

We need each other, we were both saying: I could not doubt that. And both of us were serious, about something. Less lovers than friends, it might seem, so decorous and familiar, without passion, were we tonight. Anyone, I thought sardonically, might have spied on us and found us innocent: two thickly-draped figures whose grave juxtaposition would itself suggest only such emotions as grief or consolation.

'That evening I was at the same supper-party as the Prefect,' Rufus said. 'And when the news came, of course it broke up. He invited me to accompany him – to see the Roman civil machine in action, all efficiency and justice. He wanted to consult an enormously respected prominent person – you. The Emperor was abroad, and he was terrified of scandal. . . . I can't recall everything he said, but he was certainly looking for support.'

'Which he hardly got,' I said, pouring myself some wine. 'This may be the last of the Empress's Samian,' I added with apparent inconsequence.

'Well, I don't know. He came away implying you were definitely interested – intrigued, I think was the word. He was sure you'd help.'

'I put him off,' I said indignantly, 'as Gemma might phrase it. And I made it absolutely clear I wasn't going to be involved. He had no right to imply the opposite.'

Rufus smiled across at me. For the first time this evening it was as though some shadow had been lifted from his face. His eyes seemed properly open at last, glinting as brilliantly green as Aurelia's emeralds and far more strange amid his pallid features.

'You won't like this, but he thought your coyness, as he termed it, was just a typical lady's manner, hesitant and thoroughly feminine about deciding something. He quite approved of it, you see, as part of you, Julia. In fact I think you were supposed to be in the best tradition of old Roman womanhood – silent, domestic and waiting to be told how to do your duty by a man.'

'He had no right to mislead you about me, if he did.'

His smile disappeared, like a light blown out.

'How do you mean, if–?'

'Oh, I'm weary too, tonight, Rufus. What I mean is, if you thought I was like that. But you can't have fallen in love just through Publius's description of me. You hardly saw me on that first occasion. Next, you followed me, didn't you? You were hoping for a chance for us to meet and speak – to be taken up, I expect, as Roman women were always doing with you. Wasn't that it?'

'Why the interrogation?' he asked abruptly. 'Isn't it rather a waste of such time as we've got left, going back over the past? After all, Julia, I won't be in Rome for always. When the spring comes. . . .'

'You'll go?'

'If not before.' He put down his glass with a decisive gesture almost more heartrending in its casual finality than any words.

I hadn't gambled very well, if I had been gambling. In the end, I had lacked the courage. I looked at the dice, with their eternally upwards, staring numbers. Of course I should keep them; they would probably be found among my few possessions at my death.

'I didn't tell you,' I said, consciously changing the mood,

trying to scatter my own baleful thoughts, 'why Aurelia came to see me. It was really over Pontilla Pilata's murder–'

'Not more about it?' He sounded exasperated again. 'It seems the only topic of conversation sometimes in this dreary city. For the last day or two people have been going on about it as if it had only just happened. Isn't there any other news? Perhaps when the Emperor turns up and you have your celebrations, you'll all forget about it. Really, Julia, it's hardly your concern – or mine.'

'Aurelia said much the same. That's why she came: to suggest I stopped involving myself in it. She feels very strongly on the point.'

'Quite right. I told you she was a sensible old thing.' He paused and pushed back the hair that had fallen over his face. 'Anyway, I thought you'd ceased your investigations, or whatever they were. I've never been very clear what you were up to.'

'Perhaps I was pursuing justice.'

'Whatever that might be. Instead, you ended up with me.'

'Oh, Rufus.' I ran across the room and clasped him. 'I'm afraid – of the future, of everything. I'm even afraid of what might happen to us. And I haven't yet told you other things, how I went to the Tullianum and what Gemma did . . . and all my worries.'

'Let's say goodbye now. We're both tired. But promise me this. Just come tomorrow evening in the same way. Don't send any message. Don't fail. I beg you, Rufus.'

'Very well.' He said it so neutrally I could not guess if he was pleased or angry. 'I promise.'

XIV

Sleep came to me only fitfully in what remained of the night. I woke to the thought of the temple and the hearth, forming a refuge where I might pass the time and grow calm. It was less strain to use the underground passage: not to be visible accorded with my feelings, but I had forgotten how effortlessly every step, every brick it almost seemed, recalled the first time I had ever walked that way.

How privileged I had felt, following in the foaming wake of Cornelia's rippling skirts, carefully keeping myself from either scraping against the walls or, worse offence, bumping against her. She was tall and stately, austerely beautiful under the layers of ritual garments whose names I had then only just learnt. We were to attend a sacrifice, she had told me; and indeed, a terrified bleating broke out as we ascended the steps and entered the temple itself, from a she-goat so blanched its coat looked pinkish. As it was dragged before the altar, I had tried to steady my quaking nerves, brought on by the cool dimness, the solemnity of the moment and by the desperate cries of the struggling animal, bucking and plunging on delicate hooves under a wreath of flowers interwoven and tied about its horns with coloured ribbon.

Because it was a sacrifice, Cornelia wore the purple-edged suffibulum over her stiff white linen diadem, increasing the stately effect. Her hair was banded as smoothly as the lappets which fell on either side of a face so impassive when I gazed up at it that I felt it a lesson, an implied rebuke to my disturbed sensations. Even now I could recapture the hasty way I had adjusted my own facial muscles, assuming such monumental, staring gravity that I hardly realised when the rite was finished. The air smelt of incense; the floor was wet with blood and wine; and I felt mysteriously exhilarated. Even Cornelia's rather frantic poking among the dead goat's viscera failed to upset my comatose state.

'Not a good augury,' she had muttered to me as we solemnly returned along the passage. 'A speckled liver, and before that the victim's resistance . . . I'm sorry you didn't bring us better fortune.'

'It should have gone willingly, shouldn't it?' I had said knowingly.

After experiencing the rite, I felt shocked at the insult to Vesta and the disappointing result. The goddess might perhaps be angry with me. I resolved to be even more assiduous in my duties, and I told fat Varonilla as much that evening as we climbed into our beds.

'Fancy mother Cornelia being up in time for a sacrifice,' she replied. 'I wonder what she's looking out for – a man or money. She's not usually short of either, but don't quote me.'

'Of course not,' I said earnestly, too sleepy to take in properly what she was saying. 'Anyway,' I added, more to myself, 'she looked lovely.'

Now, I was going to no sacrifice. I did not even seek to propitiate the goddess, any more than I expected to receive her guidance in my affairs. Yet it was calming to stand in the temple sanctuary, watching while a draped Vestal tended the sacred fire with a concentration that conveyed she was aware of my presence.

It blazed well. There was no danger of its expiry, and I could see we should have difficulty when March came in dousing the flames before re-kindling it to celebrate the beginning of a new year.

And by then Rufus might well have left Rome. If I had learnt nothing else that night, I had learnt that. Until now it had been a fact unmentioned between us. It was the reality I preferred to veil but which he openly and gladly lived with – as was only right. That was what I must teach myself to understand, I knew, staring into the fierce heart of the fire and feeling its warmth on my skin, alluring me to draw close, to test sensation by plunging a hand into it. Then Rufus's departure would become a reality, branded inevitably on me. The fire meant me no harm: its nature was to burn. So Rufus's nature required him to leave me, to go – almost, to grow – and any attempt to stop him would be not merely futile but wrong.

It had not happened yet, but it would come. I should be left forever wondering about him, regretting my cowardice, my lack of faith, my secret, unresolved fears. Suddenly, in the shrine of Vesta, where everything was fixed, eternal-seeming, breathing peace, promising concord, I was ashamed to have such feelings. Love should drive them out, I thought, raising my eyes without any sense of incongruity to the statue of the goddess, no flaunting naked Venus but swathed in finely-pleated robes of marble aping muslin, wool and linen. I was conscious of wearing similar robes but of having under them a body which Rufus would caress, awake and quieten; and

168

my mind too would submit, be lulled, cease to try to enter the forbidden territory of his.

I was greedy for him to bring me peace. Before we parted, I needed the reassurance of having been, of being loved. Only then could I accept the pain and absorb it. I should become firm again as I attended our rituals, impressively majestic, aloof, severe, and no longer impatient at their monotonous cycle. Dreams of going with him to Gaul had been true madness; if realised – and I flushed as I recalled the wilder aspects – they must have destroyed us both. An ageing woman in a foreign land, stripped of status and identity, and a young man increasingly despising her as an encumbrance . . .

My place was here, at the hearth of Rome. I was its guardian, tutelary spirit. And although I guessed that Rufus, even in his love, viewed me with a touch of cynicism, he was wrong – too modest, for once – if he saw himself as the first in a line of lovers. I should be faithful, simply because I wished to be. Perhaps to him I should not admit as much. I did not want to protest my virtue; I held it too strongly for that. But no one would replace him in my love.

'You,' I told the red-haired girl in the tone of an order, 'may go to bed early tonight – at least leave me unattended. And in a day or two Gemma should be fully recovered.'

She nodded without speaking. After Gemma's steady chatter, her sullen silences were disconcerting, almost suggesting something mutinous. Yet at least I did not have to think of her as spying on me: she was too little interested for that. And when Gemma was better, I had to decide her future – something I dreaded, and even dreaded having in my mind when Rufus arrived.

It seemed important that for him, on this evening, I was pure and clear: like crystal – unflawed by petty distractions and mundane problems – or, it came to me swiftly, like the clear green glass of his eyes, so that as we exchanged glances he would have the sensation I always had of being bathed in limpidity. 'No one's going to disturb us tonight,' I said vehemently, seizing his cloak and unfastening it.

I had been waiting in the lumber-room, with the door unlatched, half-open – my signal that he was looked for, longed for with more than usual anxiety. Yet I was now able to move less impulsively and be less abandoned in my

169

greeting, which I knew he preferred. It was only that the first contact with his flesh continued to excite me. The reward for waiting was always unexpectedly sweeter than I was prepared for.

'We're alone. I've seen no one, been nowhere – except the temple. We're on our own, Rufus. Are you hungry?'

'Not at all,' he said, laughing. 'Or only for you.'

'I'm glad – more than glad, relieved, blessed, happy. Last night you seemed . . . but I don't want to think of last night. You're here and we're together.'

'You're certainly looking beautiful, Julia. And now I realise how far from cold you are under the surface, I admire your beauty all the more. It appeals to me just because it's rather misleading – about what you're really like, I mean. In some ways, I feel I'm the first person who's ever known you. Does it annoy you if I say that?'

'It's true,' I said, delightedly. 'You've discovered someone even I didn't know existed. And I'm grateful, aren't I, Rufus?'

I drew his body down on mine, not hastily but in the luxury of feeling how much time there was until dawn and beyond.

'Leave the lamp,' I told him when he reached out to extinguish it. 'I want to see you, all of you – or as much as I can from this angle. I wish I could see us both, have a god's eye view of us lying here.' I locked my arms around his head and brought his lips tantalisingly near to mine. 'Now you're blurring for me, but I'm noticing your ears for the first time, Rufus. They're very wonderful in this light. One's more translucent than the other – it's a sort of pearl-colour, or like white coral.'

'One sticks out more than the other. I can't remember which it is. At home, where I wear my hair longer, nobody ever notices.'

'They must be very unobservant in Gaul,' I murmured.

'You're being absurd,' he said, kissing me. 'And what about your ears? I suppose I'm going to be told the Chief Vestal doesn't have any. She's deaf to men, has to be, of course, as part of her duties, and so they cut them off with special sacred scissors–'

'No, Rufus,' I cried. 'You're becoming revolting.'

'I can just imagine the ceremony – "auricula desecta", it's called, and it's bound to be revolting, like so many of your

170

ceremonies. We're far less superstitious and far less barbaric in our behaviour. You can't do anything here, barely cross the street, without killing something first.'

'I shan't quarrel with you tonight. But Rome will survive every criticism you make, Rufus.'

'Oh, I know. And I resent it. It's I who may not survive, I sometimes feel.'

'Why should you feel that?' I put aside reluctantly his caressing hand and tried to shift away sufficiently to see how serious he was.

'It's just a feeling – it'll pass, I expect. I'm tired of all the rumours and the gossip and the sheer triviality of what passes as life here. There's too much leisure, for one thing. And the people who are doing anything are boring people like Calvus, amassing statistics that are absolutely useless, or Afranius Dexter whom most of you look down on for being in what you call trade. Well, at least he's clever – very smart, I should say, and makes pots of money.'

'You'll survive, Rufus,' I said earnestly. 'I want you to. I've thought about it–'

'About my surviving? Good.'

'About us – and about the future. I'm clearer about it all than I was. I realise that one day you'll go away – you must – and I realise that's best, for you. I'm prepared now. I've got over my fears. When you have to go, when it comes to us parting, I shall be very calm, just because I love you.'

'That's what I want to hear.'

He drew me to him in an abrupt, passionate action, his body forcing itself against mine, stifling the response I had meant teasingly to make about his apparently wanting to hear me talk of our parting. Did the moments of tender proximity, the playing with each other's bodies as we played in speech, give me more pleasure, I had wondered before, than his actual love-making? It should no longer be so, I determined, fighting and grappling with myself as much as him.

'I haven't seen your ears yet,' he panted as we wrestled, almost brutally tugging back my hair to the roots. 'I don't know what they're like – if they exist. Perhaps they're hideous.'

I twisted my head convulsively from side to side. 'You

171

shan't see them,' I squealed, half-laughing and half hysterically tearful at the agonising intermittent pricking that ran through my scalp.

'I shall, I shall,' he shouted.

His chin was bruising as he thrust his contorted face deeper into mine, making me gasp for breath, feeling consciousness was flowing from me. I was dissolving under the repeated assault of the jerking, shuddering shaft of his whole body, aware of only a flash of his bared teeth that still snarlingly sought to sink themselves in the lobe of one ear.

A piercing pain hit me at the bite he inflicted; and then all sensation stopped. I had drifted into a hazy, twilight state, where no emotions were. It was as if my mind were wrapped in muslin – like Vesta, I thought vaguely – finely woven and being ceaselessly woven softly around me as I lay. Beside me Rufus was stretched, quiescent. The interweaving threads were binding us closer and closer, as though containing us within a single cocoon-like covering. And dimly, when I languidly turned towards him, I was permeated again with a sense of protectiveness, of guarding him while he dozed. What pervaded me was love: love as something unfocused, muffled yet glowing. It shone out, a lamp vital and unquenchable, amid all the swathes of muslin.

I gently curled and insinuated my fingers within Rufus's slack ones, interlocking our hands so lightly that he could hardly sense the contact, though there came the faintest, instinctive muscular response. That seemed the most poignant message that love could send, expressing utter confidence in the other being. My wish had been granted. As I gazed down at the two interlinked hands, merged into one shadowy, spiky shape, almost a marine creature, I was gazing at the perfect expression of our unity.

Some fresh pressure of mine perhaps, as I lay there, drifting tranquilly, insubstantial as a curtain in the breeze, made him wakeful. His shoulder twitched. I shut my eyes to prolong the floating, disembodied state, but a twinge of cramp, a crease of flesh, nagged me into equal if not greater wakefulness.

I extended a toe blindly and let it slide the length of tautening skin of his leg. Our hands unclasped as we stirred, blinking a little, looking at each other like storm-tossed lovers uncertain if they were drowned or living but content enough to find themselves unseparated.

'Hungry?' I asked, half mockingly.

He shook his rumpled head.

'Thirsty, at least? The Falernian is not mulled, by the way.'

'Only for some water.'

'I'll get it for you.'

I sat on the side of the bed while he drank, watching the movement of his throat when he swallowed.

'That was good of you,' he said. 'Thank you, Julia.'

'Oh, I'm prepared to do more than that, Rufus. For you.'

'Didn't one of your revered predecessors carry water in a sieve? Tullia. . . .'

'Tuccia, she was called. She did it to prove her chastity, so perhaps it would be foolish of me even to attempt emulation. Tullia was rather different — more like your idea of Roman women generally perhaps. I can't recall if she had a lover, but she did drive her chariot over her father's dead body. Quite deliberately, we're told — nothing to do with any traffic problems.'

'Ever since when, I suppose, no Roman lady is allowed to drive a chariot.'

'Well, most of us have servants for that sort of thing.'

'Slaves.'

'I prefer the less harsh word.'

'Be my slave, Julia. Fetch me another drink of water.'

'I will, but not because I'm a slave — or any kind of servant. I do it out of love for you, Rufus. Not out of any weakness but out of strength.'

'So long as I get the water,' he said, smiling up lazily from the dishevelled sheets where he sprawled, and reaching out his hand.

'But you don't,' I said, rapidly withdrawing the glass. 'Unless you acknowledge the distinction.'

'Oh, I do. I do. I must — I'm dreadfully thirsty. And, after all, that's because of love, so it comes to the same thing.'

A cold shade fell over me, I could not tell why; and I shivered. 'You argue badly,' I meant to answer, just as I meant to suspend the glass out of his reach. But I was silent, suddenly — amid my claims to strength — struck dumb.

It was as though shears had severed the web of threads

173

that bound us. We were two entities, separate, even alien. Yet I looked as lovingly as ever at his pale, naked body which had so recently, savagely, been coupled with mine. I gave him the water and watched fixedly once more while he drank.

The lamp was dying. Phosphorescent patches of light capriciously armoured his joints as he propped himself up in the gathering darkness of the bed, making his chest bloom momentarily like a breast-plate and laying a golden greave along one exposed shin.

It was chill in my shadowy corner of the room, and lonely. Night-terrors were pressing around me, insistent and questioning, waking my mind despite my sated, even weary physical organism. It might be I should never see him again. My love required me to know the truth before he went. Then all terrors would be stilled, however appalling the knowledge. Yet I hesitated, nerving myself to speak, to say a few clumsy words and be rid of the burden of doubt.

The longer I remained silent, the more everything seemed withering and growing remote. It was as though he had forgotten my existence, sated too, but completely so, and about to slip away into sleep.

'If you have to leave me, Rufus,' I began. My tongue was dry and the sound of my own voice was harsh. 'I've heard things, been told things.' I started again. 'Are you listening? I don't want to be left alone, unknowing, always tormented by doubting. Trust me – trust my love. All I'm asking is that I'm not left uncertain, with every recollection soured by never being sure.'

'Of my love?' He groaned sleepily. 'What more do you want?'

The lamp flickered up and went out. I crossed the room in the dark and stood beside the bed.

'The truth,' I said.

'About what?'

'Rufus, I'm not indulging some silly whim. Ever since – well, since Gemma overheard us the other night and told me–'

'Told you what?' He sounded alert now, no longer petulant.

'I've been in agony–'

'Dismiss her,' he said. 'That's my advice. I've always thought she was a spiteful, chattering, impertinent girl – slave or not – and the last person for you to encourage. Anyway, how dare she eavesdrop on us? You should have sacked her at once.'

'She's ill, Rufus, to begin with,' I said calmly. 'I am angry with her, of course. But she wasn't just being spiteful, and it wasn't only she. In fact, it's another girl who heard your voice–'

'And got a shock that there was a man in the house. Very well. I'll lower my voice in future, though I don't think I speak very loudly. Look, it's hardly worth your getting over-wrought about – if you want me to go on visiting you. There's bound to be some risk. We've known that. But I thought you had things under control here, providing we were reasonably discreet. And we are.'

'It's not a matter of discretion. That girl claims – and what she says is only one of the things worrying me. I must talk to you about them, Rufus, if only to be rid of them. Then it'll be over, I give you my promise, once I know it all. It won't affect my love: it's part of it really. Will you help me?'

'What am I to help you to do?'

'Isn't it enough that I'm asking for your help?'

'I don't know,' he said curtly. It came out of the darkness like a stab. 'Obviously, I'm involved too, though so far I'm baffled as to how exactly. Why not just leave everything as it is, Julia? We're happy enough, aren't we? I thought last night was the end of putting questions between us. Isn't it wasting the few months that are still left?'

'No, it is not. I'll be able to enjoy them properly once I know the truth. And it will mean so much to me in the future, when I'm alone, Rufus. I have to think of that.'

He remained silent, but I could virtually hear him pondering, debating in the stillness. And the silence froze me. It ought to have been the moment he jumped up and flung his arms around me in a gesture that by itself banished half the surrounding nightmare spirits that slithered and whispered as they dragged us apart.

'Can't you understand?' I burst out when the active, malign silence was beginning to stifle me. 'It's for my peace of mind. That's what you can give me before you go. Not some stupid trinket for remembrance – just peace of mind. It can only

175

make me love you more. And I'll treasure it for as long as I live.'

'You're making yourself unhappy, Julia, quite unnecessarily – and it's an exhausting process. Mayn't we sleep a little before–'

'No, Rufus. Last night we postponed it. I asked you specially to come this evening.'

'We did make love,' he said sulkily. 'In case you've forgotten. You appeared pleased enough about that. I'm not at fault there, am I?'

'You aren't at fault at all,' I said more gently. 'Please don't think that. Bear with me, late as it is. Shall I get a lamp from the vestibule? The wretched broomstick of a girl who's looking after things while Gemma's ill must have forgotten to fill this one. It shouldn't have gone out like that.'

Rather uneagerly he made a space for me beside him. 'I prefer the dark tonight,' he said.

'Give me your hand to hold,' I begged. 'I need to feel you breathing, existing, being with me – while you can.'

'Well. . . .' His tone indicated a refusal to be cajoled. 'I can't say I'm all ears, but let's get it over with – whatever it is. At least once it's done, I presume we can get some rest.'

'How shall I begin?' I asked aloud. 'I know – by calling the gods to witness I love you. Nothing will alter that. You're listening, aren't you, Rufus?

'I've got to mention Pontilla Pilata. Somehow, she comes into this – or, at least, she may come into it.'

'I thought–' he started saying.

'Soon I pray, we may indeed be done with her. Let me go on. She patronised an aunt and niece, one for her sewing, the other for her flute-playing. Tibicina is the niece's name. The aunt's dead. This Tibicina was in Pontilla Pilata's bedroom after noon – after the middle of the day – when a man came in. She heard him speaking, quite apart from the tread of his feet.'

'You amaze me. Did she see the man or just hear him?'

'She's blind, Rufus.'

'I see.'

'Fortunate you. I haven't explained how profoundly respected Pontilla Pilata was, though you may have heard something of her reputation. She was famous for the fact – among

176

others – that no man ever crossed the threshold of her house. Yet the odd thing is that we now know, since her death, that she had quantities of lovers. And we know that the custom was for them to visit her disguised as women, female friends, part of her respectable circle, I suppose, of charitable ladies. I may as well tell you that Afranius Dexter first thought up the idea of the men dressing as women.'

'Lucky Roman men don't go in for moustaches, as we do in Gaul. I shaved mine off before I travelled. I didn't want to appear ridiculous.'

'Tibicina's got very acute hearing. The voice she heard at Pontilla Pilata's was unusual, distinctive – the voice perhaps of a foreigner.'

His hand still lay in mine, inert.

'She was in this house a night or two ago, invited by Gemma. They hid in the lumber-room and she heard the same voice again – or so she claims: your voice. Of course, she could have been mistaken. I hope you'll tell me it's all absurd and untrue. Now I've said it it sounds so slight, but I'm glad to have spoken. It was best to do so, believe me, Rufus. You've only got to–'

'To deny it.' He said it without any vehemence, and that lack seemed ominous.

'Yes,' I affirmed as solemnly as I could. 'That's all I ask.'

'Very well. I'll deny it. It's rubbish – typical malevolent rubbish, probably inspired by the rumours going round. Content?'

'Ah, Rufus, I feel such a weight lifted from me. I'd begun to be sickeningly afraid. . . .'

'But it wouldn't have affected your love for me? Remember you kept swearing that.'

'Nothing would.' I turned blindly in the rush of happiness, groping for him. 'Nothing.'

My hands grabbed at air; and then I felt the bed creak as he moved, got up and must be standing over me.

'Rufus,' I breathed.

'If I had known Pontilla Pilata,' he said musingly.

'It wouldn't have mattered to me, as far as we're concerned, Rufus. Why shouldn't you have known her? In itself it wouldn't be a crime, even being her lover – one of them.

177

Anyway, come and lie down. You said you wanted to rest. Stay here a few more hours.'

'I'm not sure I shall – if I can.' His tone changed abruptly. 'Whatever you first told Publius, you did take up the case of Pontilla Pilata, didn't you? He wasn't entirely wrong, as it happened. Well, what have you now decided?'

'Does it matter, does it matter?' I stammered, not bothering to give the words any emphasis. We were wasting time talking when we should be forgetting, just reclining while there spread over and around us once more the muslin web of intimacy.

Only now did I realise my own utter fatigue. I had braced myself, held my breath, launched a challenge as dangerous as any weapon – and learnt it was unnecessary. It was as though I had fought in the arena of my own imagination what proved an invisible, ultimately non-existent enemy; yet even the relief brought weariness.

'If,' he resumed, 'I had known her, been her lover, I'd have become one of your suspects, wouldn't I? Quite a convenient one, too, as an outsider, a foreigner . . . the ideal culprit. Perhaps I was anyway under suspicion.

'Well, Julia. Have you ever suspected me? Would I be capable of what you probably think was monstrous, an outrage?'

'How can I say? You told me I was foolish upsetting myself. Now you're behaving similarly.'

'But I want the truth, you see – just as much as you did. Truth for truth. I've often wondered what you thought about me altogether. We meet, you pretend to despise me, to be grand, and then you yield – to a young foreigner about whom you know only what he cares to let you know. And some of that hurts you a lot – oh yes, it does. He's not very moral by your standards, not your class of person at all. Going to bed with him you enjoy – I hope. But what about how you see him when he isn't making love to you? Perhaps he doesn't exist outside this room. Perhaps that doesn't matter to you, whether he's got feelings, whether he's frightened, depressed, hopeful, wondering about the future, the rest of his life . . . how he'll live. He doesn't even have his rightful name for you. He's nothing – nothing at all – but a giant phallus nicknamed Rufus.'

178

'It's not so,' I cried, jumping from the bed. 'I think about you all the time.'

I blundered against him kneeling, half crouched on the floor, his skin icy. I clutched his shoulders, nursed his head, while shuddering sobs racked his body. Not his name but whispered endearments, invocations, flowed from me as I cradled him, longing to give way and let my tears too flow over him.

'Put something on,' I murmured at last, taking up some garment of my own and wrapping him in it.

'It's yours.' His teeth chattered, and he went on crouching there, immovable. 'Yours,' he sobbed.

I could not help a momentary wry reaction, a brief smile even in the midst of struggling not to weep. 'No harm in that.'

He shuddered.

'I can't hear,' I said softly as he kept on gulping and starting muffled, incoherent sentences.

'The truth,' he moaned. 'I must know. Even now you're investigating . . . still wondering . . . I did it.'

'My dearest – didn't I say I loved you? That's the only truth that matters.'

'But it's not,' he yelled, breaking from me. 'I did do it. It was me – in her room. And at the tomb . . . I was waiting for her. We had been lovers. We quarrelled. She tried to make excuses, be rid of me – for the sake of her reputation, she said. I was mad with rage – calmly dismissing me like – like a slave. I seized the ends of her scarf as she turned away. It twisted or I twisted it. Yes, I almost tore it in my anger. She overbalanced and it tightened. I went on pulling. She fell, nearly on me. And I let her fall quite gently . . . There wasn't much struggle. She was totally unprepared. It was all over very quickly – very quietly. I knew straight away, though: she was dead.

'Now, what about your boasted love?'

I sank my face against the trailing drapery that made an untidy ruff around his neck.

'Why didn't you tell me before – oh, why didn't you trust me, Rufus?' Unbidden, the name came wailing to my lips. It was not important. His name – whatever it was – would mean nothing now. There were a thousand reproaches, more bitter

179

than any he could make, buzzing in my head. Hadn't he once denied, days ago, that he even knew Pontilla Pilata? The lies, the evasions, were nothing, though, to the knowledge that this was all his love had amounted to: to need to learn whether I suspected him.

'Get up,' I said, so sternly that he obeyed. 'Get dressed – in your own clothes. I feel there may not be much time, however tired you are. We both are. I'm going to fetch a lamp. We have to think hard and plan.'

'What happens to me? Arrest, prison, execution . . . Roman justice at first hand?'

I left the questions unanswered, trembling as I entered the empty vestibule and returned with a table lamp, still trembling. When I lit it, we seemed tacitly to prefer keeping it between us, not quite meeting each other's eyes.

'I don't regret it,' he said defiantly. 'None of it. I hated her at the moment of tugging that scarf – wished her dead all right. And I wouldn't have met you otherwise, would I, Julia? I don't regret our love either. If I die tomorrow. Only, it wouldn't have lasted. We shouldn't have tested it, should we? Either of us. I did warn you, but you persisted.'

'Only because I guessed,' I said soberly. 'All I wanted was for you to confirm it. If you'd told me–' I broke off.

'On the strength of your maid's tittle-tattle? Or that creeping, sneaking blind girl's? You were glad enough to love me up till then. Oh, I've watched you, Julia, believe me–'

'I do believe you, Rufus. I'm sorry: that's the only name I have for you. If you'd watched me more affectionately you'd have seen that I meant everything I said about my love. I'm still prepared to convince you it is a reality, hasn't stopped – couldn't. I saw you clearly enough, perhaps more clearly than you wished.

'As for Tibicina, she could easily have made a mistake, honestly or maliciously – a flute-girl's evidence would never have mattered. No, what mattered was what it prompted me to remember: something I'd tried hard to bury, forget, explain away. . . . When we were in the Pilatus tomb, when you started to make love to me. . . .'

'Well?'

'Something you said made me horribly afraid – afraid you'd been there before. You spoke of an underground room. You knew it existed, because you'd been in it, with her. Then I put it out of my mind. There were plenty of ways it might be explained. You might explain it yourself, I thought foolishly. I was ready to accept anything you told me. Ye gods, how I wanted to accept you, as you really were, if only you'd confided in me.'

'You wanted not me but my confession. Now you've got it. Your case is solved.' He shrugged his shoulders with an air of bravado. 'Being at the tomb before proved nothing. Even now, you know only what I've told you. You don't know how she treated me, what I felt at being taken up, put down – like a child's toy. I'm sick of being loved for my foreign looks or because I'm so good in bed. There's a real me – a person none of you ever bothered to discover. You in particular have been asleep, really, dreaming about an impossible man. To wake you up I had to tell you about how I'd killed someone.

'Oh, I expect all the rumours and the talk of what silly servants know would have vanished eventually. It shook me briefly perhaps, though I think I'm smart enough to have survived – and got away with it. But now I'm caught, I'm not afraid, Julia. Don't think that. A Gaul can die at least as proudly as any Roman, but I'm not committing suicide. They'll have to kill me.'

'They will.'

I had listened not with hostility, just with growing impatience.

'Don't you know they've found the very man who, I suppose, drove Pontilla Pilata out to meet you at the tomb – the same man who brought you back? Trebonius Niger, her lawyer, is determined to track down the murderer. And he's clever too. Put you in her cloak again and he'll soon be able–'

'I burnt it,' he said triumphantly.

'Without anyone noticing?'

'I told the woman I lodge with a story about getting it accidentally caked with mule dung – couldn't get it off, best to burn it. I'd even bothered to rub some dung on it. . . .'

'Trebonius Niger will find her, if he hasn't already. And Pontilla Pilata's woman, Beroe, can describe her mistress's garments. Probably it's the most fatal thing you did – burning that cloak.

'By the way, how did you manage to reach the tomb?'

181

'That morning – we'd agreed to meet, much as normal . . . she used to send cryptic love tokens for meetings to my lodgings, amusing trifles. . . .'

'Of the kind you've sent me? Or perhaps the very same?'

He looked at me insolently. His green eyes shone, wild animal-like, baffling, but still capable of making me marvel.

'Similar, yes. Why not? On that morning, it happens that Afranius Dexter was driving to Capua. He took me.'

'Of course, I knew he was mixed up in it somewhere. I'm glad.'

'Don't suppose I was so clumsy as to mention the Pilatus tomb. I explained that Calvus wanted me to go out and admire your funerary architecture – as he did. I'd been out there often before. I chose the Prefect's family tomb, some miles further on . . . A neat choice, wasn't it? Then I simply walked back through the fields behind the tombs, not encountering anybody except a peasant or two–'

'They could be witnesses,' I interrupted.

'You see,' he said abstractedly, frowning as he stared down at the lamp which glowed between us. I let him go on speaking, little though I wanted to hear any of it. 'I thought our meeting was as usual – what I'd call a rendez-vous. I never guessed. . . . She'd come to charm me, at first, into accepting dismissal with a last kiss – nothing more. For once she didn't argue that we went down into that underground room – "where my ancestors aren't looking," she'd say with a giggle. This time she'd brought no food. She seemed anxious, irritable, and all the while insolent. Our relationship wasn't right . . . she was eminently respectable, a high-born lady . . . I hated her as she pursed up her tiny lips – very red and scented – and squeaked out the words.' He paused. 'I knew what it all meant: another man. She'd picked me up quick enough – noticed me at the Emperor's Birthday Games, later came pretending to want the Prefect's advice, allowed me to escort her to her litter. . . .'

'Ah,' I exclaimed, despite myself. I saw again that windy morning on the Capitoline and that glimpse of Rufus, bowing, as I dropped the curtain of my litter, his words reverberating in my ears. 'Did you love her?' I asked.

'Did she love me, you ought to be asking. She never loved anyone except herself, however many men she took to bed.

182

She'd flattered me – certainly. She was attractive, horribly so. It was sex that drew us and held us, until she found the next man. I knew there was one all right, however much she lisped about keeping her reputation spotless. She was false the whole way through, and yet in the eyes of all of you in this city she was respectability and propriety incarnate. Oh, it told me a lot about your standards of behaviour.

'And then she really turned on me when I grew angry: I wasn't going to be kicked out and told to get back where I belonged, in my dirty little village, as she put it. I was plebeian, vulgar, foreign – even my complexion was the wrong colour. . . . Another moment and she'd have been boasting of the sort of man she really lusted for.

'I meant to hurt her back, but I couldn't find words. I just seized that gaudy, fluttering scarf – it was like the embodiment of her. When she struggled, I felt excited. I'd teach her. Suddenly she stood for everything that revolted me here – everything, Julia. As she began choking, toppling, I felt I'd throttled Rome.'

'My poor, benighted boy.' I looked away. 'Man, if you prefer.'

'Afterwards,' he said hastily, as though nothing must check him, 'I nearly bolted out of the tomb, once I realised. . . . Then I stopped and thought. Outside was that mule-carriage she'd hired, waiting. I knew she always paid the driver first. She'd kept on her cloak – significant in itself. Taking it off her was the worst part. She was still warm . . . and so was it. I bundled myself up, hood and all, bent a little – and hurried out. The risk actually helped calm me. I got in the carriage and gestured petulantly just as she might. And it worked.'

He seemed dazed as he ceased speaking, and I felt if I did not rouse myself, I too would fall into a daze. I had been with him in that tomb, beside him, almost an accessory. I had allowed him to make love to me near enough to where he used to make love to her, and that loomed at least as heinous as the crime.

Later, there would be time to unravel my complex feelings: a lifetime, or what was left of it. I should never now have an opportunity to see Rufus as he wanted to be seen, even if that were possible. He was the aggressor who turned out to be the victim. Yet in either role, he was still the object of my love – or of the emotion he had first awoken and which still animated me. I could not exclaim against the circumstances that had brought us together. I did not even wish they had been different.

'You haven't much time,' I said briskly. That was one of the differences that separated us. He seemed unwilling or unable to stir.

'Do you summon a quaestor, a praetor or an aedile? Or do I rate the Prefect himself?' he asked with a last spark of defiance. 'I'm sure there's a procedure to be followed. And presumably I get lodged inside the Tullianum, as I think you once mentioned.'

'I can't hide you here,' I said. 'You must go back to your lodgings for a few hours. I'll get a message to you somehow after I've seen Afranius Dexter. No; better that he sends you the message. He'll help us. You must be ready to leave Rome tomorrow – today, rather. As soon as it can be arranged.'

'Is this a trick?' he said slowly.

'It's the only way to save you. You must go home, Rufus – where you belong. Afranius Dexter always has goods travelling north. By tomorrow night you'll be far from Rome, perhaps on board ship. . . . Anyway, safer than staying here. Now, I've got to think where and how to meet Afranius Dexter, and discreetly. I don't want to go to his house.'

'Mulciber's, the jeweller,' he muttered. 'He's often there during the day. He owns it. You know the shop I mean?'

'Of course I do. The most famous jeweller in the city – anyway, the most expensive. A shop for women like Pontilla Pilata. I suppose my visiting it wouldn't seem too odd. . . .'

'Julia?'

'You must leave, that's the first thing. Now, before it gets light. You'd be wise to get some rest. I shall.'

'Julia, I don't understand. Is it really–'

'No, you wouldn't,' I said tersely. 'And there's no time for explanation, even if you accepted one. Trust me or not – as you please. I'm not answering any more questions of yours.'

'I have to know. Please, Julia. It's love, isn't it? Oh, we love each other, after all. I do love you – believe that, I beg you. And your love for me . . . I can't say all I feel. I'm too bewildered. But, somehow, you make me happy and

184

ashamed. Forgive me, forgive me. I've been so alone. I was
mad to doubt you, but I was – thought I was – isolated, up
against everyone and everything. Now it's almost more than
I can bear, to know we are united, together.'

He stepped impulsively out of the radiance of the lamp,
coming towards me, a black figure seeking something I could
not give.

'Julia, answer, I implore you–' His voice was high and
strained, more foreign than ever, and movingly young.

I was hearing it for the last time; but I should always be
able to recall its tones.

'This way,' I said gently, guiding him and yet unwilling to
touch him.

For a moment I thought he was going to resist. Then,
docilely, he began following as I led. We crossed the corridor
and entered the lumber-room, walking warily. It had never
been easier to negotiate the piled, dusty furniture. Light
faintly indictated the existence of the door into the street. I
grasped its wooden bar, and it seemed magically weightless,
no barrier.

The door swung open soundlessly. An abrupt wash of cold
night air bathed my skin. As I turned almost hesitating, a
groaning sob broke from him.

'We part here,' I said. 'Farewell.'

XV

'Astonished,' Afranius Dexter was murmuring.

I blinked my eyes open with an effort, sat up and shook
out the folds of my dress, moving limbs that seemed as inani-
mate as the material. To mask exhaustion by a responsive
smile required only the play of a few muscles but they too
were paralysed or had simply ceased to exist.

'Charmed, of course, as well, and more than happy to be

185

of what help I can. Somehow I never thought you would – with all your sterling qualities, my dear Julia, or because of them perhaps – return to life. May I be the first to hail your revival? You come like the first breath of spring.'

'I've come on a rather less poetic mission, as you guessed.'

The atmosphere of the small, heavily-curtained room was drugged and insidious, inciting relaxation, and cloudy from some pastille burning on a tripod near Afranius's lolling, half-naked form, as jewelled as ever: an advertisement for the hidden wares of the shop, its exterior austere, that lay a wall away beyond the curtains.

I had passed through, barely pausing over the agate necklace displayed alone on the counter, conducted by a grinning negro child in a brief white tunic, who mimed a welcome with teeth as white.

'My humble den – my homely lair.' Afranius had gesticulated as he made me recline opposite him; and already I found myself struggling to keep a grip on my purpose, hardpointed like a weapon, where everything seemed chosen to disarm.

'This couch,' I said, stroking with a nerveless hand its snarling black and gold leopard-head arm, 'once belonged to Cleopatra, I presume, or at least to Alexander the Great's mother?'

'One of the Herods, I think,' he replied. 'But it's not for sale – at present. I prefer to reserve it for accommodating clients, especially those who may have come with problems. It's far older then I am, Julia, but it's equally discreet.'

'It's very comfortable,' I said banally.

'And I am so seldom astonished,' he repeated now. 'Your investigations led nowhere – that doesn't surprise me. Instead, you discovered our young Gallic friend. Well, I had wondered . . . but I never put his chances high in that direction. Other women, men too of course, he appealed to. But rarely, I suspect, for long. In any chariot race, he's a horse without staying power.

'So, if I follow correctly, he's exhausted his ability to please. He's an inconvenience and he's to disappear.'

Under the gilded lids, his eyes were studying me with mingled curiosity and amusement.

186

'I'm sure it can be arranged in some way . . . if it's what you wish.'

'As soon as possible. Today. Tomorrow night may be too late.'

'Vanishing without a trace? That may be more difficult, and anyway is it altogether wise? It's often sensible to be ready with a plausible explanation. Total disappearance overnight . . . and no body found. Unless we contrive that something's fished up out of the Tiber? It might be mutilated – artistically, of course. Lack of a corpse can be awkward. On the other hand, he's only a foreigner of no great significance. Yes, on balance, I think something sudden with no sequel should work. . . . It's satisfactorily final.'

I suddenly awoke, terrified. 'Stop. You've misunderstood. I'm – I'm desperate to help him. It's not disappearance in the way you imply. I'm not so mad as that, Afranius. I may be going mad – who knows? But I haven't come here to–'

'Commission a murder? My dear.' He got lazily to his feet. 'I never implied any such thing. You're overwrought, I can see. And, after all, I'm not sure I relish the imputation. It's one thing to pit my wits against stuffy conventions and tiresome formalities, and help other people to do the same. I'm all for love, Julia, and life. I'm neither a common assassin nor a trader in death.'

I bent my head. The void I had felt within myself the whole morning abruptly filled, flooded me, and tears gushed hopelessly down my face and into my lap.

'I love him,' I sobbed. 'If that's what you want to know. Love him – I, you may say, of all people. It's a scandal. I ought to die if anyone dies. But I can't help it. Tell anyone – everyone – you please. Only, first help me save him. That's what I'm imploring you to do. You can. And forgive me; I'm so confused and so weary, I can't think properly.'

His scented presence was beside me, but I bent my head only lower in agony. My tears were drying fast, dried and burnt away in the flaming awareness of fresh shame: to clasp that lithe, oiled male body would briefly be consoling even as I nursed the pain tearing through me for Rufus.

'Julia, you have my admiration – more than ever. I shan't insult you with pity, but you shall have my help.'

'You're very kind,' I said, forcing my face up, tear-streaked and fiery as it was. 'And after it's over – after you've got him safely away – you must use all your wits to devise how, how I can possibly. . . .'

To my chagrin, the tears welled up again like a fountain, and drenched my burning cheeks.

'When you are less preoccupied,' he said lightly. 'Something will occur. Fortunately, I don't have qualms about reminding people of what I am owed. At the very least you may want to purchase something expensive as a thank-offering at some shrine. Even a taste as refined as yours could be catered for. I'm always conscious too that we lack imperial patronage. It's a pity the Empress is quite so home-spun, I often feel, without disrespect.

'That reminds me, somehow . . . is your – our – friend in any danger? You spoke of his being saved. From what?'

'There are so many rumours,' I began, recovering myself. 'He might be accused, even arrested. He's a foreigner – a convenient culprit perhaps. I know, as you must, that he had met Pontilla Pilata. . . . Besides, he's begun to loathe Rome. Going back to Gaul is the best thing for him, and it's best he goes secretly. Isn't that enough? What's important is that he goes at once, in the next few hours. Perhaps on a boat of yours, sailing north.'

'It would be convenient, no doubt. But my dear Julia, I have no such boat. Is somebody pursuing him? I may as well learn what all Rome is going to learn, if it is, by tomorrow.'

'Afranius, listen.' I rose from the couch. 'Her lawyer was Lentulus Trebonius Niger – the Younger, I mean–'

'I know.'

'Well, whatever may be officially supposed, about the case, he's re-opening it, he's determined to – and I'm afraid of him.'

'Without reason.' He laughed. 'He's only a boy in a man's world – a lady's too, of course, now.' He bowed. 'There's nothing more, as yet? No order for an arrest?'

I looked at him, appalled. 'Why should there be? Have you heard something yourself?'

'Merely the spate of rumours. But I think you're prudent to get him away. All this could come back nastily – to say no more – on you. And it's for you I do it, Julia. I applaud your wish to live.'

188

'I have lived. I want him to live – to survive.'

'Don't agitate yourself. He shall. Just trust me.'

'But every hour–'

'This is the ostentatious tip of my activities,' he said in a leisurely way that made me want to scream. 'Where, I confess, I feel most at home. But across the river, there's a humbler, still lucrative business – a tannery. Not the sort of place you'd ever visit. Few people would. It's very smelly, for one thing. Now there he could hide for an hour or two, before a consignment of excellant quality goods – boots mostly – leaves for Bologna. In fact, two of the wagons are due, I think, to go as far as the frontier.'

'He could be concealed in a wagon. Yes, that's–'

'No. Not among my merchandise; I shouldn't care to explain that if there happened to be a search. No, he'll have to be a hired man and trudge along with the others. Somebody recruited at the last moment. We shall know virtually nothing about him. He's from–'

'Butunti,' I cried.

'Well, that's sufficiently obscure.'

'And they do leave today? In that case, please–'

He went towards one of the curtained walls while I was speaking. I could hardly bear to watch. Time was passing, and I longed to brand the very words onto Afranius's smooth skin. Yet he gave me hope. His tricksy manner, his enjoyment of his own cleverness, deserved to be indulged: they promised protection to Rufus.

He pulled back the curtain and exposed shelves of pigeon-holes, each filled with documents.

'Business,' he said deprecatingly. 'Bills, receipts . . . I must ask your pardon for having to reveal such things exist. Behind lies a rarer hoard.'

Using both hands, he swung the set of shelves open, and behind I saw the gleam of flasks and phials, ranged in a wooden rack.

'Enchanting colours, aren't they?' he said. I nodded.

From a sinister, muddy yellow-brown liquid to one purely transparent, the contents seemed almost like precious stones under glass. There was a phial of emerald-green, another as orange as a topaz. Perhaps some secret store of jewellery was what I half-expected him to disclose.

'Much more than just pretty to look at, and mainly medicinal. Opiates, dyes . . . some poisons even. That clear one, for instance, made from aconite. The green is my favourite; it's sleep-inducing but otherwise harmless.'

I found myself approaching the row of glass receptacles.

'The orange one?' I asked, pointing.

'A dye,' he said carelessly. 'But this is the one we want.' He took up the big flask, as it was, of yellow-brown liquid. 'I'll send it to his lodgings with a message – and perhaps some rags for him to wear. When he's used it, he can make his way to the tannery. He'll be quite a suitable rustic colour, head and all, by then.'

'Use it?' My voice faltered, and he smiled.

'Afraid it will harm him? My dear Julia, at any other time I'd begin to feel offended. You may taste it, if you like. It probably would be disagreeable to drink but not deadly. If it does nothing more, it will help disguise his hair. Or would you rather he leaves Rome looking his best?'

'Of course, you're right.' I bit my lip. 'I'm not fully in control of my thoughts. . . . Last night I slept very little, and the night before–'

'May I,' he interrupted, 'have a boy go now and take it to him? There isn't very much time. He knew you hoped to see me? He'll be expecting some message?'

'Yes – yes, he's hoping for something . . .'

'Would you prefer, my dear, to write a few words? You could reassure him.'

'No, thank you. Of course, send the message. It's no lack of trust, truly–'

'If you'll excuse me, the sooner this is despatched–'

'Yes, I know. Please go. And, Afranius: I shall be grateful as long as I live.'

He was absent from the room for what seemed a very few moments. I had been examining it more closely while alone and was ready, as he returned and crossed to shut up the recessed array of flasks, with questions.

'That extraordinary plant,' I indicated in one corner, a feathery-leaved, winter-flowering shrub whose brilliant purple blooms glittered waxen. 'Where did that come from?'

He half-turned from pulling the curtains close again.

'Out of my head.'

'Your head?'

'Yes, it's a creation not of nature but of art. The flowers really are made of wax. They never fade, you see.'

I gathered my draperies around me, veiling my still smarting, somehow ravaged face. Again I thanked him, but the urgency was over. My reiteration began to sound hollow and strident. How could gratitude take on reality until I knew the outcome? It was too soon to talk of any next meeting, of rewards and congratulations. If all went well, there would be time enough – years of it – in which to savour the achievement. For Afranius it could only be one stroke of cleverness amid many, and rapidly forgotten; for me it would always be memorable but tinged, blotted, stained with regret.

Other clients might have asked Afranius to spread out before them the treasures of the shop, to conjure up from the cave-like basement below some rare unfinished cup or bracelet, displayed by a half-bashful craftsman, fingering possessively the fruit of his own workmanship. What I begged before we left the room was the assurance that all would be well: to carry that away, purchased, hidden and infinitely precious. And if it failed I envisaged, beyond, nothing.

The familiar sight of our circular temple, low and modest-seeming, almost dwarfed by the mass of neighbouring arches and huge, high-pillared façades, reminded me of the life that lay ahead. My steps would resume their circumscribed path, while my thoughts lingered far away, forever following Rufus as he trudged at a cart's tail, the stench of fresh leather in his nostrils, down a dusty road to a destination I could not descry.

Here, under that shallow dome, where the fire burnt eternally, was the earth's centre. According to fable, a primitive structure of thatch and willow had risen here, to roof in the first sacred hearth, now ringed by marble walls. Certainly the site was as ancient as the city. Women had tended it even then, as they would go on doing, whatever my fate. Something vital would continue, and that was oddly consoling – a spark of warmth in the coldness which invaded my mind at the prospect of the future.

To live on is to grow fragile, I thought, seeing the old door-keeper hastily drop his polishing cloth at the appearance of my litter and put his tremulous hands to the great bronze handles of the door. He was hunched so deeply as he concentrated that his mouth and nose seemed almost slobbering against the metal, but the door yielded at last and he cackled happily to himself.

I entered the house and remembered Gemma. So much had happened since I had seen her. But I could only send to enquire if she were better, and the news brought impassively by the red-haired girl that she hoped to resume her duties tomorrow made me inwardly sigh. I gave commands that I was not to be disturbed: by no one, I emphasized, and the girl shook her mop at me as she withdrew.

I slept almost as I stood, sinking into a sleep that promised to be seamless until the noise of voices nearby, bickering and growing louder, ripped open my robe of oblivion. Still I lay there unheeding as though bandaged against intrusion. It was peaceful, despite the expostulations outside; I sensed I had been asleep for several hours. To bathe and eat and sleep once again were the goals ahead of me.

Even the sight of a Vestal whirling into the room, writhing in the red-haired girl's long freckled arms, as if in some obscene dance, was no more than mildly provoking.

'I told you Madam's orders,' the girl panted. 'She–'

'This is important, you idiot.'

The Vestal rushed to my bedside, falling clumsily onto her knees.

'Why, Valeria,' I said, recognising the bulging eyes and the headlong, over-eager manner as she thrust something at me. A token – from Rufus, or at least from Afranius Dexter – was the hope that swept me before I saw clearly.

'From the Empress herself,' she gasped. 'An imperial guard . . . the Empress's own seal. You had to have it straight away, didn't you? A communication from the palace – it could be something desperately urgent. And, anyway, it's bound to be of tip-top importance.'

'A gracious message of some sort,' I agreed, toying with the unopened missive bound with spidery purple thread.

'They say,' Valeria went on at my elbow, her face still flushed from the struggle and excitement, 'that the Emperor will enter the city in exactly four days' time. It's going to be the most smashing triumph ever. We'll be involved, won't we? And if I hadn't been on the spot this ghastly girl would

actually have kept Her Majesty's communication from you.
I think that's pretty steep.'

'No, I never; she said—'

'How dare you contradict me? I'll—'

'You both did right,' I said wearily. 'I had asked specially
not to be disturbed, Valeria—'

'But when the Empress herself—'

'Quite so. And now, I'm about to take a bath. . . .'

She looked down at the ivory tablets, dismayed to see I
had glanced cursorily, closed them and put them aside.

'If there's any news – you know. Anything I can do.'

'Thank you, Valeria, but nothing needs to be done – except
for me to bathe.'

'Will you be seeing – I mean, are you invited . . .? Sorry
to be so nosey but I'm such a tremendous admirer of the
Empress – as a woman and everything.'

'I'm sure you must be. And I'm sure you appreciate that
I have to respect the Empress's confidence.'

'Oh, absolutely.'

I smiled at her dismissively.

The peremptoriness of the summons from the Empress
was unmistakable. Of course it would be pleasant to adopt
Valeria's conjectures, but common-sense made me doubtful.
I could not see the Empress consulting me or troubling herself
inordinately over the protocol for the Emperor's triumphal
entry into the city. The nice question of the appropriate type
of animal to draw his chariot would merely bore her. Few high
personages were less likely to have sought or been affected by
advance information of the state of the heavens, either divi-
nely or atmospherically. And whether the Senate, led doubtless by Valeria's father, had voted that the Emperor might
be dressed in both a palm-decorated tunic and a gold-embro-
idered toga would be a matter of total indifference to her. 'As
long as he's home in one piece,' I could almost hear her
growling. 'I don't mind if he's naked.'

Whatever awaited me, the procedure of reception at the
Palatine was as well-jointed and as well adjusted as it had,
on the last occasion, been almost flagrantly awkward. Marcus
met me with precisely the right note of not excessive deference
or friendliness but as someone expected.

Again I slid into Marcia's practised hands – hands that

193

kneaded and massaged so expertly that, against every instinct, apprehension dropped from me. Under such relentless anointing, my mind weakened, and I even obediently paused when we reached 'Gorgon Corner' and she pointed to the empty niches.

'Sorry you find us stripped,' she said, with a simper, 'in a manner of speaking. Between ourselves, it's being got ready for a group of Dacian artefacts – gifts, I gather, from some grateful tribesmen. Of course, one doesn't quite know what to expect. It's so far away, isn't it? I do hope there's nothing – er, unsuitable. . . .'

'But the dear Empress,' I said, 'seems so robust in her tastes. I shouldn't have thought–'

Marcia looked round conspiratorially and then gave me a playful nudge. 'It's *him*,' she muttered. 'Easily shocked. But when Hadrian was out in Lower Moesia he sent back something that really . . . well, I thought, if that's what they call art in Lower Moesia. Still, perhaps I'm old-fashioned. And,' she said more loudly as we walked on, 'the dear Emperor deserves every consideration. We are looking forward so much – let's only hope the weather plays its part. We've been lucky so far, haven't we? Just that one big thunderstorm. Something tells me we're going to get through the winter without snow, and that's a blessing.'

'What's a blessing?' The Empress called at once when Marcia showed me into the room I knew. 'Is it Julia perhaps? You're indeed most welcome, especially coming at this late hour. But poor Marcia has so many blessings, it makes her life even with me quite delightful.'

'Oh, ma'am. . . . It was only about the snow, you know,' she added.

'It melts, I believe, and then doesn't grass return to the fields? I'm no poet but it happens every year – always assuming, of course, that it has snowed.'

'I foresee a mild winter,' Marcia cried. 'Imperially mild, and then the coming of spring.'

'My dear, you're inspired. And now, Julia is about to help us, I'm sure, to another happy outcome.'

'Your Majesty commands,' I said, bowing where I stood.

The Empress gestured at a couch. I sat down and Marcia

handed me a glass of wine ('Dacian,' she whispered warningly, making a face), before fading from the room.

'If it tastes like hemlock,' the Empress said composedly, 'leave it. Patriotism and victory are affecting us all, Julia, which is why I sent for you. In two days' time my man will enter the city, in triumph. It's no longer a secret. You see how short the period is before I embrace him again.'

'I congratulate Your Majesty – and His Majesty as well. The Vestals–'

'The Vestals? Oh, I needn't ask if you have them prepared to join in the celebrations. That is quite understood. No doubt he – perhaps we – must visit the shrine. With you I don't waste time enquiring if the sacred fire is in good order.'

She gave a heavy, snorting laugh and sat back regarding me fixedly. Tonight she was as plainly dressed as usual, with scarcely any jewellery, but the effect of her dress was rich in the lamp-light: tawny and silky and worn so carelessly that it might have been the pelt of some exotic animal wrapped around her. Against it her skin showed hardly less tawny, and the black of her lustrous hair seemed to glow. That homely air of hers, and even something of her normal placidity, had been replaced tonight by a sense of impatient command. The pelt-like dress might have come from some quarry she had slain and skinned as efficiently as killed. She sat there, apparently unoccupied – without any needlework distraction – but concentrated, intense and somehow fiery, unless that was merely an accidental association fused from the colour of her clothes and her last sentence. I barely lowered my eyes under her gaze, and I felt a purpose burning within her. And to her I, dressed as I was, seemed perhaps a bar of white metal which heat would bend.

'The death of Pontilla Pilata,' she stated brusquely, 'was why I sent for you first. You recall? I say "death" – it was murder, and it has gone unpunished. Now I am told terrible things about her, and perhaps they are true, but she is unavenged. Rumours increase. Our good and great Prefect has not managed to stop them. But I mean to have the whole affair finished, cleared up and closed, before the Emperor enters Rome. That will be my greeting and my gift to him.

'I should never have accepted Publius's version of events. You, Julia, were quite right. I judged wrongly. But the gods give me the opportunity to end the matter, and end it I shall. Your interest was firm, I remember, when mine wavered. You set out to investigate, without my support – which was foolish of me. Now, I shall make up for that foolishness. Tell me what you have learnt and you will see me swift to act.'

'Well, ma'am, I reached no conclusions. . . .'

'I am surprised. None? I shall be frank. Stories have reached me that you were going here and there, speaking to this and that person. I can't think you of all people were just indulging idle curiosity. What you did or even whom you saw is not my concern. What you found out, however, is my concern.'

'I didn't mean to imply I did nothing,' I said hastily. As I hurried on, I was wondering – guessing I was meant to wonder – how much the Empress had heard. 'I talked to some of Pontilla Pilata's household, her woman, Beroe, for one.'

'She is, I am told, under grave suspicion, in prison.'

'Wrongly, ma'am. I can assure you at least of that.'

'Then she must be released – when we learn the real criminal's identity. She told you nothing except that she was innocent? No names of those men – the lovers – who it appears were welcomed by that so outwardly respectable mistress of hers, our friend? Am I astray in supposing that among them we should look for the murderer? You, of course, I feel sure, have already done so.'

She sat unmoving, her hands loosely in her lap. Whatever emotions she was suppressing, she was enviably free of any tendency to adjust her hair or straighten a pleat in her dress. She neither smiled nor frowned.

'May I,' I asked, 'be allowed to be equally frank with Your Majesty? Perhaps the wine is a little rough at first taste, though possibly drunk on the spot. . . .'

'Then let Marcia bring you something vintage. I've such a coarse palate, I can't pretend to mind. My man's the same. But Hadrian, I expect, will agree with you.'

'I mustn't trouble you, ma'am. As for the Pontilla Pilata case, I confess I've ceased to take an interest in it, if I ever seriously did.'

'I regret that, Julia, very much. You grew discouraged perhaps – and yet I would not suspect you of giving up easily.

Nobody would dare intimidate you. You simply felt you were getting nowhere?'

'That is what I certainly felt when I came uninvited to the Palatine one morning,' I said warmly. I also could burn, and if a few flecks of hot ash fell on her they would serve as a warning not to come too close.

'I failed to see your imperial majesty, but perhaps it's just as well. My accusations would have been wild . . . disrespectful even. I didn't know anything of what I now know. After that, it stopped being important to me . . . I no longer wanted to learn what happened. I understood no good could come of it, only pain – pain and grief.'

'Yet,' she began impassively, 'it seems to stir you, Julia, still. It stirs me, too. I love my husband, and he is also the Emperor. In his absence I have ruled Rome, though no one may have noticed. He has won great victories. He will enter the city in triumph, and I am too proud to think I have lost a battle in his absence and failed to punish a scandalous crime. Ah, they will mutter, we had to wait for the Emperor's return; it takes a male to deal with those things. A woman is weak, when she is not wicked. Isn't that how Roman women have always been – because that's how Roman men have always wanted them to be?

'I'm not like that, Julia. Nor, I believe, are you. We're not content to sit supine and be hailed as virtuous because we keep silent. But then we are not monstrous like Agrippina and Messalina, are we? In the East we should have been far more welcome. Either of us, let me say, could easily have been another Semiramis. Why, who has even heard the name of her husband, if in fact she was married? It is he – or them perhaps – for whom history has no time, but the whole world is aware of her and her achievements.'

'Your Majesty is too modest,' I said. I could not help smiling faintly as I spoke, stirred a little despite myself, even softened, by her vision of us both as ruling women. 'Posterity will surely honour a happy marriage and a happy reign enshrined in our ruler and his dear consort. It's unusual enough, I grant, ma'am, where Roman Emperors are concerned.'

'No,' she said. 'I shall be forgotten. Did the Emperor Trajan have a wife, posterity will ask, if it enquires at all.

And that will be partly because he had no children: she, rather, had no children.

'Well, forgotten or not, I will act while I can. However brief my reign, it shall be strong and effective. You will help me make it so. We can show Rome what real women are made of.'

I sat trying to appear as composed as she. I forbade my hand to stray to tuck back a tendril of hair that almost whispered while it vibrated at my ear: my ear. . . . I had a sudden, insane impulse to shout his name in one ringing, defiant farewell, hailing a departure as triumphant in its way as the Emperor's imminent arrival.

'When I came unbidden to the palace . . .' I said slowly.

'It was a morning I had given instructions I would see no one. I say I love my husband, Julia, but I also love my brother. News had come that the Emperor was returning and I knew he would not relish finding Sempronius in Rome. I instigated the rumours, using whomever I could, just to keep Sempronius privately with me for a few more days. Now, he has gone – away to Spain. That is the truth. We had our days together; we were happy. Now I shall be all the happier to welcome back my man, our ruler – and happiest to hand back to him Rome as it was when he left it.'

'But nothing, whatever you do, can bring back Pontilla Pilata.'

'Do I wish her back? She is better dead, though I do not forget how she died. Let us find the killer, deal with him and we and the gods and the city will be appeased. That is all.'

'When I came that morning, it was really your brother, ma'am, whom I hoped to see. You have heard I was seeing people, and it's true that up till then I thought – hoped – I might solve the affair. Had I seen dear Lord Sempronius. . . .'

'You believe him guilty? Perhaps you still do?' She put the questions without urgency, looking across at me for answers as calmly as if she were a judge.

'Guilty of loving Pontilla Pilata – yes, if that were a crime. But no, I do not think he killed her.'

'So what would you have gained by seeing him?'

'Oh,' I said, with an instinctive smile I extinguished as I felt it strike some dangerous spark from her dark eyes. 'I might have lost rather than gained. It was better to be

198

discouraged. I found – other things to do. . . . I am content to leave things as they are. No harm will come to Rome or to any other person. The Emperor may be assured. You too, ma'am. The gods speak through me when I say that.'

'Most gratifying,' she said dryly. 'But I am human, Julia. I need to know more – and to act accordingly. And Rome is human also, let me remind you. People are talking. Suspicion is rife and nobody is free from it. Why, next it will be that you and I are guilty – of hushing up matters, if not of the actual crime. Shall they be permitted to say that of us?'

'Your Majesty mentions love of your dear brother, but what if he had been guilty? If I had come to you, requested or not, and told you I had found the culprit – the criminal, the man who did it? After all, he was her lover–'

'Among many, as we now know,' she said contemptuously.

'But he alone felt real love for her. Perhaps in his anger at finding out her true nature, he strangled her. It would be no premeditated murder – no murder, perhaps, in any sense. They would be meeting as they had often met–'

'Where?'

'Perhaps at her family tomb. When he declared how much he loved her, begged her to be faithful, even to marry him, she just laughed and turned away. He caught at the ends of her floating scarf and she struck him and that made him wild with rage. He seized her by the throat. You know how strong he is, ma'am, and quick-tempered, you'll agree. He must have meant to hurt her, be revenged but not commit murder – and it all happened so quickly. . . . You would call him guilty?'

'Of course,' she said.

'I denounce him, then,' I cried. 'Lord Sempronius, your Majesty's own brother, is the person whom you would have to punish. If that is the position, you see how nothing is gained – nothing. And how much pain and misery are caused – to you yourself, above all!'

'Nevertheless, if it were so, I should proceed.'

'Oh, it's easy to say, ma'am, though even saying it is a betrayal of someone you love. Pardon my frankness or not, but listen. If you love him, you can hardly condemn him to death – and for what? Accidentally slaying a woman you too now recognize wasn't worth anything, who virtually brought death on herself by her slippery ways. And for that death a man must in turn die? Someone close to you, whom you state you love – it's horrible and mad and perverted. I doubt if even Messalina at her foulest would have behaved like that.'

There was a pause. I was breathless, silenced only by inchoate thoughts. Now, irrevocably our roles had been reversed. She it was who enshrined every extreme of outraged chastity and revenge to be associated with a virgin goddess: something must die, and the more appalling the sacrifice, the more blood spurted, the deeper her joy. I could see her tawny skin and dress daubed with blood as she bent to embrace the bleeding victim she was stabbing. Only killing would sate her. It was left for me to speak for life and for the experience, painful enough as I had felt it, of love. It had its sacrifice to make, but something lived as a result. And if any spot of blood fell on my pure robes, it would be my own, secretly wrung from my heart in the effort to keep another heart beating.

'But I'm bound to point out, Julia,' she said at last, speaking rather rapidly and with heavy, guttural emphasis, 'that you know perfectly well it is not so. Sempronius, you have admitted, is not the guilty person. I am not called on to be the creature of your virulent denunciation.'

'But you would be. That's enough.'

'You feel all this very strongly, I must also point out: very personally, it seems. You don't love Sempronius, do you? We are alone. We need not apologise to each other for frankness. You will not shock me, say what you will. The forms between us are meaningless. We are two women in a world of men.'

'If I loved him – but I don't – I should defend him, protect him – save him, if possible. That is all.'

She made no response, brooding as she sat there, apparently impassive. The turbulence of my own thoughts was dying down. Now I had spoken, I began to feel a growing calmness. Two women we might be, but utterly separate and distinct; and in that seemed to lie safety. I had only to sit on a little longer, letting silence part us further, and soon there would be physical distance between us.

'Julia.' When she spoke my name it was as sudden as a rap on a table. 'There are things you don't tell me. Perhaps I might insist, but I don't. Yet it was in this very room that

200

you swore to me that if you uncovered the murderer I should know. And didn't I warn you that even if it was my own brother, I should punish him?'

'Fortunately, as you pointed out just now, that doesn't arise.'

'No, but we are left with your involvement. You took up the case. You dropped it. You discourage my pursuit of it, Julia, if I understand correctly. Yet I do not feel you are quite unconcerned, for all your disclaimers.

'You see, I tell you exactly what I feel. Don't assume it is easy sitting here, being the Empress, thinking of everything except what Rome supposes I am thinking of – my costume for the imperial triumph. I'm not asking for your pity, still less any envy. But insinuations reach me, people crowd round me . . . our good Publius has his reputation to consider. . . . Lentulus Trebonius Niger urges me–'

'What?' I exclaimed. 'He has dared approach you?'

'While we are talking, poor Marcia is doubtless offering him a glass of Dacian which in the interests of loyalty and enthusiasm he is – shall we say? – sinking as he toasts the empire.'

'He is here – in the palace?'

'He seeks a solution to the case. I too do. He is young, Julia, eager–'

'Merciless.'

'But to whom should we show mercy? Give me the answer, and then we may see what is appropriate. Otherwise, who can escape his suspicions? That wretched woman attendant of Pontilla Pilata's is only one person he suspects. He talks of her husband's involvement also. He is plausible, even if he would like to incriminate us all. The best way I can counter him is by the truth.' She stopped and allowed a pause to develop. 'Are you sure you are unable to help me?'

'I should be sorry to be supposed not to help, ma'am,' I said, reverting deliberately to the usual address; it played its part in the distancing I sought, waiting for the signal of dismissal. 'I fear the facts will never now be known, and it's best to close the case. The Emperor's return provides public opinion with more agreeable topics. Even your Majesty's wardrobe for the occasion may divert speculation. . . .'

'Trebonius Niger is less easily diverted. He will think me

201

weak in not acting, Julia, should I not act. You understand me, don't you? People you suppose innocent may suffer – unless you're prepared to help. I still feel there is something you know and you haven't told me. If so, be careful.'

'Is that a warning, ma'am?' I asked the question almost casually. I had suddenly realised how little she could harm me – harm us, I amended. She could set in motion the might of Rome: send Publius marching ponderously along the sacred way of his duty. Or she might listen to the insidious schemes of Trebonius Niger, darting agilely among witnesses and suspects, leaving a sticky trail which would culminate in the law-courts with a trial, an accused and perhaps a sentence of death. It was all faint to me now; I had lost any sense of indignation. Whatever threatened, Rufus and I would have eluded it.

I was unprepared for the Empress rising, moving almost stealthily, so that before I could myself make a move she was seated by my side. Close to, her appearance was rather haggard, despite her composure. A trace or two of silver showed in the lustrous black of her bushy hair. More strongly than ever, I was conscious of our physical disparity. To me the closeness of our bodies on the couch was uncomfortable, but I felt that she no longer had the power to frighten me.

'I am not monstrous or perverted,' she said, strangely echoing my own thought. 'You misunderstand me. Perhaps we are doomed to misunderstand each other. Nor am I divine, Julia. At this moment I'm confused, I'm worried – and I'm tired. Also, I am alone. All I ask is for you to remember that.'

'I am – or have been – all those things.'

'But being alone is your place. It's your function. You're strong tonight in resisting every appeal I make. We can't even talk together, can we? Do you hate me, Julia, or despise me?'

'Neither,' I said.

'You're very proud and very confident. As a virgin Empress, you perhaps should and could have ruled Rome.'

'I have no ambitions. I am content with things as they are.'

'So you have said. But outside your cloistered existence, life does not stand still. It's going on while we're exchanging

202

these sentences. Don't believe you can stop that process. None of us can – not even you.'

She put her brown-skinned, stumpy hand on my knee. It clung there briefly, incongruously, amid the white folds, inviting some touch or answering pressure, and then she lifted it off with a resigned gesture, taking it away as she herself took her place again on the opposite couch.

When Marcia bustled in, we were sitting silently. Silently I rose and bowed. The Empress half-opened her arms in an embrace that did not attempt any contact, only signalled farewell.

Outside, the evening air came swirling round me with the assurance that I was free – had escaped and had triumphed. Plunging down the hillside, I wanted the litter to tilt more steeply and excitingly, careering on as it bore me away from the palace and the brooding figure of the Empress, encircled by sinister or ludicrous creatures and tortured perhaps by the decisions she was pressed to make.

'Faster,' I might have yelled, sending the bearers staggering on into the night and almost disappointed at the shortness of the journey. I was still travelling when we halted, still buoyed up as I stepped to the ground.

From the glow of the atrium disclosed by the hastily-opened door, I turned on the portico, reluctant to go inside while my heart throbbed with the awareness of all that the day had achieved. The servants waited – Gemma among them, I could see, a pale, subdued sprite, waiting to come alive again at a smile of recognition.

Instead, it was another face I seemed to have a vision of, glimpsed at the bottom of the steps, lit by a torch's flare: at first hardly recognizable, an illusion, and then unmistakable and actual. Light and darkness were clashing in my head, and Rome rose up in a great buzz of noise. I reeled but turned back, wildly staring. From the black gash of face that the torchlight inflicted, there sprang out a brilliant beam from the wide, glittering green eyes. It was Rufus.

XVI

I pushed past the gaping, puzzled servants, not waiting to listen to their babble. My visit to the Palatine need scarcely have brought the whole household out to stare, late though I was in returning.

'Tomorrow – tomorrow,' I muttered into Gemma's imploring face, as I brushed by. 'Tonight I must be left alone.'

By the time I had reached the corridor, out of sight, I was running. I heard, or I imagined hearing, Rufus first scratching and then, more desperately, drumming on the outside door.

My dress caught, and something fell with a metallic crash as I got a hand to the latch and wrenched open the flimsy panel. That Rufus was standing there, dressed in rags, his hair and skin dark blurs, halted me. Even in running, I had not quite believed I would find him solidly present, a palpable figure loomed up out of the dusk and blocking the doorway.

'Why are you here?' I cried, dragging him inside. 'What's gone wrong? You should have left Rome hours ago. It's Afranius, isn't it? He's betrayed us. Oh, I knew it – I should never have trusted him. We must think of another–'

'Nothing's gone wrong,' he said calmly. 'Except some axle's broken and we aren't starting until the morning, when the gates open. Now, don't worry and let me talk to you in your own room. I've come back to do that. It won't take long, but I couldn't bear us to part as we did before. We aren't ever going to meet again, Julia–'

'I know, I know,' I panted, almost hiccoughing as I fought to recover my breath and my equilibrium. 'But you must get away, Rufus, not stay near here. Anything can happen. Nobody's to be trusted,' I gasped. 'Nobody.'

'Including me. That's what you were thinking, isn't it? Well, I've been given the chance, by the grace of your gods or mine, to come back and tell you – swear to you – that the truth is different. . . . Won't you hear it? Or do you want me to step out into that alleyway without another word? I've dodged a long way across Rome to see you, Julia.'

'You shouldn't have done. The risk's too great. I can't talk about it all now, Rufus – never, I suppose – but this is madness. You must get back and hide in the tannery and leave as soon as possible in the morning. I can't rest till I know you're safe.'

'And what about me? Suppose I can't rest thinking how underneath you doubt me and despise me – even though you've helped me? I don't want you to go through life thinking I never loved you. But that is what you think, I'm sure. Don't you?'

'For a few moments, then,' I said, after a pause. 'Only a very few moments – for both our sakes. As you're here, though you shouldn't be. But I'm terrified, Rufus, I don't quite know why. I felt so convinced – so happy, even – that you'd got away . . .'

'I have a charmed life,' he said.

'Don't boast of it, if so.'

Instinctively I took his hand and led him through the darkness to my room.

'You're glad to see me,' he said flatly, when I went to trim the triple lamp that stood on the table by my bed. 'You know, I had an awful feeling as I hung around outside that you wouldn't recognize me like this. I only hope it will all come off eventually; it makes me feel dirty.'

'Oh, I should always recognize you,' I said.

'Shall we sit down? I feel rather absurd, making a speech across a room to a woman I know as well as I know you. Put me at my ease, Julia. I hardly thought we should be meeting like this.'

'Don't you see,' I exclaimed. 'We can't be at ease. We've got to be on guard. I've just come from the Empress. She's dangerous – and I'm afraid. Oh, I'm touched, I suppose, that you came back, insane though it was. Perhaps you came just because it was insane. But I've spent all day saying goodbye to you in my mind, Rufus – if I may still call you that. Apart from feeling shocked, and shaken, I've no more emotions left. Above all, don't try to make love to me. I'm virgin – barren, anyway: an old priestess of a lonely, fierce, female cult.'

'Whom I love,' he said smiling.

'I am no more nor less than the Chief Vestal.'

'Whom I love.'

In the silence I smoothed down my robes. They still seemed fresh, unlike their wearer, though I felt I stood bravely unyielding under the persistent gentle hail of his litany. He might worship me, if he wished; I did not forbid it, as I gazed gravely at him in his rough-dyed state. The crest of his hair rose and fell exactly as before, though lank now and tinted a muddy brown, as were his thin cheeks. As a method of passing unnoticed, the disguise failed: he simply looked more exotic than before – more exotic and to my eyes more vulnerably beautiful. He seemed almost quivering as he stood confronting me, appealing mutely. But I was apart, enshrined, mute myself.

He would never again reach out and touch my body, nor I his. At most, perhaps, our hands would briefly come into one final contact at the impending moment of farewell.

'You've saved me, protected me,' he said at last. 'But wasn't it done to teach me a lesson? To show me that you were really better than I am and more truly loving? I've come back to assure you that, whoever's better, I did and do truly love you, Julia. Don't go on thinking that it was only because of your – your investigation, that I made love to you. It was you I wanted, even if I also wanted to know how close you were getting to the truth.

'I couldn't go away letting you believe I hadn't loved you – that it was all a pretence. I didn't want you to live with that image of me, and you can call that vanity. I don't care.'

'You should have gone,' I said sadly. 'That's all I know. It didn't matter what I thought . . . I'd gone beyond thinking. I don't want to be disturbed, that's my only prayer – to you, to the gods, to everyone. Your being here disturbs me. You must go.'

'You'll sleep the better for this visit – wait and see. I'm a good dream, Julia – and that's how you're to recall me in the years ahead. Whatever else I was and am, I was your lover, true and faithful. I may never be able to say the same again to anyone. Isn't it worth knowing that?'

I shook my head. It was too complicated, therefore too delaying, to explain my thoughts. I should be faithful, but I did not ask it of him: it was absurd, unreasonable – unlikely. A young man moping his life away in Gaul for an ageing woman he would never see again . . . my love never expected nor wanted such a sacrifice. 'Live,' I breathed, uncaring whether the injunction reached him. It would be the faintest breath on the back of his neck as he toiled days later beside a laden wagon; the breeze that ruffled his hair and pricked his eyes open with its salty tang when he reached the harbour of his home.

'Julia,' he said, taking a pace towards me.

'You must go,' I said, stepping back. 'I've told you – I'm afraid of the Empress.'

'It sounds mad, I know, but come with me. We've got the chance – been given it. We're lucky. Get out of those clothes and come with me. We can–'

'Elope? Rufus, you certainly enjoy creating scandal. If I weren't so tense, I'd have to laugh. No, leave me with my dreams, good or bad, and my memories. I'll have this visit to treasure, once I know you're safe. I'm glad you came – or, at least, that something in you wanted to come. Don't ask me for any other tribute. It's all too serious – and urgent – for words. We've seen each other again. That's enough; and now go.'

'It's not how I saw this meeting. You still don't tell me if you realise my feelings and then you relapse into half-mocking me when I'm desperately earnest. Why don't you come with me? Even if it's a risk, we'd take it together.'

'We are parting, Rufus,' I said. 'To survive, we have to. That's all there is for us. Now, you must be stoic, if not exactly Roman – a stoic Gaul going where his duty lies.'

'Do you think I'm a coward?'

'I'm sure you'll be brave enough to follow me – to the lumber-room door. Once you've gone I'll have it blocked up. It'll never be used again.'

'When I first saw you,' he said, 'it was in this house. The Prefect brought me. You paid no attention to me, did you? I was just some underling, an attendant, a slave. But I noticed you. I don't claim I fell in love then and there – yet I felt a challenge, if you like. Someone so stately, almost inhumanly lofty, was going to be made aware of me and to care for me. Maybe it was half a game, for myself. I can't tell, even now. But when we actually met, when Calvus was patronising me and showing off to you, then I felt a real impulse of love. It was you I wanted. I said so, too, didn't I? After that, I determined we'd meet again. And we did – we have.

'So, in the end, it became no game, Julia. I utterly banished the shade of Pontilla Pilata. I couldn't have spoken about her to you, whatever had happened. And still I don't feel regret or remorse. It's as if a different person lived then. I've never, I suppose, experienced the emotions you've aroused in me. I'm not usually the one who falls in love. I've surprised myself. But this is different – truly. My feelings for you are deep, intense, real. That's what my farewell message amounts to. Say you believe me and I'll go – and go quietly.'

'I want to believe you,' I said.

'It's not the same thing.'

'No.'

'Even though I've risked everything to come back? Just for this very purpose.'

'Even so.'

He stood there immobile as if absorbing the meaning of the words we had exchanged. Then he shook himself. With one hand he twitched his rags around him in a decisive way. 'Will you kiss me, Julia, before I go? Here, before we leave this room.'

'I'd rather we just shook hands, as friends.'

'Roman to the last, I suppose.'

He extended his hand. I reached out and seized it, clasping his arm so painfully that he grimaced. Yet I felt nothing: not even consciousness of whether his grip was exerted on my flesh.

Moving together, almost with military precision, we went to the threshold and paused, as if saluting the room in farewell. I had thought that we were going to separate without another word, but as we crossed the corridor and entered the lumber-room, Rufus stopped and spoke.

'Let me stay, until dawn.' His voice was low, but eager. It had never sounded more individual – more, I suppose, foreign. 'Just stay: sit in your room, do anything, nothing. Sleep, if you like, though I'm too alert to sleep. Let me stay, Julia. You can sleep – truly – and I'll watch over you. It's only for a few hours, and after that. . . .'

'Don't,' I said. 'Don't beg and don't keep making me out some superior, inhuman being. Nobody knows better than you that I'm not. But I've got my life to get through.'

'I wanted tonight to be memorable – that's all. It's not much for a lover to ask, at the end of the day.'

He seemed still grumbling resentfully as I opened the door. How domestic a departure it was – like that of a husband relieved to be escaping a scolding wife. Or he might have been a beggar repulsed from her portals by some aristocratic matron.

Outside it was misty. The black walls that formed the alley rose vaguely into the night sky. Almost angrily he elbowed by me, his face down and his body hunched in the ragged clothes.

'I wish you well,' I said fervently. 'For ever – Rufus.'

The mist and darkness absorbed him. He had gone. I slammed the door to and leant against its rough surface for support. Sudden, violent pounding on it made my ear vibrate. I snatched my ringing head away at the impact. Outside men's voices were shouting, Rufus's among them. Unthinkingly, I scrabbled at the wood, pulling open the panel so desperately that it swung back on its hinges with a shriek I thought might be my own.

Down on one knee Rufus was struggling in the grasp of three burly soldiers, while behind four other soldiers, their swords drawn, were closing in on him.

'Stop,' I commanded, trying to force my way into the group. 'Release this man.'

They had him pinioned now, and as they dragged him upright I saw his knee was bleeding through the rags.

'Release him,' I said even more sharply.

Out of the mist an officer appeared, flanked by armoured torch-bearers, bowing slightly as he came forward.

'I regret the disturbance, Madam–' he began.

'Regret it? It's disgraceful. This man must be released. At once, do you understand?'

He smiled with an official, fleeting smile that halted me. The glint of his teeth was more forbidding than all the array of steel and leather gleaming in the flaring light.

'A criminal being arrested, Madam,' he said curtly. 'A civic matter of no concern to your ladyship, and I am sorry you were awoken. It was thought he might attempt to break into your sacred premises–'

'What!' I exclaimed. I knew I had gone pale.

'Yes, indeed.' His smile was as tight as the strap of his helmet. 'Your ladyship may be thankful we were forewarned.

209

He's a murdering young foreigner who's due to die tomorrow. Two hours after sunrise, to be precise. I'm almost sorry I won't be on duty. Nasty-looking bit of work, isn't he? We'll get him out of your ladyship's way, with renewed apologies for any inconvenience caused.'

'Wait.' I spoke with deliberate haughtiness.

Ringed and roped by the now relaxed, jocular soldiers, Rufus was a dim, slumped figure, hardly human in his tatters, whose head had fallen on his chest.

'Wait,' I repeated. 'Some mistake has occurred. On whose orders are you acting?'

'Those of the Empress, my lady.'

'The Empress? A common criminal would scarcely merit intervention by the Empress. And this is some poor, wretched fellow, foreign possibly, whom your men have—'

'No, no, my lady,' he interrupted confidently, indifferent to my glare. 'My orders were clear – remarkably clear, I may add. To arrest any man lurking in this area. It was feared he might break in and threaten your ladyship and the other Vestals. He's killed one woman – a lady – and he'd do it again, given a chance. Not that he's getting one now.'

'But you received a description, didn't you?' I said despairingly. 'A fair-haired man, and this one's dark. He's just some foolish drunk, I expect. You're making an appalling mistake. You'll pay for it and meanwhile the real criminal is loose in the city.'

'I had my orders. And this one's foreign all right – jabbering away he was. If it's a mistake, they must sort it out at the Tullianum. That's where he's going. Come on, lads. Get him moving.'

'No,' I cried. 'Wait. Do you hear? I order you to wait.'

I tried to thrust him aside but his body resisted stoutly and he gave a frowning glance at my flailing arms; I felt them weaken and drop hopelessly, as my will-power seemed to falter in the dark, dank alleyway. I could hurl myself at the brick walls around and make no more impact on them.

The soldiers had closed about Rufus, looking impatiently and curiously over their shoulders towards their officer and my no doubt strange, almost demented figure. Rufus I could no longer see. He was lost, crushed in a giant, mailed fist I was impotent to prise open.

210

'The Empress's orders must be obeyed,' the officer said. 'By everyone, my lady, whatever their rank. Quick march, lads.'

Barely saluting, he turned away. The torch-bearers moved off, taking the light with them. Darkness swept over me, but something burst out of the centre of the packed group and for a moment the torches' flare illumined Rufus at the rope's end, jerking and gyrating as he strained back towards me. A high, bubbling, incomprehensible scream came from him.

'*Je t'adore, je t'adore!*'

Then a soldier's scabbard chopped at the back of his knees. He stumbled. The rope tightened and he fell. Spears pricked him up again. Helmets and shields flowed together like molten metal, swallowing him totally.

I could hear the steady tramp of feet well after they had rounded the corner of brick wall and gone from sight. A stench hung in the air, compounded of burning resin and bodily smells. As the soldiers had waited behind the officer's back, even while I was desperately fighting to assert my authority, one of them had stood and urinated against the wall.

I had to leave the scene, but I could think of nowhere to go. There must be things I could do – should do – but it was difficult to stop the whirring, beating wings that blurred my mental vision, wheeling like bats around me in the darkness. I felt I would never grow calm enough to plan until I knew how we had been betrayed.

The broken axle, the forced delay, a word of encouragement possibly fostering Rufus's impulse to break out of hiding . . . all pointed to Afranius Dexter. Every aspect was known to him. By going to him, by confessing as I had, I had compounded the possibility of treachery, which for him would be no more than fresh proof of his own cleverness.

I left the door hanging derisively half-open, an invitation to assault. It seemed no longer to matter if some late-night reveller strayed that way. More probably, soldiers still guarded the house invisibly, less to protect us than to watch what happened next.

I could not bear the thought of my bare empty room, and it was comforting to remain amid the obscurity of the dusty, piled furniture of the lumber-room, where time had ceased.

I fingered the cracked pedestal of some statuette and set upright again the candelabrum earlier knocked to the floor. Each of my predecessors had lovingly chosen objects that had in turn become neglected, discarded, relegated here and then left to tarnish and decay.

Yet now, as I sat virtually unaware whether I was awake or dozing, the presence of these broken things seemed strangely soothing. Did Gemma look in on me once and then flit away? I could not be sure. The awful image of Rufus dragged bleeding, screaming, from me was still there, but now I felt less desolation than rage. Out of the darkness was flowing some message to stir me to one final effort, depending on myself alone. Up on the Palatine there was the Empress, and dawn might find me beating at those doors for admission. Or, better, there was the Emperor: camped outside the Flaminian Gate, and so shortly set to enter Rome in triumph.

I rose, feeling borne on and up by a rush of purpose. I could have seized a gong and summoned the household from sleep, as I sped through the corridor and embraced the expanse of silent, marble hall where my sandals slapped on the polished pavement with the rousing effect of hooves.

A white-robed figure abruptly confronted me. It checked any sense of lonely exultation and made me tremble for the fragility of my hopes and visions.

'My dear Julia.' Publius was as unctuous as if he were my host, welcoming me as a guest in what was my own atrium. 'I had been anxious to see you – most anxious. This is gratifying indeed. Your people didn't wish you to be disturbed, and only urgency, given the lateness of the hour–'

'Why are you here?' I asked.

He let his surprise at my tone be apparent.

'My dear . . . I come at the express wish of Her Majesty.'

'But why?'

Like me, he must be recalling that previous evening visit and our standing in this actual place. Then he had been gathering his dignity and his sobriety, and I had been effortlessly cool, even cold, a little amused and utterly unaware of what was to unfold for me by receiving him and learning of Pontilla Pilata's death. I had scarcely noticed his attendants, those shadows he had conversationally disposed of as I led him towards my apartments. What had he said? 'A young

Gaul temporarily staying in the city . . . in my service. . . . A Gallic youth . . . some young foreigner. . . .'

It was odd to have listened so indifferently.

Tonight Publius had come from no supper-party. Ostensibly at least, he was alone. But he was, for all that, heavy with official power; and any tipsiness he showed would derive from a draught of conversation with the Empress.

If he expected me to propose retiring from the hall, he gave no sign. Its space suited him well enough, perhaps, to deliver whatever announcement he had. I, too, preferred its impersonal air and also the authority it exuded in my favour.

'The deplorable incident which took place this evening has depressed Her Majesty, indeed us all, greatly. It was of course essential to act swiftly. You will be the first, Julia, to agree. The scandal must be disposed of before the Emperor's entry, and again you'll understand why. Execution takes place publicly in the morning. I flatter myself that that will be the end of the whole affair.'

'And you've come to tell me as much?'

'I've come, in no reproachful mood, I assure you, to explain how any scandal is best avoided. My dear, the situation has its awkwardness all round. Don't think I don't partly blame myself. After all, he – I need name no names – was as it were under my aegis. Like you, I'm deeply shocked, I feel culpable even, but the Empress has been all that is gracious – most gracious.

'You, I'm sure, will appreciate her thoughtfulness and indeed her wisdom. A shrewd woman, allow me to remark, my dear Julia, without disrespect. An asset to Rome.'

'Publius, as you're here, tell me please exactly what has happened. I'm very much afraid that someone innocent and foreign is being wrongly–'

'There,' he interrupted, raising a solemn hand. 'You may have no qualms. He's guilty, all right.'

'Of what?'

'Do you need to ask? Of murder, in the first instance – and of a patrician lady.'

'But can you prove it?'

'Well enough for our purposes,' he said smoothly, crossing his hands on his chest and giving me a benevolent smile.

'How?'

213

'Oh, my dear, I scarcely think that is your concern. The facts speak for themselves, and even if they didn't, we have the extremely grave crime of breaking into this holy house this very evening. In itself it is punishable – need I remind you? – by death. The Empress herself takes the most serious view of that incident.'

'I can believe it,' I said tersely, 'if that is how it was represented to her.'

He frowned. 'That is how, for everyone's sake, it has seemed proper to represent it, publicly at least. Scandal, let me emphasise, will benefit no one. No one. In any event, it has been established that he was intimate with Pontilla Pilata and visited her disguised as a woman.'

'So did many other men, Publius. That also has been established.'

'In his case we have a witness. Thanks to the assiduous work of Lentulus Trebonius Niger–'

'Ah,' I breathed.

'The name, I see, is not unknown to you. I refer, of course, to the Younger. Thanks, as I was saying, to his patient work, some senior female slave employed by Pontilla Pilata revealed the name of a certain Tibicina, a blind musician of the humbler sort. She it was who told us of being frequently required to play to Pontilla Pilata and on one occasion detecting the voice of a man in the bedroom. And she was able to identify that voice for us.'

'And so?'

'It was, I admit, a shock. I had looked on the case as long ago, and satisfactorily, closed. But the lodgings were searched and he had vanished. At first we assumed he had fled.'

'Fled,' I echoed.

'The Empress thought it conceivable he might attempt to break in here, perhaps hoping to hide himself – unknown, of course, to you, I should add. She was thinking of you and for you, Julia, and forbade me to question her further. Indeed, my own feelings might otherwise have led me–'

'Where?' I demanded. 'Are you presuming to insinuate–?'

'Not at all, my dear Julia. Not at all. No breath of scandal shall ever attach to you. It is, admittedly, unfortunate that somehow this house of all houses should have been polluted by his presence. I don't even presume to suggest a ritual

214

purification to someone of your experience. But it has been – frankly – a narrow escape.'

I stood pondering the various implications of his last sentence. Perhaps at another time I could have smiled at the faint but distinct disclaimer of personal interest in me. I was not destined to be pressed again to consider marriage with Publius. Even my status as a twin pillar of the state had been undermined.

'He must die?' I said, not attempting to hide the bitterness in my voice.

'He is guilty, my dear Julia. Do you deny it?'

'Not every guilty person has to die. There's to be no trial, no evidence – no justice.'

'This is justice. Believe me, it's better altogether this way, avoiding scandal or a long drawn-out trial, with reflections upon highly-placed personages. This way it will quickly pass and be forgotten.'

'The Empress wanted me to know this?'

'She values your discretion, Julia. I might go as far as saying she admires, even without approving, the silence you displayed when she summoned you. She asks no more questions – wishes to know no more.'

'But–?'

'Her Majesty anticipates that you might be tempted to consider laying down your exalted, indeed unique office and retiring into private life. It's not without precedent and perfectly respectable as a course of action. Some – er, pension rights accrue, I would assume. The state would always be eager to recognize in due form . . . it's a point our indispensable Calvus could undoubtedly advise on, if it arose.'

'I see,' I said, but the words were meaningless, the exact opposite of all I had envisaged.

Only by an effort could I keep my body from tottering. To have this snatched from me, at this moment, was like being felled.

'It is the Empress's command,' he was saying portentously, watching me apprehensively as he spoke. 'And of course must be obeyed. Her Majesty requires you to continue in your office. She forbids you to retire. I am charged to convey that imperial command . . . are you, my dear Julia, quite well?'

* * *

I knew I had not spent the night in a fruitless vigil in the hall, and yet the morning found me there.

Publius must have summoned some of the servants, to lead me away. I could remember nothing except his voice flowing on, passing me by as he drifted imperceptibly out of my sight even while I thought I was listening with fixed attention.

I felt as stiff as if I had been left to lie stretched out on the hard pavement; but stiffness suited my mood and my few, slow actions and the void I seemed to be carrying in place of a mind. Over and over I repeated my instructions to myself.

No emotions flowed through my arid heart. I had ceased to exist as a figure of the present. I was already part of history: even what lay before me brought no quickening sense of anticipation. Already, for me, the future had become the past. I felt I had lived it and would merely perform a series of gestures no more meaningful than some twitches of a corpse. I might have read about such a person, rather than being it. This, it seemed, was how my life had been ordained, from the first. It had been written so. Only I had not read and understood.

Despite my somnambulistic state, I had ordered the double doors to be opened so that I could see, from where I sat, the sun as it rose over Rome. Coughing and heaving, and still blear-eyed, the aged doorman managed at last to swing back the studded doors on which the sunlight hammered a thousand glittering golden nails. I had missed the actual moment of the sunrise itself. Less than two hours remained before Rufus began to walk the public road from the Tullianum to execution.

Above the city the sky was burnished into a pure, colourless radiance, cold and apparently infinite. Rome was barely astir, and this morning it looked not old but wonderfully new, purged of human presences, risen from the shadows to greet the sun as though marble had thrust its way up overnight through the earth to form the temples and palaces that crowded on my sight. From the doorway I could turn to see the Palatine, a pinkish blur along its hillside, while intense light seemed to blaze out the way I must take through the Forum.

I thought of Rufus waking, woken no doubt, in the depths of his prison, unable to tell day from night. They would manacle his arms and legs, and by the time he set off, stunned, bruised, half-reeling under the impact of brightness and noise, Rome would be fully awake. A crowd would gather. It would be mysteriously known that a criminal – a murderer, a foreigner, a fitting sacrifice – was going to slaughter. Human blood was to be shed but dried before the start of the next spectacle: the Emperor's triumphal return and entry into the city.

I was prepared and dressed. Gemma, wan-faced, smiling with an effort, and yet uncomprehending, had helped me, at her own wish. She did not venture to ask why I was up so early or where I was going. Every so often she peered into the hall, nodded as if to reassure herself I still existed, and then was gone. To her, I hoped, I appeared as stainless as the early morning sunlight, and purged of most mortal associations. I must leave the house as freshly and firmly as if it was my first day as Chief Vestal.

So I should manifest myself to the crowd, the city – and Rufus. When I stepped from my litter into the sudden, total silence, he would probably be too broken to understand. The halt of the escort of soldiers, the lowering of the lictors' fasces, the moment of my uttering the words of pardon and release might have no meaning for him. How it had happened, who had achieved it, would only gradually become clear as sullenly they freed him and let him pass, beginning to murmur perhaps against me even as I resumed my own progress.

The woman Rufus had known was rightly obscured under the Vestal dress. It was better that he did not raise his head, just stumbled away with no backward glance.

For me it would be harder. The actual incident of release I knew I could perform if necessary under the gaze of all Rome. I should be obeyed. But then I too must give no backward glance. No tremor could mar the solemnity of my appearance or my speech. I should never again see Rufus, but that knowledge had to impel me onwards, away from him. To falter and weaken would be despatching him once more to death. Love had to fuse me into being the impersonal vessel through which he survived: that, and nothing else.

One penultimate experience, most unexpected of all, was to be granted me. It was equivalent to an act of giving birth. Perhaps, in releasing him for life, I recognized that he had

217

all along been not only my lover but my son. Any mother would feel herself blessed in giving up everything for her child – accepting even that he should never know her.

Suddenly, I seemed to be filled with understanding. It would no longer be hard to carry through my whole purpose. A strange excitement banished all feelings of aridity.

At the next popping out of Gemma's head I beckoned her towards me.

'Yes, mum.' She was too patently eager. She went on tacitly asking a pardon which I would never be able to extend.

'The suffibilum,' I said, 'lying in the upper drawer of the chest in my bedroom – I've decided I shall wear it this morning when I go out.'

'I know it, mum. I'll get it straight away. You just sit tight.'

After all, I recollected, the Chief Vestal should be arrayed in it for a sacrifice.

Gemma's absence gave me time to rehearse the further step, when I climbed into my litter again, going solemnly and without haste on towards the Flaminian Gate. My thoughts would by then be concentrated on myself. I should beg, I should obtain, an audience with the Emperor. To him I should reveal all. It was necessary, for my own purging, that someone heard what I had to relate. Not the Empress. Increasingly, as I recovered consciousness, I savoured the precise nature of the price she exacted by requiring me to remain at my post, to behave as though Rufus had never existed.

And yet I had foreseen, dimly, that all might probably end in this way. Only the Emperor's notorious clemency made me pause. He too might bid me live.

'Here we are, mum,' Gemma exclaimed, with her old animation regained, pattering into the hall holding the purple-edged veil by one corner and flicking it to make sinuous shapes as though it were a semi-sacred duster. 'Not much warmth in it, you know. Wouldn't you rather I got you a shawl? It's a mimsy bit of a thing, for all that it's pretty.'

'Help me put it on,' I said absently.

While she happily fussed around, I sat up straight, settling my hands in my sleeves. I was being decked to sacrifice and be sacrificed. Even the Emperor's most merciful tendencies would be eluded. My fingers touched and gripped fast the slim glass object I had instinctively secreted among my clothes as I dressed.

Its presence gave me ultimate confidence. I felt convinced I could trust the efficacy of its contents; and before the day was over I would put that to the test. It was the phial of aconite I had stolen on impulse from Afranius Dexter. Only, of course, I should never learn now, if he had noticed its theft.